Sweet Waters

Sweet Waters

An Istanbul Thriller

Harold Nicolson

Cornucopia in association with
Sickle Moon Books

To my Mother

First published by Constable in 1921.
This edition published in September 2000 by Sickle Moon Books,
3, Inglebert Street, Clerkenwell, London EC1R 1XR
in association with *Cornucopia*, the magazine
for connoisseurs of Turkey.

ISBN 1-900209-08

The print on pages ii and iii depicts picnicers enjoying the view across the Upper Waters of the Bosphorus, looking from the European shore towards Anadolu Kavaği crowned by the Genoese castle. The map of Thrace on pages xii and xiii is from the Russo-Turkish war of 1878, both reproduced from the Barnaby Rogerson collection.

The cover is taken from the celebrated 1909 portrait of Enver Pasha by Fausto Zonaro (Painter to his Imperial Majesty Abdul Hamid II from 1896-1909), from the archives of *Turquoise* magazine with the permission of his daughter, Signora Mafalda Zonora Meneguzzer.

Cover and verso designed by Mick Keates, printed and bound for the publishers by GraphyCems.

Contents

Foreword

Harold Nicolson wrote some forty books, only two of which were novels, *Public Faces* and *Sweet Waters*, which was first published by Constable in 1921, and re-issued by them as a Constable Miscellany in 1928. It has been out of print ever since. So it is with much pleasure that I welcome this resurrection of a book that has been undeservedly forgotten, even during his lifetime by its author. To the best of my recollection he never mentioned it to me. But there can be little doubt that he was fond of it, since it was the legacy of the most traumatic period of his early life when he was wooing my mother, Vita Sackville-West, and serving as Third Secretary in the British Embassy in Constantinople in 1912-14, the years of the Balkan wars.

He did not write the book at the time, but after seven years had elapsed – the war years, and his involvement in the Paris Peace Conference of 1919 and the founding of the League of Nations. By 1921 he was serving full-time in the Foreign Office as First Secretary in the department that dealt with Central Europe. At weekends, and during short holidays at Long Barn, our house near Sevenoaks, he worked on two books, a biography of the French poet Verlaine, and then *Sweet Waters*, both published in the same year. He was indefatigable. The novel must have been written almost without pause or correction, for how otherwise could he have completed it in so short a time, when his profession, his busy social life and family concerns occupied so much of it?

It is a love-story and an evocation of Constantinople before it became Istanbul. He loved the country of the Turks. He had been happy there in the pre-war period, but his happiness was marred by doubts whether Vita would return his passionate adoration of her. They had become half-engaged before he left England, and now their separation by the full width of Europe, and her distraction by other lovers, other occupations, caused him infinite anxiety. Their surviving letters record his tenacity of purpose and her vacillations. Eventually he won through, and they were married in the chapel at Knole in October 1913. She accompanied him back to Constantinople, after a short honeymoon in Italy and Egypt, and they returned to England in time for the birth of their first son, Benedict, in August 1914, two days after the outbreak of the First World War.

His personal drama in those years is only marginally reflected in the book. He introduces himself as Angus Field, a lowly employee in the British Embassy, and Vita as Eirene Davenant, who was living in Constantinople with her widowed mother. They are by no means exact portraits of their originals, but that their resemblance was intentional is put beyond doubt by the insciption that Harold wrote in the copy he gave Vita, which is still in my possession: "Eirene from Angus. Long Barn. Nov.1921".

The novel covers the period when Bulgaria, Serbia and Greece united to crush Turkey, and nearly succeeded. Although a junior, Harold was deeply involved in the diplomatic drama that ensued. It was his professional baptism-of-fire, in more than a metaphorical sense, for he was in some danger. His visit to a field-hospital just behind the Turkish front line, and his return in a launch filled with wounded, was an incident that finds its place in the book. It is historically accurate that the Turkish army was decimated by cholera, and that Enver Bey, the leader of the Young Turks, burst into the room where the Turkish Cabinet was sitting, and shot dead the Minister of War. The mood of the Embassy in this crisis is faithfully described. So are some of its characters, though fictionalised. Hugh Tenterden, the chargé d'affaires, is Harold's idealisation of his own Ambassador, Sir Gerard Lowther – cynical, experienced, highly intelligent and masterful – a character which Harold, aged 28, wished to emulate, but to which he later reacted.

What had not changed in the seven year interval between conceiving and writing the book was his love of literature, landscape, architecture, history and the diversity of human nature. *Sweet Waters* contains magical descriptions of Constantinople before it was ruined by modernisation, and he worked into his narrative quotations from his most loved poets – Homer, Byron, Mallarmé – among them. It is an intellectual book. One can detect his acute observation of the idiosyncrasies that define a character, the way people dress, move, talk, their possessions, their habits. He is quite unsentimental, even in his love-passages, determined not to sweeten them. When Eirene refuses Angus, she in no way softens her rejection of his proposal. "Well, I won't", she says, "So there!". It was the answer that he had constantly feared from Vita.

When my father came to read the proofs of the book, he was sickened by what he considered its superficiality. "When one turns the page", he wrote to Vita, "one always hopes it will get better. But it flops and one flops, and there comes nothing but despair when one turns over." He need not have worried. The reviews were adulatory. The Foreign Office forgave him. He was their rising star, his literary gift an enviable addition to his other talents, even though, in *Some People*, five years later, his colleagues were to become the targets of it.

Nigel Nicolson, Sissinghurst, 1999.

E. G. Ravenstein.

CONSTANTINOPLE

AND ITS

APPROACHES.

0 5 10 15 20 Miles.

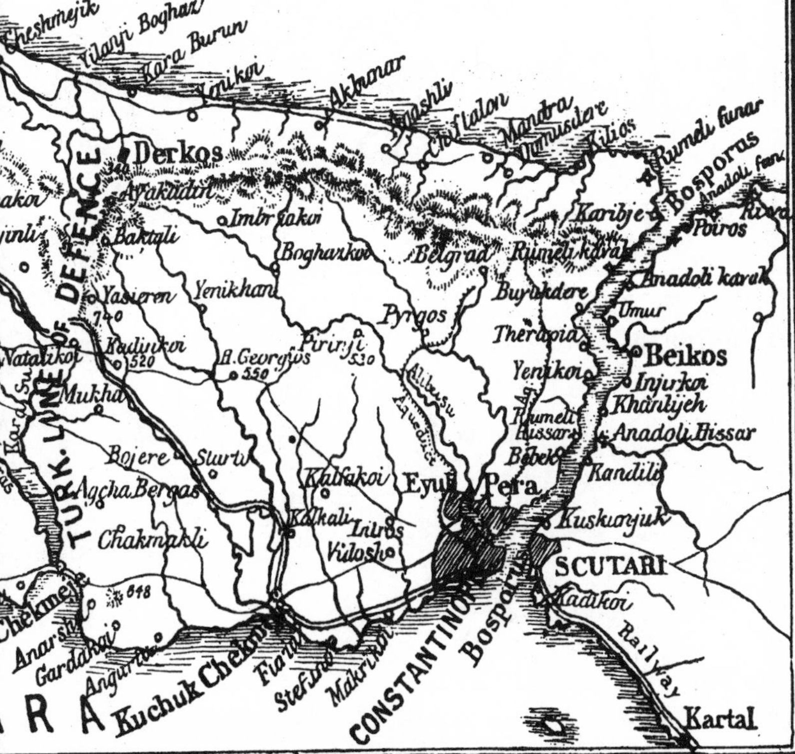

Sweet Waters

CHAPTER I.

June

(I.)

SHE spoke to her daughter in the languid French of the Levant. She said: "Eirene, you must come in now, my little one; you must come in, and you must close the window." Eirene stepped back listlessly into the room. She closed the upper half of the window and pushed the bolt: she then released the lower sash from the brackets which supported it: the sound of the waves was hushed suddenly as the frame slid home in its socket. "There is a breeze to-night," she said: "it comes straight across from Kavak; it is quite cool upon the balcony."

"Yes, it is cooler to-night," her mother answered, "but you know that I do not like to have that window open. It makes a draught and the lamps smoke. Why even now, you see, little one, the shade is shaking——"; she pointed to the pink silk fringe which swayed gently against the lamp-light. "You see, little one?" she repeated.

"I see, mother," Eirene answered; "yes, it is better with that window closed, we can open the others upon the garden: the magnolia is not in flower yet, it will not give you a headache."

Her mother was lying on the sofa with the large lamp behind her: she was reading an illustrated paper, and the light cast across the page the oblique shadow of her piled and tidy hair. Eirene stood for a moment looking down upon her. She noted, half unconsciously, the unwonted gracelessness of her mother's pose, the stiff-sleeved elbows holding up the paper, the two tight-buttoned feet protruding rigidly upon the cushion. At her scrutiny the little white thumb that held the paper jerked in irritation. "May I play something?" asked Eirene.

"As you like, my little one," her mother answered, and she cut out irritably between the glossy pages of her paper. The sheets had stuck together. It was so damp there in the old house by the water.

Eirene turned back into the shadows of the wide, low room. The felt of her bedroom slippers made no noise upon the matting. She let her hands rest listlessly upon the cool lid of the piano.

She closed her eyelids and sought again to catch the thread of sensation which had begun to vibrate for her out there upon the balcony. Her mother's voice had snapped it suddenly; and yet, she remembered, it had been interesting, stimulating in a way; yes, even after she was back in the room she had felt a small fibre of her heart still glowing. It had not been a thought exactly; it had not been as definite as a thought, and yet it had possessed an outline. It had been distinct and stimulating, as a puff of night wind from the Black Sea: now she was gaining it again; the Black Sea, that sudden line of horizon between the two capes of Europe and of Asia. It was noon, and she had climbed up to the cliff, the cliff behind the garden, and she had lain down among the thyme and gum cistus; how silent it had been up there, how hot and silent—not even the trilling of the crickets in the sand! The sun beat down upon the soft and steaming hills, uniting everything into one fierce and intent monotone. The smell of crushed thyme startled the silence as the scream of a hawk. In the little village down there by the water the dogs lay panting in the shadows, twitching at the flies which clustered at the edges of their sores. Suddenly the clatter of a barrel-organ had sprung up from the quay-side; gaily, buoyantly it had soared up to her, some old Greek love song set to the swing and flutter of the Phrygian mode. On and on the tune had whirled, clean-cut against the captive somnolence of nature, presumptuous and virile, gay and unremitting. Eirene had laughed; a lizard, grey as its shadow on the stone, flicked back into the dappled bushes. Again Eirene laughed; shading her eyes she looked out to where the clear horizon of the Black Sea drew its cool line between the hills. How seldom she laughed! It was that, really, which had stirred her consciousness. She had been thinking of it on the balcony, when the breeze began to blow. Why could she not laugh—suddenly, defiantly, as the Greek tune had laughed? Her throat tightened for the experiment, and then relaxed. No, she would startle her mother. Her mother would say, "Mon Dieu! My child, how you startled me!" Her hand, quick at the exploitation of a grievance, would fly to her heart. "How you startled me!" her mother would say.

Eirene opened the lid of the piano, and her hands dropped gently upon the cool glimmer of the keys.

(II.)

It was always the same! Always the same procedure. They would come up together to the large sitting-room that stretched out over the water. The pink lamp would already have been lighted: Eirene would go to it and turn up the wick, while her mother settled down petulantly among the cushions of the sofa It was always the same!

Eirene did not resent that hour: it was perhaps the easiest of all they spent together. At the end she could escape; she knew that. She could escape to the little room with the magnolia outside. A few days now, and it would be scenting the whole garden. Already the buds glimmered like unlit candles among the leaves.

Eirene sat there at the piano, pressing aimless chords, waiting for the moment of release She thought of her own little room with a stir of affection. Her gentle little room, where she was safe and alone. A locked door. Her little room that loved and understood her. Since it shared the secret.

The thought of the secret! A warm and intimate pulse twitched suddenly within her heart; yes, there was always the secret. Mother did not know of that; it was her secret and father's, and it came at night, there in her own little room, her own, own little room, when mother was asleep. Mother asleep! A stilled, unusual mother.

For years now Eirene had nursed the secret. For seven years since that fierce year of anguish when her father died. It had come gradually during those long nights when she had lain in bed, the sheet tight between her shivering teeth. She had been sent away to Moda when her father fell ill. And then one morning they had called for her, and taken her up to the town house in Pera, into the corner room which looked out upon the sunset.

The sun was flaming that evening when she entered; it made two oblong patches of red upon the wall opposite. Her father was in pain, but he had smiled at her; she remembered the creases of the smile cutting down from the eyelid And then a sudden spasm had seized him, and he had flung his head back into the pillow, his teeth clutching at his lower lip. He had smiled at her again when it was over. He had said: "Well, enjoy yourself, Meirene!" That was his name for her. Then they had taken her away; the cab had rattled down to the quay, and she had gone back to Moda.

How well she remembered it all! It must have been in April, for the Judas trees were in blossom. Her aunt had come in early in her dressing-gown, and had drawn the curtains. She had taken her hand and she had said: "I have bad news for you, dear. You must be brave." That was how she had heard of it. She had said to herself: "Your father is dead, Eirene, and they will put him in a wooden box in the ground, and people are sorry for you. They call you 'dear,' and they stop talking when you come into the room."

Sweet Waters

It was all a dream; it wasn't true. The real Eirene did not believe it. It was only that pale girl who wore black gloves and came in and out of rooms who believed all they said. Eirene, the real Eirene, knew that it wasn't true.

They had all stood there in the British cemetery at Haidar Pasha, and there were little red and white tulips in the grass. Eirene had looked out between the cypresses to where the gulls screamed and fought for the garbage which floated in long lines upon the oily sea. There were three barges in a row, and there were men working in them, emptying the dustbins of the city on the waters. And the gulls wheeled and flapped. Also, there was a steamer that came in from Europe. It swung quickly round the Point and on into the Golden Horn. Some of the gulls followed it, and mother cried. She had a black edge to her handkerchief.

It was only afterwards that it had all come to her. Weeks afterwards, when she had joined her mother at Therapia. At Pera, in the town house, it had been different. The Pera house, at the corner there where the trams scream at the bend down to the Petits Champs, was mother's house; it was never *theirs:* it was not a house which belonged to her or father. No, it was mother's house, the large foreign drawing-room with the parquet and the gilt furniture. It meant winter, and heavy curtains and a closed stove and silver things on the sideboard: it meant rain upon the sodden pavements and people in coats and umbrellas and a fierce bar of sunset at tea-time behind Stamboul. Therapia was different. Therapia was spring and the sound of water; and then summer, with the thunder grumbling over the forest of Belgrade. That was the real home, the place where she would meet father at the landing-stage when he came home in the evening. They would walk back along the quay and watch for porpoises. It was at Therapia that it all began to hurt so terribly. It was there that those long white nights of agony had come to her, night after night, as she lay there damp and shivering, the hot sheet between her teeth. It was at Therapia that she had found the secret. She sat there by the piano thinking back on all these things, and a faint smile drooped at the corners of her mouth.

(III.)

Her mother laid down her magazine and raised the weight of her hair with the paper-cutter. She yawned openly. Eirene glanced at her and looked away: she did not like to see her mother ugly.

"Come here, little one," her mother said, "I wish to speak to you."

Eirene closed the piano carefully and crossed the room. Her dark hair seemed to touch the ceiling as she walked. She knelt down beside the sofa, repressing the familiar recoil evoked by her mother's arm upon her shoulders. Her mother's voice was gentle, almost insinuating: she stroked Eirene's shoulder as she spoke. "Tell me, little one," she said, "tell me: yesterday, when you came in—yesterday afternoon you remember; you stood in the doorway before we noticed you—before I noticed you. But tell me, little one, did you see anything?—tell your mamma."

"What do you mean, mother? When I came in from tennis? When M. Paniotis was here? I noticed that he was shy when I came in: he is generally so polite."

The hand on her shoulder gave two quick little taps in succession. "My good little Eirene. That is well. I had broken my brooch, and Paniotis was trying to mend it. See, little one, it is there, the brooch, on that table. You see that it is broken?"

"I see, mother——"

Her mother rose and turned down the lamp. Eirene kissed her on the temple where the hair sprang from the forehead. "Good-night, mother." "Good-night, little one"—and then, stridently, in Greek—"Eléni, we are going to bed: you can close the windows."

Eirene took her little lamp outside in the passage and went slowly to her room. "Had she noticed anything?" How strange that mother should have ventured such a question!

And in the lower room, the room that was underneath the drawing-room and looked upon the sea, her mother stood clutching her little jewelled fists in nervous irritation. "Quelle dinde," she was murmuring, "toucher à vingt ans, et être dinde à ce point là! Franchement!"

(IV.)

The secret had first come to Eirene, suddenly, almost accidentally, at the end of a sleepless night some months after her father's death. She had come back to Therapia, and in a drawer of the little table where the smaller lamp stood she had found an old cartridge case made into a pencil. She remembered how her father had shown it to her on his return one year from Salonica. They had been on the small steamer coming up from the town: he had pulled it out from his waistcoat pocket and had shown it to her.

"Look, Meirene, this was made by prisoners," and he pulled out the bullet to show her the pencil within. It had given her a pang when he was gone to find it thus again forgotten in the drawer. She had slipped it hurriedly into her pocket, and the same evening she had locked it away with her other treasures in an Italian box in her bedroom. And one hot night of misery she had taken it to bed with her, clinging to it with fevered fingers, clinging to it through her sobs. And then the secret had stolen in upon her. An impression of sudden concentration, an impression of increased identity, and of herself rising rigid through mists to something unrealised but clear. Almost at once her father stood beside her. She knew him because he took her hand and interlocked their fingers. Only father did that, and his fingers were strong and hard. It was not more than that at first; not more than the knowledge that he was there and she could speak to him. Nothing else would happen at first, except the feeling of warmth and security and father. And then the gentle anodyne of sleep.

During those seven years—those seven adolescent years—the ritual of Eirene's secret had become more complex. Gradually, as the mists cleared, she would find herself always at the same place, out there on the hilltop at Tchamludja, above Scutari. She had been there once with father. They had climbed up together to the pine trees on the summit, and they had sat by the old tomb looking down upon the meeting of the seas, upon the great city, immobile amid its waters, and out beyond the islands to where Olympus wavered as a cloud above the lower mountains. Impulsively he had taken her hand and locked her fingers. He had turned her to the north and to the west, to the east and to the south. "Look, Meirene," he had said, "up there is Thrace and all the Balkans, and there across the seas is Europe, and England right away there in the corner. You understand, Meirene, your England, my England; and there behind the hills is where the Russians live; but look you here, Eirene, look you at this red road below. That, Meirene, that is the red road to Baghdad."

It was up there always that she met him now, under the little group of pine trees beside the Turkish tomb. And she had nursed the secret, her own intimate ceremony: carefully she had nursed it; screened it, not against her mother merely—that primary and most instinctive defence—but against the world; even against her own indulgence. . . .

"Had she noticed anything?" Her mother's question echoed in her ears, disquieting and sinister. She put down the lamp and let her hair fall loose upon her shoulders: the call of the frogs quivered up from the garden. "Had she noticed anything?"—the water lapped upon the quay. The wind had turned to the south, so gently to the south—and it had set the current lapping against the stones.

Her curtain swung softly against the open windows: yes, the wind had gone south, it carried a breath of fever to the room: the cry of the frogs was insistent, querulous; could nothing still the menace of the frogs? She knew what they were saying. The frogs screamed, "Did you see it?" and the water lisped at her; it lisped, "What did you see?" And then the wind came warm and insidious to her very room: it came to spy on her, and there was none to help. Still standing there she fumbled for the key of the Italian box: she wore it on a ribbon at her neck, and it was still warm as she fitted it into the lock. She drew out the cartridge case and thrust it beneath her pillow. Even then the chill of fear remained with cold consistency beneath the fever of her skin. How slowly the veils began to lift! As the pine trees of Tchamludja swam down to her, she saw that they were bent and straining in a phantom wind.

"Father!" she screamed, "Father!" and something laughed, and then she felt the smell of his rough coat and clung to it. "Oh, father, I was frightened!" but he did not answer her. He took her by the shoulders and bent her downwards, he forced her downwards till she fell upon her knees, and still downwards, till the wind-swept heather brushed and rattled in her eyes. He came close to her, his lips came close to her ear. "Did you notice anything, my little one, did you notice anything?" and the trees howled and laughed again.

She woke and stretched with shaking fingers for the light.

She rose and hitched her dressing-gown from the bed. It was the first time he had failed her.

The first time the secret had failed. The window was still open, and she leaned out into the night. The moon had risen above the hills. "Had she noticed anything?" She turned and flung herself sobbing upon the bed.

"I saw it!" she sobbed. "I saw it! I saw it all!"

(V.)

Eirene woke next morning to find the wind, the soft, wet wind, still panting from the south; the little waves beyond the lip of the French Embassy chopped and sparkled in the current. A thin mist hung about the lower reaches of the garden, but already the higher branches of the plane tree stood up clear and sparkling in the sun. She dressed dreamily, noting these things as in a haze; while within her, as a lesser weight upon her heart, was the consciousness that something warm and infinitely precious had been lost. She walked across, still dressing, into the drawing-room. The east windows, looking towards Buyukdere, flung their bright square across the matting. Soon, she knew, the south windows upon the water would catch the sun, and then Eléni would go out upon the balcony and close the shutters. The room would become dark and silent then; only the smell of lilac. She went out on to the balcony and gazed across towards the gap where the Black Sea showed its sudden horizon between the capes of Asia and of Europe. Eirene loved that line of cool horizon; it gave her confidence and courage: it was clear and hard and straight, it was not curved, or veiled or shimmering like the rest: it opened vistas, it was not enclosed, not captive. Yes, that was it, her world was captive—a prisoner to its own soft loveliness. There was no escape, and no wish to escape—no will for anything. Only the barrel-organ beside the quay-side had possessed the courage. Courage! Had father possessed courage? He had been too gay for that: courage was a stern and glowering quality. It meant doing hard things quickly: it meant being very unhappy, and rigid and contradictory. One could keep the secret safe from mother; that was not courage. It was self-defence. Eirene leaned out over the water. Already she could see the little steamer leaving the landing stage at Buyukdere, its smoke black against the green hill of the Russian Embassy. Soon it would be lost to sight behind the corner, and then suddenly it would appear again, quite close now to the balcony, and one would see the people on the decks, the red fezes, the baskets in their hands. So close, in fact, that she would hear the engine-room bell tinkle to the stoppage signal as it approached the pier at Therapia. And then, the smoke trailing back upon itself, it would drift away round the corner on its own impetus, the paddles suspended and dripping, and there would again be silence; and in a few minutes a figure or two, and then three more, basket-laden, coming back along the quay below. Eirene stood looking out upon this familiar morning scéne, the stillness and the movement of it all, trying to force herself to go to her mother's bedroom and face the ordeal of the daily encounter.

Since she was quite small Eirene had always dreaded these morning visits. They entailed, she knew, some grievance which the morning letters had brought, some old complaint, repeated volubly, her fluttering attention pinioned by the endless "You hear, little one? You hear what I am saying?" Always Eirene would leave those interviews with a sense of defeat, with a sense of revolt and contradiction surging but suppressed, with a heavy consciousness of weakness and humiliation. Her mother would appear indeed to be feverishly busy at these early hours, to resent Eirene's visit as an interruption. And yet the visit had become a ritual which neither thought of breaking. Eirene would pause outside the door, and in her low voice would say: "May I come in, mother?" And always her mother would appear surprised at her coming and a little irritated. Eirene would cross to the window and look down upon the water splashing nearer now than in the drawing-room above. It was always the same.

With slow feet she descended the wide staircase, and knocked at her mother's door. The voice from within was brittle with irritation. "Oh, come in, my little one; you are early, are you not?"

"Oh no, mother, it is past ten."

"So late as that? But how pale you are! Why, you look ill, my child. You are black under the eyes."

Listlessly Eirene went to the window. She sat down on the little sofa there with the pink ribbons. Her mother was reading the local paper. "I see that the French are coming up late this year. They are not coming till next week. The English must be coming sooner. That young Secretary with the long legs rode over yesterday and went back by the steamer. He has left his ponies."

Already the sun was creeping round to the southern windows. Eirene could feel the woodwork warm beneath her touch. "I shall go out," she said, "I shall go up to the village."

"Go out?" her mother echoed. "In this heat? To see Emily, I suppose? To see your aunt? What a strange idea, little one! Comme elle m'agace, cette femme! No, my little one, it would be better for you to remain indoors this morning."

The newspaper rattled ominously. Eirene crossed to the door. "I shall go out," she repeated, "I shall go up to the village. I shall see Aunt Emily." Eirene closed the door. She carried with her an impression of her mother's delicate and painted eyebrows raised for a moment in astonishment. The impression made her smile. A hard smile. Unlike Eirene.

(VI.)

She turned to the right along the burning quay, past the French Embassy and round to where the village clustered down to the little harbour, a group of wooden Turkish houses, disreputable in contrast to the white façade of the hotel glaring up there upon the hill-side behind its fringe of pines. The walls that flanked the quay threw back the heat quivering upon the dust of the road. The village street was empty even at that early hour, and the sun-blinds of the café were continued to the ground by hanging curtains, which, as they swayed in the wind, gave glimpses of blue syphons dotted upon the shadowed green tables. Eirene turned round the corner of the café to climb the hill. The little lane between the walls felt cool and damp after the white glow of the quay-side. Halfway up the hill she stopped at a gateway in a wall with steps up to it. She groped for the bell among the wisteria. "Madame was in," they said, and she climbed the steps on to the terrace garden.

She found her aunt sitting in the vine arbour at the edge of the terrace. The work-basket and the scissors were spread upon the green top of the tin table. Her aunt had fixed a length of holland into the sewing-machine, and glanced up, her hand suspended on the wheel, as she heard Eirene's step upon the path. Eirene had come intent upon her purpose: she kissed her aunt perfunctorily and sat down beside her. "Aunt Emily," she said, "I want to talk to you. I want to talk to you about mother."

The little fat woman by her side twitched from her like a startled wren: the mottled hand fluttered down to the length of holland. Then she twitched back again, and her small eyes darted sideways at Eirene, the head inclined away from her, at once furtive and inquisitive. "About your mother, dear? But what about her? Your mother is still a lovely woman. And such a figure, as I always say."

"No, it's not that, Aunt Emily. I know all that. You see, I want to *help* mother. You know how fond I am of her; you know what we are to each other. She is all I have—she and you—Aunt Emily."

Her aunt began to turn the handle of her

machine, her eyes steady for once and fixed upon the fabric as she guided it under the needle. "Go on, my dear," she murmured, "tell me all your trouble."

Eirene hesitated for a moment. Her eyes were fixed on the little strip of horizon, visible always, even up here at her aunt's villa, between the vine leaves and the roof of the houses below. "You see," she continued at last, "you see, Aunt Emily, there is so much that I do not know about. There are so many things which one can't say to mother, or even ask her. It is not that I don't understand her. I know exactly what makes her cross, and what she really means when she says things. I know all that. But I can't talk to her as I talk to you, Aunt Emily. I try sometimes, and then she looks surprised and asks me what's the matter. I tell her nothing's the matter, and she picks up a book, and then it's all over. It's so difficult to begin again. She calls me 'my little one.' It's silly, when I'm so tall. And she makes me curtsey to Ferid Pasha when he comes as though I were in the schoolroom. And then I get on her nerves, I think. Yes, I know I get on her nerves. I can hear her tapping the cover of her book when I am talking to her. If I talk she becomes irritable, and if I'm silent she says that I sulk. She is restless when I am with her. What can I do, Aunt Emily? Is it my fault?"

Her aunt turned the wheel a little faster, and bent down carefully to readjust the fabric as it puckered under the needle. "You're frightened of her, of course," she mumbled, keeping her eyes away from her niece.

Eirene raised her head slowly, gazing out to the Black Sea. "I don't think it's that, Aunt

Emily. Not now. Not lately. She's so small and slim and delicate. And I'm so tall. You see, she gets so nervous about things, and I give way. It helps her for me not to explain things. She hates explanations. She doesn't understand them. She so often blames me for what I haven't done, and if I explain there is a scene. She says I am being impertinent. So I say nothing, and then she quiets down and is nice again. No, I don't think it's fear exactly—not exactly fear. It's habit, I think. And then I hate noise. You know what a noise mother makes when she's angry. Her voice screams at one: it gets hoarse and shrill and grates all at the same time. You see, you don't know mother really: you so seldom see her: you don't understand. You're not on good terms with mother."

"Your mother's a woman of great charm, my dear. I always say so. I say 'Zoe, my sister-in-law, is a beautiful woman. You may say what you like about her, but she has great charm.' I always say that. Of course, she's Greek and you're English, like your dear father—all except the looks of you. And the laziness. But you're your father's daughter through it all, my dear. Your dear father——" And Aunt Emily's voice trembled a little as she bent to readjust the cotton.

"She's so kind, sometimes," Eirene continued. "You remember when she went to Paris last winter? She brought me such pretty things back with her—she brought me this parasol. And then she's so thoughtless sometimes, so, so—*cruel!* She threw my stick into the water. Father's stick with the horn handle. She snatched it from me suddenly and flung it into the sea; it sank because of the handle. And she was angry. You know how her arms twitch when she's angry. It was dreadful that day. I screamed at her; I screamed —'You beast!' and her eyes fluttered; I think that for a moment she was ashamed."

Eirene paused; her mouth set in a sudden firmness; her voice as she continued had a lilt of triumph; her aunt stopped and snatched a timid glance between her eyelids. "No, not ashamed exactly," Eirene went on, "I think she was surprised; yes, surprised and—afraid." The last word fell like a challenge on the hot air. Aunt Emily bent nervously to her work, and for a space there was silence.

"And then, the other afternoon, when I came back from the village, I had left my purse in the drawing-room, and I ran upstairs: it was dark, and the shutters were closed: all the shutters were closed—it was dark in the room——" Eirene checked herself, disconcerted by the wave of shame that had risen to her cheek. Her aunt was leaning forward, the little face turned eagerly towards Eirene: the eyes behind their sparse lashes blinked eagerly; her lips were open.

"Go on, my dear," she whispered, "go on, my dearest one—tell Auntie of your trouble."

Eirene looked down at her aunt, shocked instinctively by her vehemence, by the sudden curiosity that had lighted in that vague and shambling face. She recoiled from her; she put a firm hand upon her shoulder. "Oh no, Aunt Emily. I can't go on. It's wrong of me to tell you. It was all so horrible, so—horrible—so——" she hid her face shuddering.

The machine was turning again now faster and faster, and as it turned Aunt Emily began to whimper a little: "My poor child," she murmured, "your dear father——" She snuffled—

and the steel of the needle quivered into the stuff as it was pushed tremblingly along the slide. Eirene stretched out a puzzled hand.

"Aunt Emily," she said, "Aunt Emily, what has happened? You're trembling. Oh, Aunt Emily, I've made you cry—I am so sorry—please stop, Aunt Emily," and she clutched the little arm that turned the wheel. Her aunt dropped her hands into her lap and lay back panting. And then suddenly she became very odd indeed; she swung round at Eirene, and her little face flashed into a glint of courage. She gripped her niece above the knees and leant forward: "Look here, Eirene," she panted, "you are afraid of her: afraid, and you hate her. Yes, you do, child, you hate her—hate her—hate her!" Her voice grated to a higher key. "You hate her—and, by God, so do I!"

Eirene rose slowly and as in a dream walked down the path, shutting the gate behind her.

CHAPTER II.

July

(I.)

THE little ferry boat swung out from the landing stage at Candili and beat across to the European side, catching the full glitter of the current as it passed the shelter of the Point. Even at that early hour it was hot under the awnings. Angus Field rose and thrust his note-book into his pocket. He watched the blue smoke of his pipe float out into the sunlight between the stays of the awning. He sat down again on the bench that ran along the taffrail. From time to time the paddles stopped, and the boat, lurching for a few minutes against a landing-stage, would be off again, breasting the current. He drew his note-book from his pocket and turned the pages. He had tried to write last night. It was prose that he had tried to write, something "which might come in useful later." It had begun all right; at first he had been pleased with it. It would certainly come in useful. He had read the beginning aloud to himself, and it had sounded well enough; a little self-conscious, perhaps, and a little precious; but he could continue in a simpler vein. He could conclude on a firm note of creation. He re-read the beginning. The thing had become involved; the heavy music of the opening sentences had thrown an atmosphere of metrics over the rest: the words grouped themselves into blank verse. He coped with this at first by adding syllables here and there to break the scansion. Then he read it out again, and it read like trochaics. "'Locksley Hall,'" he murmured, "Damn!" And he clipped and patted the words and read it a third time. It was all wrong; it drawled in places, and in places it snapped at one. And yet it was something that he had really wanted to say—to put into words. "No good to-night," he had said to himself, "read it to-morrow on the boat."

The pages fluttered a little in the draught; he held them down together with his thumb. He found the passage he wanted, scribbled over with corrections. He looked up under the awning. They were approaching Bebek. Yes, there would still be time to read it again before he reached Therapia. He smoothed the pages. He whispered it to himself:—

> "Oh Languor of the East, to what sad lute you tune your lethargy! Oh subtle apathy, with what soft touch you steal upon our strength! Twelve amber beads upon a silken string, a puff of spices in a narrow lane, a lilting song flung suddenly across the water. Oh, lambent East, and all our wisdom, all our courage purposeless!
>
> "Oh padded silence of the East! Your sanded ways, unhedged, unheeding: a world untenanted, and there above, your somnolent stars; a jackal's cry; a speck of fire high up upon the mountain; and in the dawn the wheel of vultures, the water oxen wallowing in the reeds.
>
> "Oh patience of the East! Timeless and secure: and we outside who fumble through the busy-fingered years: we thrust and wound

and whimper; and you smile to know that we, like you, shall come upon decay.

"Oh wisdom of the East, that saps our doctrines!

"Oh squalor of the East, that mocks at our array.

"Oh deleterious East! You hold us gently as you suck our veins; you seize upon us and you lull, and pander. Your soft wings beat about us, somnolent.

"Oh various East! To some you open as the great adventure; for some you shine as freedom; others yearn after you as peace beyond their dangerous world; you lure the curious, you entice the young. But, East, you catch the dross of us, you do not keep the gold.

"Oh Ignorant East!

"We know, we understand! We fear the poison of your opiates, and we are wise. A summer day, no more you hold us; for we resist, oh ignorant East.

"For we, oh languorous East, are strong!

"Oh, slothful East, you cannot enter ——"

He turned the page. There was more upon the other side. The end bit, he remembered, was the part where he had begun to write more simply. But the beginning! "Precious!" he said to himself, "that's what it is. Futile! Worse than Wilde." And he tore it viciously from the book. The little pieces fluttered along the deck, caught for an instant, and then disappeared. The ship breasted the Point at Yenikeui, and with a wide and practised swing sidled up to the wooden landing-stage at Therapia.

Mechanically the two sailors on the pier fitted the wet loop of the hawser round the bollards. The dripping rope strained for a second and then slacked. The gangway was run out on to the planks, and in a moment the little floating platform was crowded with a rush of passengers.

Angus knocked out his pipe, and, thrusting his tattered note-book back into his pocket, went down to the lower deck, joining the end of the crowd upon the gangway.

(II.)

It was not till he set foot upon the gangway that he saw Eirene. Their eyes met across the crowd that seethed between them: "An Englishman," she said to herself; and her look rested on him with a momentary interest. There was a press at the barrier; people were fumbling for their tickets; and as the crowd struggled out through the office on to the quay Angus and Eirene approached the wicket together. He made a motion to allow her to precede him; he murmured a few words in French. She answered with a smile, in English, but as she stepped behind him the smile checked itself with a sharp intake of her breath. A sudden giddiness. Something so strange had clutched upon her heart: a pang had come upon her, a pang of startling intimacy, at once familiar and remote. All this had happened before. She closed her eyes, her brain hung suspended—the mist; there was a mist upon the waters, but up there at Tchamludja the sky was cool and gentle: the trunks of the pine trees glimmered in the sun, and the road shone below them, the red road to Baghdad. She reeled back against the gangway: he turned and saw her vacant eyes, her opened lips. He noted the clear line of her teeth, the pale olive profile against the blue. He stopped and turned to her.

"You are not feeling queer at all, are you?" he asked. "You are feeling quite well?"

With a sweep of her dark lashes she returned to consciousness. She laughed a little nervous laugh. "I am quite well, thank you," she said; they came out together into the sunshine.

Eirene hesitated. "You are going to the Embassy," she said: "we can walk together. I live in the house beyond."

"Oh yes, of course," he answered, "you live in the other house," and they turned along the quay together, walking slowly in the glare of the white houses and the dust.

It was Angus who broke the silence. "I have seen you once before," he said, "but from a distance. My name is Angus Field. I work at the Embassy for the moment, till I can get a post up-country. I keep their beastly papers for them."

She did not answer him. Surely this had all happened before? He was so familiar, so intimate. He belonged to the other side. He belonged to the secret. Angus was talking easily as they went along. "Yes, I found a cottage out at Candili. Quite a rough place, of course, but rooms are so expensive at Therapia. And one gets more air there, I think, don't you? Certainly one gets more air."

They were passing the French Embassy, and his voice lowered a semitone as it resounded under the wide eaves stretching across the narrow strip of quay. She forced herself to say something. "Then you stay up all day and go back in the evening?"

"Oh yes," he answered, "I bring sandwiches with me and I go up to the top of the hill; I lunch there; there is a spring, you know, and one sees through the trees and out to the Black Sea. The spring comes out of a rock. It's a jolly place."

"Oh, I know," Eirene answered. "Our own garden runs up next to it, and we've got the key. I get water from the spring when I have tea in our summer-house. There is a gate, you know, and Sir Henry gave my father the key. I have always kept it."

They passed the main door of the Embassy and paused beside the further gateway on the point where the Secretaries' House stood in its own garden, a *pendant* to Eirene's own. The Chancery was on the ground floor. He swung in awkwardly between the gate-posts.

"So long," he said.

She smiled and said, "Good-bye."

(III.)

The Bosphorus flows from Black Sea to Marmora, as a river twisting out and in between the wooded banks of Asia and of Europe. On each side the Bithynian and the Thracian downlands soften suddenly as they reach its gentle valley and fringe their crude limbs with pine and ilex, with fig and Judas tree, slipping thence softly to the water's edge. The teeming city at the river's mouth has flung its tentacles along the shores. At first but a continuance of the city itself, stuccoed, terraced, and tram-infected: a mosque here and there; a white palace here and there, the current drawing blue lines across its reflection; and then the villas and the villages begin: little clustering homes by the water-side; a landing-stage built out on rotting piles; a plane tree on the village square; the glint of marble fountains, and then the paddle-boat swings out again, zigzagging from shore to shore across the stream. A road runs along the quay-side; a road narrow and unparapeted; at moments, so close to the water that the wash of the larger steamers splashes the little cabs that jingle by; at moments cutting off a headland, it passes under the reverberation of a tunnelled arch. The smell of lilac and laburnum, the pungent smell of burning sage, the smell of frying butter, the smell of fresh-cut cypress wood, the smell of vanilla, the smell of open drains. And at the end one comes to Therapia, backed by its low hills and wooded gardens, and beyond Therapia the Bosphorus sways out into a bay, as if a lake, closing abruptly into the twin bare peaks, their surf-flecked rocks, the old Symplegades, joined by the sharp line of the Black Sea.

Upon the narrow lip of land that lies between the quay-side and the terraced gardens glitter the Embassies of the Great Powers, the villas of the richer Europeans: a strange community, isolated and important, polyglot and yet united by a common function. And there among these gay and gracious companions, stands the other house, Eirene's home, an old Turkish house of bleaching wood, rising in three untidy tiers above the lowest storey.

The face of it stood flush with the quay-side, the first storey projecting sharply above the square, grated windows of the ground floor, and the topmost storey, in its turn, pushing a balcony out on wide struts above the water. The garden wall continuing the line of the ground floor, was pierced here and there by old iron gratings, and by the entrance gate on the left flush with the house. The western windows looked down upon the square of level garden, with the big plane tree, the magnolia, and the terra-cotta fountain tinkling in its circle of parched grass. Her mother did not care about the garden. Eirene preferred the hill behind. There were some dusty roses on the wall, and a stunted ceanothus. It was not a successful garden. Behind it rose the hill, ilex and Judas tree, and at the top the little summer-house which her father had built for Eirene with his hands. "Our summer-house" he had called it, and one evening he had brought some cretonne down from Pera, and they had nailed it upon the boards. And he had made a cupboard for the corner.

They dined at seven, the mother and the daughter, alone together at the table under the big plane tree in the garden. It would be damp of an evening and the wood of the old table was soft and porous to the touch. There was a sheet of oil-cloth between the yellow diapered cover and the wood, and as the meal wore on it would begin to coil upwards, bulging the linen cloth below the table.

Her mother ate nervously, but not fastidiously. At least, not when they were alone together. They were generally alone. She picked at a dish of olives by her side, dropping the furry stones one by one into her finger-bowl. The water clouded. The trick was one that irritated Eirene. She had had the courage the other night to protest against it; her mother had raised pencilled eyebrows and puffed a cloud of cigarette smoke at Eirene; a strange, defiant gesture; almost coy. Eirene had been surprised; it was a surprising thing for mother to have done. A different atmosphere; a sudden rift in the clouded monotone of their relationship; a vista of something else. Eirene had registered that gesture at the time; she had analysed it afterwards; she had asked herself why, exactly, it had filled her with surprise, why it had opened as it were a sudden rift of blue in the bank of clouds. A little puff of cigarette smoke in her face. A defiant puff; that was not wholly odd. A petulant puff; that was customary. But a coy, feminine puff: yes, that was the facet which had filled her with surprise. She knew the gesture well enough. She had seen it often. It was thus, sometimes, that her mother would counter the glutinous compliments of Paniotis. And of the others. It was part of the other mother, the drawing-room mother: it went with the cigarettes, and the little French shoes, and the big bottle of scent and the long doe-skin gloves. It was not part of the mother Eirene knew, the dressing-gown mother, the bedroom-slipper mother, the strident, yawning mother, who picked her teeth. Yes, that was it, mother had puffed her cigarette at Eirene as she would have puffed it at someone else: at some man, probably; at someone on whom she wished to exercise her charm. Mother had charm, everybody said so. Eirene was proud of it. She admired it. Eirene had no charm: she was a "lump," her mother had told her so. A lump physically and morally. "Dieu," her mother would say, "être cruche à ce point là!" It was a pity. Poor Eirene! No charm, poor girl, and so conspicuous! Her thoughts wandered off again upon their lonely road. Her analysis of the incident with the olive stones had come to no conclusion.

(IV.)

Her mother dropped the end of her cigarette into the cup of coffee by her side. It spluttered for a moment, leaving a thin scent of caramel upon the air. She stretched herself and looked at Eirene. She looked at her curiously, with an air of investigation.

"Tell me," she began, "who was that man you were walking with this morning upon the quay? I could not see him properly."

There was no irritation in her voice, a note only of curiosity. "His name is Field, mother, Angus Field. He keeps the papers at the Embassy. He's a clerk of some sort. He's not a regular secretary. He has a soft coat like father's." She spoke mechanically in her level voice, but her own last words sent a little wire of thought vibrating within her. "A soft coat like father's?" Could *that* be it? The smell of Irish tweed in the sun? Yes, that was it—of course; the sense of intimacy, the feeling that it had all happened before. The feeling that he belonged to the secret. "How grotesque!" she said to herself, and endeavoured to dismiss it. But it would not be dismissed. She half-closed her eyes and saw again the line of his neck above the collar. His hair grew down so silkily until it reached the line of his neck, and then it stopped abruptly, and the skin below was sunburnt. The smell of tweed in the sun? How silly of Eirene! How mawkish! Father had worn a coat like that the time he had taken her shooting to the gulf of Ismid. It had rained and they had sat huddled together under a rock. He had told her stories. The smell of wet tweed! He had told her stories of the Iliad and the Odyssey and he had recited certain lines in Greek: he had accented it like modern Greek: she had caught a word here and there which she recognised, words like "foam" and "wind," and "wine-dark sea." She had laughed at that.

Her mother was speaking again. "He is not one of the Secretaries then? He is not really of the Embassy? Tell me, tell me, little one, he is a gentleman, is he not?"

"How should I know, mother? I only spoke a few words to him. We came off the boat together. He speaks French differently from most Englishman. He is quite poor. He sleeps at Candili; he has a house there, a cottage. Quite a rough little place, but rooms are so expensive at Therapia. He comes up here on the steamer."

There was more, of course: there was the bit about his having luncheon up there above the cliff in the Embassy garden. The place where the ilexes stopped, and the spring shot out over the big stone. She did not tell her mother about that. That was part of the other side: it was part of the secret. One never told mother things about the other side.

Her mother was speaking again. "I think it foolish of you," she began, "to talk like that to a strange man upon the quay, where everyone can see you. He is not even of the corps diplomatique.

You must not speak to him again. Do you understand, little one? You are to pass him next time as though you had never spoken."

"I see, mother," Eirene answered. It was the old habit. The habit of acquiescence: it was no use explaining to mother. She would get angry, especially if she were in the wrong. This time she was not in the wrong: she was in the right.

"I see, mother," Eirene answered with sullen eyes. And then she continued. Something within her made her continue. Just to annoy mother: just to see what would happen: to see whether this time Eirene could be brave and defiant like the barrel-organ had been brave. "But you are wrong," she began, "but he is not a strange man, you know. I have spoken often to him before. I have met him often up there above the hill in the Embassy garden. His name is Angus Field. I go up there when you are having a siesta."

Her mother was looking surprised and flurried all at once. And *interested*. She was not getting angry. It was silly of Eirene to tell lies like that. She had only meant to be defiant, and mother had believed her. Mother was looking interested. It was very disconcerting. Eirene blundered further on the road.

"And I have arranged to go up there to-morrow. I am to meet him to-morrow while you are asleep, mother."

She paused: there was a little smile on her mother's face. A smile of understanding; a half-smile of confederacy. Eirene was puzzled: she felt her feet sinking in a morass. The only way to get back to land was for mother to be natural, to get angry.

"And I am not a child, mother, I am grown up now. You have no right to interfere. You have no right. . . ." Even that did not make mother angry. It was all very disconcerting and futile, and unnecessary. Mother was almost pleased. And it hadn't been true. How silly of Eirene! What a fool's road to have embarked upon. Not necessary, not dignified.

"Petite méchante, va!" Her mother's laugh rang out under the tree. "But be careful, Eirene, do not go too far. Be careful, little one."

That was the end. A bungled performance. Eirene did not understand how it had been so bungled. Mother had disconcerted her; Eirene had acquiesced at first. Generally mother became irritated when one acquiesced. This time she had sat there, a little puzzled, a little interested, and *pleased.* Yes, she had enjoyed it. Not amused; no, mother was never amused, exactly, by that sort of thing. Mother was only amused by physical things: not by mental processes. She had laughed when the horse fell into the sea. *How* she had laughed that time! She had lain back in the chair with her legs thrust out straight in front of her, and she had laughed and laughed. "O! Mon Dieu! Mon Dieu! La tête qu'il fait! Regarde donc! la tête!" Helplessly she had laughed. It had puzzled Eirene. Eirene was sorry for the horse. She had looked at her mother puzzled and disapproving.

No, mother could not have been amused. She must have thought it true what Eirene said about meeting that young man. It wasn't true. Never, never could she see him again after having lied like that. She would pass him next time as if they had never spoken. She would be very cold and proud and distant.

Yes, *that* was a consolation. That was something she could do. How provoking of mother to have put her in a false position like that! She had made up the story to annoy, and it had failed in its object. She was left with the story, with mother's acceptance of the story, on her hands. How *could* mother? How *could* she? But mother was like that: she had no self-respect. Only vanity, vanity. Well, Eirene was above that sort of thing. Why should she mind what mother thought? What did it matter? She would go up there to-morrow, through the gate at the top of the garden. She would go up just to show that it didn't matter; that she didn't care.

One had one's pride.

(V.)

The little wooden house which Angus Field had rented for the summer lay round the point of Candili, nestling into the fig trees between the water and the hill. The sun had already set when he climbed the path from the landing-stage and rapped with his cane upon the door. His servant opened it; he held it open, a black outline against the gleam of the six windows beyond. Angus spoke to him in Turkish: "It is too late to bathe to-night, Hamsa, I shall dine at once. You can light the lamp."

He went on into the room and stood leaning

against the window. The Bosphorus shimmered green and purple in the afterglow. Angus murmured to himself as he changed into his slippers: "I shall write to-night. I shall remodel what I tore up this morning. I feel it in me to-night." It was dark in the room, but the windows still gleamed like white sheets against the water. Above the hill opposite a single star throbbed through the haze, and in the distance the spires of Stamboul were pencilled against the gleaming West. The lights of the ferry-boat crossing from Ortakeui to Scutari clustered close together, tremulous in the hot air. The fireflies flitted between the fig trees and the oleanders. Angus leant there against the window.

Yes, certainly he would write to-night. "Oh, Languor of the East. . . ." the phrases were beginning to regroup themselves in his memory. He reached for a pencil, and wrote it down, "to what low lutes you tune your threnody." No, it was "lethargy" that he had said at first. He made the correction. He scribbled "lambent" between "Oh" and "Languor," and then he read it against the failing light, waving a slim hand to mark the cadences. "Oh, lambent Languor of the East, to what low lutes you tune your lethargy?" It didn't seem to scan; or was it that it scanned too well? And had it been "low" lutes that morning, or "sad" lutes? He would try "grim" lutes. Angus always had a liking for the word "grim." But could a lute be grim? And what did "lambent" mean? The Bosphorus down there was definitely lambent. He was not sure. He must be careful not to use words for their sound alone. Mallarmé had done that in poetry, but Angus was no good at poetry. But he could write prose. *Could* he write prose? How dead it seemed the moment he had written it! But there was more to come. He must try again after dinner. He was tired now. Perhaps, after all, it would have been better to have had a bathe.

He sat down discouraged at the table. He opened a book under the lamp and read while he ate: if he did not do this he felt he had to talk to Hamsa, and the prospect irritated him. He had some beer. He felt better after that. And a glass of Benedictine. By the time Hamsa had brought the coffee he felt much more competent.

"Oh, Languor of the East——"

Angus strode over the matting declaiming the phrases. They recurred to his mind, carrying with them a sense, at first of pleasing achievement. The sonorous words were tremulous upon the quiet room; he said them softly. He hurried to the chair and wrote them down. And then he read them louder, and as he read a note of hesitation, and on its heels a note of defiance, crept into his voice. A note of anger—and even before he reached the end his attention wandered. He winced before what was coming: he was facing the reaction, facing the fact that what he had written was again meaningless. It was no use trying to brave it out. Slowly he ground the point of his pencil into the soft wood of the table.

How familiar had become for him that inevitable reaction: the sense of incompleteness: the conviction of insufficiency. The twigs and shavings of his inspiration would soar and crackle into brilliance: for a moment it would seem certain that something bright and vivid was to be secured. Then suddenly the flame would flicker, a tongue or two of fire would dart up listlessly and then subside, an ember falling on the ash; and only the black logs of reason to show how he had failed. It was always the same, the end was always the same. It approached him, it was true, by different processes: there were several distinct analogies to which he likened its approach. Sometimes he felt as if some intent spirit of malignity lit up in the recesses of his brain, a small, cruel light that derided and denied. It would squeak at him and disconcert: it would say mean things to him that cut across his inspiration, and that checked the flow. "There's *atmosphere* for you," it would say; or, again, "What need have people nowadays of poems in prose?" Angus would desperately endeavour to ignore this little voice: he would continue writing: and the little light would nod at him with the heavy-lidded eyes of a reviewer; it would say, "Mr. Field has a nice taste for the more recondite intricacies of our language." It would say, "The subtleties of Mr. Field do not convince us. We doubt whether, with all his faculties, he has the gift of creation." *We doubt!* It would say things like this, and Angus would feel the pencil falter in his hand.

At other times he visualised his brain as a machine, glittering, intricate and perfected. The thing would turn at first, cog within cog, transmitting motion till the small wheels buzzed in unison, and the slim, slow piston rose, and sucked, and fell. Four times, five times, the sleek shafts of the piston would rise up, precise and, to all seeming, inevitable. But at the sixth time they would pause; drop a foot or two; cease.

"What you want, Angus, is a fly-wheel—that's what you want." He would say this jauntily at first and try again: a feeble, flaccid movement, a slight jerk of the piston, and no more. Motion was dead. Angus would gaze detachedly at his machine, despairing and aghast.

To-night his failure enveloped him with a peculiar dejection. He had been so sure to-night that the impetus of his inspiration would not flag. He had been so certain that at last he had seized upon the edge of truth. Only a few hours back, on the boat from Therapia, the whole scheme had seemed so close within his grasp, so easy and so tangible. Yes, he would use what he had written yesterday, but as a velvet case whereon to lay the bright hard object of his message: a challenge to lethargy, a steel arrow-head of thought, incisive, permanent and clean: how crisp and challenging it would echo: a clarion upon the mountains: it would encourage and stimulate: it would be strong. Yes, even to himself he varied his metaphors. Angus sighed and re-read what he had written. The velvet case was there right enough. Or was it plush? Plush—green plush! He pushed his note-book from him, and went down to the little garden by the water. The night was very warm. His soul revolted against it.

Up and down he paced between the two fig trees. He did not ask for genius, he flung out his renunciation to the stars. He knew what genius was—a thing uncontrollable and apart:

a vast reservoir, a store of pressure that with incalculable and unwilled action sets the little wheels of mechanism whirring to creation; a force unavoidable, unrealised, impersonal and dominant: the pen should fly along the paper, a tiny thing driven by an extraneous and extravagant motive: oh, Angus! His pencil! He looked at it, the slim pencil in his hand. It was but a brush of camel's hair: a brush poised intermittently, dabbing little purple words upon the page. A touch of colour; and then a pause to judge of the effect. No force! No motive force! And why? Surely he was no feeble creature. He was "physically magnificent." They had said so at Marylebone when he had been examined. The doctor had put up his glasses. He had said: "Why, my dear young man, you should be cast in bronze." And even mentally he was not decadent. Angus assured himself of that. He strove continually for action. His senses shied at preciousness How angry he became at his own cadences. Why was this so? And so often—so inevitably? Was it experience that he lacked? Education? Scarcely. His mind seethed with the air bubbles of other people's quotations. Of Life? Perhaps. After all, what did he, Angus, really know of life? Tonbridge and Wadham: a white figure with a megaphone panting along the tow-path: a little pine-wood inn up there in the Niederwald: the lights of the Café Royal clustering in a double brandy: a tired strumpet playing the piano in a Brussels brothel. Would it come easier when he was alone? Could even Flecker write at Candili? Too soft, this Bosphorus valley. Not the East even; only the Levant, "too Hellenistic"—even at that moment his mind caught and registered the phrase. Yes, if he ever got away; *when* he could get away. . . . At Erzeroum, perhaps, the clean air, the snow in October. Or the pink uplands of Teheran. "A jet of water in the sun-cracked marble: the thirsty irises." Damn! Words, again, words! Phrases that minced across his vision. It was the tide he wanted, high and flush; some ultimate force: the wind upon the bare hills. Or else a cause? What did all these people mean by a cause? Angus could think now of no cause which would win him to concentration. A cause was politics, and politics to him were but a fat ledger, in which he registered the works of others. A cause? Love? He paused beside the pomegranate. Love? He had never been in love. There was the girl there at Eridge in the green house. "A petulant lip" —he had coined the phrase at the time: it was all the incident had given him. Love? How curious that he had never been in love! A Cause? The moon slid up behind the cedars. How silent, how impassive! She had been so statuesque, that girl there by the landing-stage Her eyes had turned to him with the calm immobility of a statue. How lovely she had been! Her voice had been so gentle and so passionate. Oh God! the peculiar inflection of her voice. Yes, she had been detached, remote, and formidable. Her name, they told him, was Eirene. Eirene! Peace? And such force somewhere; not obvious, not blatant, but remote. Eirene! His heart quivered at the recollection. He gripped the tree suddenly, and suddenly he stepped forward to where the moon flung its white waters on the open garden. He raised his eyes to that soft and sinister flood of light. He raised his arms. "Bethink thee," he murmured, "bethink thee, Mistress Moon, whence came my love?"

CHAPTER III.

August

(I.)

EIRENE went up to her room and closed the shutters. She locked the door and lay upon the bed. She lay quite still upon her back, her hands behind her, gazing at the wooden slats of the ceiling. A deep silence enveloped the house, intensified by the soft lapping of the water outside. The afternoon sun was blistering the wood of the shutter: Eirene drew the curtains. Those sharp bars of light had always irritated her. She was tired, and her head throbbed dully. She had not slept the night before. She lay there and the reflected light in the room soothed her. There were rooms in her brain that were closed and shuttered even as this one. There was the little black hatred room and the Paniotis room, and the large muffled room of the secret The secret! Her hands stole to the little key on its ribbon. She toyed with it, and then she rose deliberately and opened the Italian cabinet. With a little laugh she slid back across the room, the cartridge hot within her palm. Dimly from outside she could hear the water: the noise of the waves against the stone edging of the quay, and beyond them the crisp plash of the smaller waves, caught between breeze and current and leaping gently among themselves.

Sweet Waters

The pine trees were motionless that evening up at Tchamludja, and the red road across the mountain stood out clear and warm through the haze. Eirene lay there waiting for her father: waiting confidently, and soon she felt the touch of his rough coat upon her cheek. At last, at last, the secret had come back to her: she gripped the arm and ran her slim fingers down till they were locked in his. Her father stood behind her, but he bent his face down close to her, so close that when he spoke her own lips moved at the contact: he said, "You will kill her one day, you know. You will go down when they are all asleep: you will go down to the little room under the grain case. You will take your little lamp. There is petroleum there, and you will throw your little lamp at it. And you will lock the doors, you will run from door to door, locking them with your silver button-hook. And I shall kiss you at the corner of the lips, I shall kiss you like this," he said. His mouth pressed closer. It was the mouth of Angus Field. She screamed and strained away, but his arm was round her: he bent her backwards to him, crushing her body in his arms: and she was falling, falling, till the veils came up again and hid the evening sun. She struggled to return, her muscles struggled to get back to him; she tore at the veils as they rose past her, struggling up to where in a pin-point of light above the well she could see the lips of Angus. He was speaking down to her: he said, "In summer, where the stream leaps out over the stone," and his smile widened into the roar of waters and the glint of sun behind the shutters.

She stirred restlessly in a half-slumber, and

then turned again and slept, a dreamless sleep, awaking to find the sunlight tinged with pink upon the curtain rings. Eirene rose and smoothed her hair carefully. She looked at herself with narrowed eyelids in the glass. Yes, of course she was beautiful, they had so often told her so. And now there was a flush of colour in her olive cheeks. She would go over behind the hills to the clear uplands beyond. There would be a breeze there, and she could think. Her mind was eager for thought: she felt the cells in her brain throbbing for the relief of quiet thought. Hurriedly she ate the food that they had brought her.

She walked up the winding path, and through the gate behind the summer-house to where the Thracian moorlands rolled bare above the fringe of trees. Beyond the crest, the Forest of Belgrade threw out a green tentacle nestling down into the valley below, and billowing away again east to Dercos; or to the left, with one soft sweep, it traced the westward line, the line to the Valley of Sweet Waters. A group of cypresses on the summit and a stone tomb beside them with a little railing. She sat there looking down the slope she had ascended. The ilexes and the stone pines of the gardens fringing the Bosphorus showed up grey and green against the ribbon of dark water: the villas and the lower gardens were hidden by the sudden dip towards the quay. The hills opposite in Asia threw their purple shadows across the valleys; and beyond, between the two capes, stretched the line of the Black Sea, a line longer now, as viewed from the heights, than when it showed, a short familiar bar, down there upon the water's level.

How seldom these last months had she been able to think! How seldom had she been able to seize a thread of thought and feel it single and continuous to her will! It was so silent up there: the rustle of the breeze among the cypresses, and in the hollow, the dry tap of tortoises amorous in the hush of evening. She took her head between her hands and hung her hat upon the little railing. She had been unhappy recently: she had lost the secret; she had hated mother. She had lied to mother. So foolishly, so gawkily. A school-girl lie. A pointless lie. Something had taken hold of the calm, confident Eirene whom she knew: some hidden lobe within her mind had become inflamed and venomous: things had come to her in fantastic semblances, ideas half-realised had bent across her vision and then shrunk away laughing. It was clearer now that the windows had been opened. What had she seen of Paniotis? There was nothing really. Only a sudden look of terror in her mother's eyes. It was disconcerting to see her mother frightened: her mother, so small and nimble and unabashed. And frightened of Eirene—her little Eirene. It was unseemly and grotesque; she saw it now, she would put it all out of her mind: she would put it out of her mind. For why need she trouble now that the secret had been recovered? What mattered every day and all day if she could shut herself away from it for the intimate comfort of the road beyond! Only Eirene knew about it: only Eirene knew—Eirene and her father.

"And father," she murmured happily, and as she did so a wave of colour flooded her upturned face. She stood up suddenly and faced the wind from the Black Sea. Her breath caught in her throat. She remembered now, it had *not* been father. It had been the man on the landing-stage. The young man with the rough coat and the soft hair about his neck. Eirene took a few steps forward: it was coming back to her. He had put his face so close to hers, she had felt his lips moving as he whispered. She put her hand to her mouth: her heart raced wildly. "How horrible," she murmured, "how disgusting!" Her mind flamed with anger: "How *dare* he!" she exclaimed: she tried hard to substitute her father for that burning picture: but her father's features were blurred to her. She dropped upon the ground. "Oh, father," she sobbed, "come back to me, come back to Eirene. She's afraid!"

She lay there sobbing among the thyme. Her anger left her, and gradually the sense of shame was stilled. "Be sensible, Eirene! it was only a dream" Her consciousness adjusted itself and, like an elder sister, soothed her nerves. "Be sensible." Yes, it was only a dream. "An unpleasant dream," she said. "A nightmare," she repeated. "A nightmare," she said again, almost crossly; and her brain cleared. After all, it was the road beyond that mattered. The road beyond and the feeling of calm. It would come again. And even Angus was not terrible: she would see him soon, perhaps to-morrow. Why should she be afraid? He had locked her fingers like father's, and his arm had been safe and strong. His lips had frightened her; that was not part of the secret. That was the nightmare. Of course it was a nightmare. She would see him again, perhaps to-morrow, and she would show herself that she need not be afraid. He was alive and young like her. It was silly to be frightened. And deep within her a little fibre throbbed and sang like a cicada on the wall. Yes, she had recovered her secret, and she was happy. How happy she was! She would go straight to mother while she was still happy. She would show mother that she was no longer afraid.

(II.)

Intent on her purpose, Eirene cut down across the terraces and up through the kitchen entrance and the low-stepped stairway to the upper floor. Her light shoes made no noise upon the matting: the drawing-room door was in front of her, and she opened it quickly, afraid, if she hesitated, to lose the impulse of her mood. The room was dark as she entered: her mother was speaking to someone and did not hear her. She was speaking Greek, and Eirene paused in the doorway.

"You see, she is so innocent," her mother was saying, "she does not know. She knows nothing. I have told her nothing, and she has no friends."

"Don't you believe it," Paniotis answered. "She is of the age, you know. In fact, she is already past the age. It comes early in this accursed climate." He leered across to the sofa. "And then she is your daughter."

"You say that, but I wonder. She is so strange, so silent. She is morose, you know. I tried once to tell her, but she put on her silly face. You know her silly face, Ion, when her mouth opens like this," and her mother's dry little laugh trilled into the room.

Eirene closed the door silently. What was it that she did not know? Why was life so complicated and so hostile? It was obscene! She had read the word somewhere, and she repeated it: "obscene." She walked down the staircase slowly with the inward pain gnawing at her heart again, numbing her brain. She felt humiliated chiefly: a child again. And with the feeling came a wave of the heavy ennui of childhood. It was six o'clock. At seven there would be dinner. The drawing-room was closed to her. She was tired and yet she was afraid, now, to go back to her room. She went out into the little brown garden and sat on the edge of the terra-cotta fountain. Through the gratings in the wall she could see the waters dancing in the current. Yes, she would go up and see Aunt Emily. There was just time before dinner. She opened the garden gate and walked out along the quay. Past her own garden wall she walked, past the small yard of the British Embassy, and along the wall of the Secretaries' house. One of the shutters on the ground floor was open on the road, and through the bars she could see the wide, low room; the click of a typewriter, the flash now and then of a white shirt-sleeve crossing a band of sun. Eirene passed on under the arching red eaves of the French Embassy, and then up into the sudden damp and darkness of the little lane.

Aunt Emily was again sitting there at the edge of the terrace under the vines. For a moment she was flustered by Eirene's arrival, but she laid down her book upon the green table.

"You are late, Eirene; they have taken away the tea-things."

Her aunt sat there, hunched and nervous, glancing slyly at Eirene through her fluttering lashes. The girl was so disconcerting. And to-day particularly it was irritating to have been taken by surprise. She had let herself go the other evening: she had gone too far. It was Eirene's fault: Eirene was so impassive. One said things suddenly like that to wake her up, and then afterwards, when she was gone, one felt sorry.

Aunt Emily picked up her book again. It would be a help. She tried to make conversation; but there was so little one could talk about to Eirene: she would say, "Yes, Aunt Emily," or "No, Aunt Emily," and Aunt Emily would know that she was not listening. Eirene sat there with her long, cool hands upon her lap, looking out across the water. She said slowly: "What is it, Aunt Emily, that I do not know? What is it that I do not know that I ought to know?"

Her aunt's head twitched suddenly, and her eyes fluttered sideways at Eirene. "I don't understand, my dear; I don't know what you mean."

"But there is something, something which is behind everything: something which you are all thinking about—even you, Aunt Emily—and, of course, mother and Paniotis. They know, and they know that I don't. I heard them speaking about it just now. The room was dark, and I heard them. Paniotis said that I *did* know really, as I was of 'the age.' What did he mean by 'the age,' Aunt Emily?"

Aunt Emily winced in her chair. After all, it was not her business to tell Eirene. Or *was* it her business? It was unwise that a girl of the age should be so ignorant! It was dangerous; Eirene was so strange. One never knew where one was with Eirene. Her mother ought certainly to have told her: *she* knew; the egoism of that woman made Aunt Emily's head twitch three times in angry succession. She ought to tell her niece herself: it was her duty: but it was so difficult. These things had to be learnt gradually or they came as a shock. One could express it delicately: vague similes of flowers and bees and pollen floated for a moment in Aunt Emily's mind. But it was not her business, and it was too hot to-day in any case. This strange, solemn girl was, after all, not Aunt Emily's responsibility. She patted the cool hands that lay in Eirene's lap. "Don't worry, dear. Don't worry about these things. You will know soon enough. When you're married, dear; then you'll know it all."

Aunt Emily settled back into her chair trying to ignore a little flicker of conscience. And Eirene sat on beside her, her wide eyes fixed, expressionless, on the short, blue line of distant horizon.

(III.)

The last week of June. Therapia in the cloudless end of June; a monochrome of blue. Dark blue, the blue of gentians: light blue, lighter than the blue of harebells. The blue of morning: the dark cloths of night. The rose-red blue of evening. Blue, pencilling the outline of a minaret, capping a distant dome. The blue of cypresses. A child flying a kite in the meadow. The wake of a steamer cutting across from Beicos. The dip of a gull's wing. The wheel of porpoises.

The sea.

Slowly Eirene unlocked the gate that led into the other garden.

He was surprised to see her coming towards him through the ilexes. He was sitting there with his sandwiches and their white paper spread upon his knee. The spring beside him leapt out over the wide stone.

"I thought," said Eirene, "that I should find you here. You told me, you remember, when we met upon the quay."

She did not notice his surprise. He was so intimate to her. She did not realise, she did not choose to realise, that for him she was but a chance acquaintance of the quay-side. His coat lay beside him on the thyme; he was in his shirt-sleeves. He did not rise to meet her. He sat there looking up at her; surprised.

Eirene sank down beside him among the thyme. Her eyes narrowed as she looked out to the dark glitter of the sea. She did not speak for a moment. Angus was embarrassed. He was pulling down his shirt-sleeves over his arms: his fingers fidgetted, as he fitted in the links.

"It is quite dry up here," said Eirene; "one does not notice the damp."

"Yes, it's a jolly place," he answered. "A very jolly place," he added. He was becoming irritable. This large lump of a female beside him. Difficult to cope with. Not at all easy to cope with. He wished that she would go away. Should he offer her a sandwich? Could he eat one himself while she was there? Why not? He had not asked her to come. She had come without being asked. An impertinent thing to do: a pert thing to have done. The girl was pert: six foot of pertness. Most incongruous. "Bethink thee, Mistress Moon." He must have been drunk last night. So incongruous.

The silence was becoming oppressive. She did not seem to notice it. She was rubbing a spray of thyme between her wide, white palms. The scent of it rose pungently in the hot air.

"There are some eagles over there," he said, "above Buyukdere."

"There always are," she answered. "Sometimes only two, and sometimes three. I have seen five there. I like them."

The subject dropped: it was not an expansive subject.

She had picked up the book he had been reading. The "Everyman" Edition of Byron. "Rubbish," he commented, as she opened it. She looked up at him, with her eyebrows raised in enquiry and surprise.

"Rubbish," he repeated, "all that Byron business."

"What *do* you mean?" she said. "Byron—rubbish?" She looked shocked, as at some indecency.

"Mere bawdy sentiment," he commented. She did not understand the word. A slight frown gathered on her brow, a frown of concentration.

"I thought so once," she said, "until I read the letters. That explains it all, you see, the humour, the sincerity, the sincere unrest, the flow of impulse and sincerity. They have been for me quite different since I read the letters."

"What letters?" he asked.

"Why, the Byron letters. Those blue volumes, you know."

"I haven't read them," said Angus, "and I don't want to," he added sulkily.

"But you won't, you can't, call Byron rubbish till you have." A note of protest only, not a note of criticism. Angus was ruffled. He manœuvred on to firmer ground.

"You see," he said, "I don't care much for English poetry. I suppose I read too much French."

It was *not* firmer ground.

The discussion, as it developed, left him ruffled.

"But what an amount you must have read; what an amount you know!" She did not notice the thread of petulant irony in his remark. She echoed his last word.

"Know?" she repeated. "I? I know nothing. Mother said so yesterday."

He was filled with a dull resentment. It was that which inspired, and subsequently justified, in his eyes at least, the way in which he told her; the fact that he had told her at all. She had asked him, of course; that was some justification. He had not understood, at first, what it was she wanted him to explain. She had told him what it was. She had told him quite naturally, with a calm precision. And then he had explained. He had enjoyed explaining. It had given him a curious, stimulating pleasure: he had not minced his words: he had not shirked the details; not *all* the details.

And when it was all over, she looked at him, calm and unabashed. "Oh, *that*," she said. "But I know about that. You see, I used to keep rabbits."

Coarse! That's what she was. Most unpleasant. An unpleasant taste in the mouth. Angus was shocked: the dull resentment had not been allayed. For the moment, while he himself was speaking, it had been allayed: he had felt like an elder brother, pointing the road. Or *had* he felt like that? An unpleasant picture floated in his mind of an afternoon ten years ago at Hastings with a cousin, a cousin from St. Paul's. Angus had been twelve then. He was to go to Tonbridge next year. The cousin had "explained": Angus had disliked him ever since. And then to go so far, to help the girl like that, and to be told at the end that she had known all the time! It was extremely unpleasant. It made one feel a cad, somehow. She did not seem to notice anything. She did not notice the false position in which she had placed him. She must be obtuse: obviously she was very obtuse.

She was speaking again, pulling at the thyme around her. She looked away from him as she spoke, out across to the Black Sea.

"No, I didn't mean that," she said. "I meant something more important. I didn't mean just having children and all that sort of thing. I meant the thing that interests people: I meant love. What is love? I don't know, you understand."

"Oh, love . . ." said Angus. "Well, love . . . you see . . . love——"

He looked at his watch. "I'll tell you some

day," he concluded. "I must be going down again."

"When?" said Eirene, "to-morrow?"

"Yes, to-morrow," answered Angus, and he stooped to pick up his coat.

(IV.)

The month of July passed slowly, fœtidly across the waters, borne upon the damp breath of the south wind. Up there in the great city the wisteria sagged limply across the alleys, its leaves blackening against the sky. The flies crawled thick upon the muslin of the meat-shops; from time to time a boy would wave at them with a whisk of dried and yellow grass; for an instant they would rise, quiver, a mass in the shadow, and then settle again; coagulated, clustering, obscene. Only the bells of the water-sellers, a flash of polished brass passing from sun to shadow, broke in upon the silence. Down by the sweltering port, the dock hands laboured at their work; the clank of derricks, the soft thud of bales, the sudden grunt of ropes tightening to the strain. Above them in the Customs house the clerks toiled listlessly, the ink upon their ledgers clogging as it left the pen. In shop and warehouse, and up there in the languid Ministries of State, men gasped and panted for the hour of release, and when it came, and the sun showed scarlet in the windows of Kadikeui, the golden dust would rise under the feet of thousands trooping to the bridge, packing upon the steamers which would bear them up the

Bosphorus, or out across the Marmora to the Islands. Black-coated thousands, straw hats and fezzes bobbing in a queue: a man there with a green sunshade; two young Armenians mopping with white handkerchiefs; again the tinkle of the water-sellers; a shambling crowd; the sobbing of a tired child. And with the fall of evening the city sinks to loneliness: no alien cry to break its native silence: the real Stamboul: a light there below the mosque: an old man in a doorway fingering his chaplet: a donkey in some distant garden braying at the moon.

Therapia in July! The splash of the hot thunder-drops upon the Bosphorus, the roses bursting from bud to tired petal in a single day, the green and yellow water-melons heaped upon the quay. The memory of June, the dread of August. The heavy, tired leaves upon the trees. The passage of July.

Day after day, with the sun high above them, they would meet up there beside the spring. Eirene and Angus. A prolonged, repeated assignation. He used the word deliberately, knowing full well how little it applied. Eirene? Assignation? He smiled at the disparity between these words.

How intimate, yet how unreal, was the relation which evolved between them! For him apparently a deliberate, self-conscious gésture of emotion, a fictitious attitude, an impulse irritating even to himself by its very lack of spontaneity. When he was away from her, in his own little house by the water, the emotional side would seem sincere enough. "Eirene," he would murmur. "Eirene," the sound of her very name was soothing, the thought of her stole into his heart as something strange and penetrating and remote. Soothing? Remote? That was not the flame that he had sought for. And yet it was sincere. It was not what he had expected, but it was sincere. Yes, when he was away from her he was not troubled by unreality. He saw himself kneeling there before her with the gesture of offering, while her eyes, unmoving as the eyes of a statue, would look out beyond him to the sea. A humble gesture of offering, the very humility of it gave him relief and satisfaction. It never came to him that the offering was more than a gesture of homage: he would have been dismayed almost by the thought of acceptance. No, she must stand there indifferent: she must reject and refuse according to her rôle. And he would be purged by the emotion, purged and inspired.

But when he was with her, up there among the grey ilexes in the noonday heat, it would be different. They would be close together, and she would be natural: a wise and gentle child, a child intimate and confiding. He was disconcerted by this confidence, it disturbed the proportions by which he had justified his own attitude. He would be disturbed by the gulf which stretched between the clear simplicity of their actual relations, and the purple clangour through which he wished to envisage them. Or *was* it that which really angered him? Was it not something even more essential? Was it not her sex, her very virginity which played upon his nerves? His senses winced at the fierce functions of the male: conqueror and captive, was he capable of these? It seemed an outrage. And yet surrender on her part would have chilled him equally. He felt ashamed. And sometimes when the imminence of climax would fret his nerves, he would be grateful to her for not noticing the problem. She would talk to him gently and naturally of unimportant things. And he would be soothed and interested. A figure strange and penetrating at the feet of which he laid his homage? A citadel which he was to storm and to attack? Not this; not that. It was "the friend," sexless, confiding, and intelligent. That's what it was. Intelligent. How could he have ever thought her stupid? Impassive, perhaps: she was not nimble-minded. But she had a sure, simple gesture of judgment. She was so clear and calm and frank. It was that which was important to him.

And for her, primarily and gaily, he, too, was "the friend." The first friend, the only friend. He would smile at her when she spoke to him. He made her laugh sometimes. He said funny things, and sometimes he said things which she thought funny. He didn't like it when she laughed at the things she was not meant to laugh at. She could not tell him why she laughed: she would say, "Because I'm happy." She was happy and serene. Companionship—but under it, away in the recesses of her thoughts, there was something else. . . . Something else. An impression, derived, secondary, but always present. Was it as much as an impression? Was it more, at first, than the mere medium of an impression? The wire of an electric current? The conduit for the flow? Could an emotion, a mere stirring of emotion, an emotion so unvisualised, so almost wholly impersonal, be more than a mere hesitating medium for the expression of something else? It *was* more than that. There was the line of his neck: that was visualised. The muscles of his forearm, the slim strength of his thighs, the texture of his hair. *They* were visualised; they recurred to her sometimes; when she was alone they would recur. But not the face of him, not the expression of his eyes. It was difficult for her to recall his features. Or his voice. His voice was a little flat, she remembered, a little over-labial: a soft voice; not a very manly voice; not enough stress upon the harder consonants. No, she did not like his voice. She disliked his voice: it was the worst thing about him.

Eirene, for she had the habit of such analysis, would resort to self-examination. Was it merely as a potentiality that he obsessed her thoughts? A potentiality of what? she wondered. Of Love? She would laugh at the idea. Yes, she was happy, and she could laugh. But underneath it all was something else. Something persistent. A little flame of fear. Attraction? Repulsion? She was frightened sometimes by that little flame; it would shoot up suddenly and still the laughter on her lips.

She told him about her life; about everything. She had told him of her mother, and the secret, and Paniotis. He had been annoyed at first. He had said: "But why do you tell me all this? It's all so very morbid and unnecessary." And she had looked surprised.

"But don't you see," she said, "don't you see I am afraid of mother, and I hate her? It will end in a tragedy."

"Rubbish," said Angus shortly, "schoolgirl rubbish."

" But you said yourself, you remember . . ." Eirene checked herself. She was getting confused. " But Aunt Emily said . . ." again she paused.

" Your Aunt Emily's a fool," said Angus. " I know her, she's an obvious fool. A sparrow-brained person."

Angus was at his best that afternoon, he was feeling confident. That afternoon he was less self-conscious than usual.

" All girls," he said portentously, " some time or other think they hate their mothers. And their sex comes along and they both become fellow-conspirators against the male. Leagued confederates: cronies." He turned sharply to Eirene. " Hate your mother? That's mawkish. It's unintelligent."

" But you don't *know* mother," Eirene interrupted in a puzzled voice: " I don't see . . ."

" Oh, I know about her. Everyone knows *about* her. Scarcely maternal, I should say. Scarcely the type to be at her easiest with a daughter."

Eirene looked at him in astonishment.

" Mother not at her ease with me?"

" No—shy of you, frightened of you. Always in the wrong." He dismissed the subject petulantly. But it germinated. It bore fruit for Eirene. For once Angus had sown the seeds of wisdom.

And then one day he had drawn his note-book from his pocket and read to her what he had written. Perhaps she would give him an idea. She had a knack sometimes of saying simple things which opened a new window. She had laughed her low laugh when he had finished. She had said: "Why, it's verse like." That had annoyed him, and Eirene, noting this, had begged him to read it again.

> "Oh, lambent Languor of the East——"

When he had read it he paused—pleased to note a look of sudden concentration on her face. She said, "Read the beginning part again." She put her hand upon his arm and stopped him.

"Low lutes," she murmured, and her eyes narrowed. And then suddenly and gaily—"Oh, of course, I know—it was what father used to like. It was low lutes. Low lutes of love complain." She rose excitedly. "Oh, I know," she continued, her voice rising, "I remember now. I remember——"

> "Glad to know the brine
> Salt on his lips, and the large airs again . . .
> And see the stars, or feel the free
> Shrill wind beyond the close of heavy flowers,
> And through the music of the languid hours
> They hear, like ocean on a western beach,
> The surge and thunder of the Odyssey."

"Oh, I had forgotten that," she said, and clapped her hands. "Oh, I'm so glad to have found it again." She was standing there against the sky and sea. He was too surprised to be annoyed: the words, "Oh, Lang! but it's a fake really—it's a crib on Keats," had died upon his lips. She stood up straight against the sun: a flush of sudden colour in her cheeks. He lay there in the thyme amazed and admiring. He said: "But you look quite different. What is the matter? You look so different suddenly. You look so—English."

(V.)

England?

English?

Did they mean anything to her? Why did they mean so much?

She was alone in her room, alone with the window open to the night.

She had been there once, to London, when she was a child. The policeman in Hans Place had shown her his whistle. A funny smell when one blew out the candle. The sheets had been cold. That afternoon at Folkestone they had sat in a shelter under the Leas; she had picked some wild mustard plant; it had tasted different from mustard, a sour, narrow taste. A swan hung from the gas-bracket on an elastic string: it jumped up and down when one pulled it. She kept her hoop in the conservatory.

England? Governesses; Kings of England; Queens of England; dates; 1216; the little princes in the Tower stairway; William Shakespeare, the scene between Prince Arthur and Hubert; Macaulay, the Armada; Nelson; sums; fractions, compound fractions; geography; counties, rivers, towns, the Lizard, Morecambe Bay, Portland Bill, the Wash.

England? The Illustrated London News; King Edward; Mr. Ainley as Paolo; The Oxford Pageant; Miss Gertie Millar. Round lumps of trees. Coaches.

England? The Ambassador; the flag on Sundays above the Embassy; lemonade; the white ensign on the yacht, the sailors; father; church.

England? L. T. Meade; The Talisman;

Dickens; The Idylls of the King; Harrison Ainsworth; Excalibur. A book in crushed morocco for her birthday. The hundred best pictures. The boyhood of Raleigh; Aunt Emily.

England? Kipling; In Memoriam; Chaucer; Philip Sidney; Mrs. Humphry Ward; Hardy; The English Men of Letters series; a picture of Hardy in the papers. Gosse. Everyman.

Shelley. Keats. The Shropshire Lad.

Byron.

Shelley, Keats, Shakespeare; John of Gaunt; the Sonnets. The English Review; the stream which runs through the Forest of Belgrade; half-a-crown: Chaucer. The Shropshire Lad.

Swinburne.

The Times.

Shakespeare.

Barrel-organs.

The wind from the Black Sea.

The horizon of the Black Sea.

The Black Sea.

The frogs down in the garden were screaming at the moon. Eirene closed the window.

CHAPTER IV.

September

(I.)

THE old Emporium of the East, the Golden Horn has lost its dignity: the commerce of the East is choosing other highways. Danube and Volga, Tigris and Euphrates, each in its turn has tapped the flow of merchandise, and in our later age the brain of man has drawn a straight blue line of water through the desert. No longer now the camels grunt and bubble under the plane trees of Scutari; the caravanserais of Stamboul are crowded only with the refugees from Turkey's sundered provinces. Some basket-workers under the arcades, some skeins of coloured wool drying upon the parapets, and in the courtyards pigeons murmuring among the grass-grown stones. The greater vessels of the world choose other highways: London and Liverpool, New York and Hamburg, and the wide thoroughfares of trade flow out to other continents, through other oceans. The ships that ply to India and beyond, from Tilbury past the light of Ushant, the rock of Cape St. Vincent, and the white cliffs of Trafalgar, swing up to Marseilles and then across to Alexandria and the rest. Only the lesser ships pass through the Dardanelles and up the Marmora. The Messageries that ply from

Marseilles to Naples, the Piræus and to Smyrna: the Paquet line; the Khedivial Mail steamers from Port Said. Black and indolent, they swing round the point of the Seraglio and sidle up to the quay at Galata, the smoke trailing across the minarets. And then they turn away, back into the Ægean. The Bosphorus beyond sees little of them; it has its own tenuous and familiar traffic. The oil-tankers from Batoum, clanking slowly by, low in the water, their funnels set far back in the stern, the long ungainly bulk of the vessels, rusty and disproportioned, protruding out beyond. And now and again some tramp steamer from Odessa, or the slim outline of a yacht bound for the Crimea. More intimate, and more unceasing, comes the splash and bustle of the little ferry steamers, puffing across from landing-stage to landing-stage; squat, busied and appropriate. And in a different key, the sailing ships beating against the current, hugging close to the shore, or hanging motionless in the fairway, waiting for the breeze.

For those who lived beside the water, the passage of these ships could be told by the echo of their wake upon the quayside. The oil-tankers, keeping to the Asiatic shore, would send four languid waves to break upon the stones that fringe the dusty road. The little Bosphorus steamers, audible at first by the clank of their paddle-wheels, and the tinkle of the engine-room bell, would leave behind them the crisp, small splash of water churned up close within the shore. And sometimes would come the clearer beat of waves from some less usual vessel, and in the little wooden houses by the quay people would raise their heads and glance up across the water.

Perhaps a boat from Varna, drab and rusted like the rest of them, foul and slow-moving, with its low-grade fuel. A shabby, second-rate procession, redeemed only by the colour of the sea and sky.

Three mornings in the week, however, would occur a break in this monotony of movement. The people sitting in their shuttered rooms would start to the sudden noise of a more violent passage. A larger, more determined, wave would skim across the Bosphorus, with four others following behind it, approaching quickly to the shore. It would strike the large stones by the quay and send up a fountain of spray, flinging salt drops across to the hot plaster of the walls that fringed the gardens. The white dust of the road would be dappled and mudded like the shade cast by elm trees across a lane, and little pools of water would collect in the crevices of the stones, while the flat surfaces steamed and evaporated in the glare The people who lived beside the waves well knew what this betokened. They would smile at one another and murmur "The Rumanian steamer." And out there would come a flash of movement as the slim mail steamer from Constanza dashed arrogantly up to Constantinople, its clean white flanks flashing in the sunlight, and the clear blue and yellow of its flag fluttering behind. They liked the Rumanian steamer, these people who lived by the waters. It meant Europe to them and efficiency, and the Orient Express. And the Rumanian steamer, for its part, relished this sudden and dramatic entry into the Bosphorus, the wide sweep round the Point of Kavak, and the rush of full speed through the calm water. Three times a week it would swoop into the Bosphorus, fluttering the row-boats in the little harbours and splashing the curtains of the cabs which sheltered by the landing-stages. Three times a week, and yet always with dramatic effect. The thing had become a demonstration. People would take down their opera glasses from the nail by the window and scan the decks. One could see the passengers in groups looking at the shore; clean, tidy passengers, who but a few hours before had been in Paris, in Vienna, or in London; rich, important passengers who came from outside, and who had leather luggage and valets and eau-de-cologne. The ship would flash past the Point, and the people of the Bosphorus would sigh and hang their opera glasses back again upon the nail.

It was thus that on that September morning Therapia looked out envyingly at the Rumanian steamer, and that Hugh Tenterden, proceeding from Paris to take up his new post as Counsellor of Embassy at Constantinople, sat in a deck chair on the Rumanian steamer and gazed back idly at Therapia.

(II.)

The steamer slid round the Point of Rumeli Hissar, and the fretted outline of Stamboul was disclosed suddenly against the sky-line. A babel of excited admiration came from the deck below. Tenterden rose and stretched himself.

"We are approaching, Exellenz," said the Captain; "we shall be alongside in twenty minutes."

"And you do not want me on your bridge any longer," laughed Tenterden, "and I am not an Excellency." He went to the railing and looked down at the passengers below. A flash of interest lit his eyes as he leaned forward. "Bela Lukacs!" he murmured, "so there may be something in it." A large man in a Tyrolese hat was leaning against the bulwark below him smoking a stout cigar. "Lukacs," Tenterden called down to him, "Bela!" and the fat man started and looked up.

"Ah, Mr. Tenterden, I heard of your appointment. This is indeed an unforeseen pleasure."

"You wait there," Tenterden answered, "and I shall come down to you." He said good-bye to the Captain and thanked him for his hospitality. The passengers were grouped together by the railing. Tenterden passed through them and shook hands with Lukacs. "I thought you were at Tokyo," he said to him.

"And I," Lukacs answered, "imagined that you were in Paris."

There was a pause. Tenterden threw back his head and looked at Lukacs with laughing eyes. That was the worst of Tenterden, one never knew when he was serious. "So there is something in it, my friend Bela—first Berana, and now Kochana. They have thought it worth while to send you. You and me. Two of the vultures, eh?"

"Not so, Mr. Tenterden. I am here for pleasure this time. You remember that little girl at Ernest's? The time Mayol was there. Well, she has come to Constantinople. She is to dance at the Jardin d'Eté. I found a letter from her when I reached Berlin: but such a letter! She was on a tournée to Buda-Pesth, Bucharest and Athens. I missed her at Bucharest and found she had come on here. What do you expect? The heart is unwrinkled."

"And of all this," Tenterden answered, "of all this the Neue Freie are ignorant? Oh, you are a gay dog, Bela! A very gay dog. Eh, Bela! And at your age, too!"

Lukacs winked back knowingly, but in his pink-lidded eye was a look of irritation mingling with a look of curiosity. "Now for you, my dear Tenterden, this sudden appointment, and when you were so well installed in Paris, must have been provoking; and so suddenly like that! And in this weather!" He panted and padded at his damp bull neck with his handkerchief.

Tenterden laughed again, a laugh challenging, infectious and boyish. He always laughed when he was going to be indiscreet. "Ah no, my dear Bela; for me it is different. I have come on business. These massacres, you know. They have taken them so seriously at Cettinje and Sofia. They have taken them seriously in Downing Street. Why have they taken them so seriously? Tell me that, Bela."

The fat man blinked back at him. "But to what do you refer, Mr. Tenterden? Massacres? There are always massacres in this country. Surely your Government . . ."

"You are right, Bela, my Government is not over-sentimental. Nor is the Neue Freie Presse. What, to either of them, is Kochana and a few peasant girls wounded in a market-place? These are straws, Bela, but they show the direction of the wind. Yes, the direction of the wind. And that is why, my dear Bela, you and I are here, and why we shall, I hope, meet often in the months that there are to follow."

Bela Lukacs passed a little red tongue over his lips. "Then your Government think . . .?"

Tenterden stopped him. "Of course they do, and so does your Government, and your Neue Freie, and you, my dear Bela, and every soul in this ship." He paused and looked up. They were entering the Golden Horn. "And every soul," he added, "in that doomed city."

Lukacs was murmuring to himself as if he had made a discovery. . . . "So the British Government think there will be war."

(III.)

Tenterden waited till the other passengers had disembarked. There was no hurry for him. He had arranged for the Embassy launch to take him up to Therapia in the evening. It was to be at Topkhané at four. He would go up to the Embassy at Pera and fetch his letters. He would lunch at the club, he would do things comfortably. He always managed to do things comfortably. It was not egoism exactly, not exactly self-indulgence; but experience, foresight, and a certain habit of being obeyed. He leant over the side of the upper deck watching the turmoil on the quay below him. There was Bela Lukacs with a green sunshade shouting at the porters. How strange that Bela, that much-travelled man, should show such lack of balance. There he was, prodding a young Kurd with his sunshade. An unwise thing to do. Bela Lukacs of all men should know better than to prod a Kurd. Tenterden puffed a thin stream of cigarette smoke into the sun: behind him waited Giuseppe, his Italian valet, and the Embassy cavass, with the luggage. On the quay, in the shade of the warehouse, stood the motor prepared to take him up the hill. The sun blazed upon the sweating babble on the quay. The cab-drivers shouted their fares at the passengers, thrusting out their brown fingers in twos and threes to indicate their fares. From time to time a cab would jerk and rattle off over the cobbles, the heated passengers bumping back upon the cushions. Tenterden eyed the motor and the two servants waiting behind him in the shade. He could go now if he wanted to. He would only have to walk along the deck and down the gangway there. He could sit in the motor till the luggage came. But it would be noisy there until the crowd had dispersed. The guides would come and leer at him through the windows. He loathed guides. He pulled out his watch. Better get the luggage on first. He signed to the Customs official, who came up saluting. "They can take my baggage now," he said, and Giuseppe behind him stooped down to lift the dressing-case. He watched them pile his luggage on to the motor: the chauffeur threw a strap over the top and made it firm. He saw that it was ready for him and still he lingered. Not indolence alone, not only the languid vanity of the practised traveller, but a certain hesitation to set foot again in Turkey. A new chapter, this, in his career: perhaps a decisive chapter. The Ambassador was ill and in a week would go on leave. He, Tenterden, would be in charge: and at a vital moment. He turned his back on the railing and looked across the deck to where the terraced hill of Stamboul rose above the harbour. The cypresses of the Seraglio Point, the mass of St. Sophia, the stucco of the Sublime Porte, the houses and the minarets. Stamboul? Tenterden smiled and threw away his cigarette. "The doomed city," he murmured, and his white flannels caught the sun as he strolled down the gangway to the shore.

The vast Italianate Embassy on the heights of Pera stood deserted in the noonday heat. The staff were in their summer quarters at Therapia. It was cool down there in the shuttered corridors: his tennis shoes flapped silently upon the marble. The under-porter recognised him, and made him welcome. He would find his letters in the Chancery. It was twenty years since, as a young attaché, he had worked in that dark, cool room. And the under-porter had recognised him! But of course he had been warned. The man had tried to kiss his hand, a revolting custom. He glanced carelessly at the photographs on the walls. Generations there of former diplomatists, young attachés, bearded councillors. His own photograph was there, with his bold Elizabethan signature across it "Hugh Tenterden," a little faded now. He picked up the pile of letters on the green-baize table, glancing at their addresses. His eye wandered round the room. No change in twenty years! A few more photographs, that was all, and on the table the familiar, inevitable incidents of the Chancery, identical with other Chanceries throughout the world: the typewriters, the Foreign Office List, the envelopes, the paper-baskets, the punches and the little green silk tags: the familiar cameo upon the writing paper, the tobacco tins, even to the golf balls in a bowl on the mantelpiece. It was always the same. Stockholm and Adis Ababa, Peking and Bogota! What was the use of going anywhere? No change, no change; always that cameo on the notepaper, always the "Stateman's Year Book" and the Foreign Office List upon the table! "Stale and unprofitable," he murmured. He must go to lunch. He would go to the Club, to the Cercle d'Orient. He had been a foundation member twenty years ago, but they would not know him now. He would have to give his name and they would keep him waiting while they looked in a book. That would be tiresome: Tenterden hated things that were not smoothly arranged. He would be kept waiting in the anteroom where the hats were, and the secretary would have to be fetched. He might be lunching, and it would take time to fetch him: that would be very tiresome. The alternatives were the Pera Palace or Tokatlian. But they were noisy, and promiscuous. Perhaps he could telephone and warn them of his coming. He looked round the room for the telephone. There was none to be found. Twenty years and no telephone in Constantinople! That was something at least! That was something to cheer him. Yes, he would go to the club. He walked out almost gaily into the glare of the streets.

They had been warned right enough. Someone in the Embassy had possessed the intelligence to warn them. Tenterden was pleased at this: it was the particular form of efficiency which pleased him. He sat at a little table by the window in the empty room. The diplomatists were all absent at Therapia: there was no one in the club besides himself and the two waiters. This also was gratifying. He knew what it would have meant: meetings with former colleagues. The forced intimacy of such meetings: the stereotyped phrases. " Tiens, mais c'est vous, mon cher! Mais je vous croyais à Buenos Aires." And then the reply: "Ah, mais, vous le savez bien, la carrière, c'est une vaste famille: on se retrouve toujours."

"La carrière!" Tenterden grunted and swallowed some melon. He would read the papers after, and then his letters. He was bored by the thought of his letters. He could feel them, a fat, square wad, in his pocket. He knew what they would be. Invitations to balls, which were already over, in other places. Letters from women: they would have to be answered with gallantry, intimacy and humour. He must preserve his reputation; or at least he presumed that he must. Must he? Why preserve these vapid relationships? Damn! He had not slept well on the boat: that's what was the matter with him. He would sleep again after luncheon in an arm-chair. There would be no one to disturb him.

At four the motor came to take him to the quay. The launch was there, a contrast strangely English, with its white ensign and its sailors. Giuseppe was there also with the luggage. The coxswain saluted and the little boat swung out into the Bosphorus and up again towards Therapia. He watched the white palaces slip by between the stays of the awning. Their names recurred to him: Dolmah Baghche, Tcheragan, Beylerbey. . . . A sailor came aft and began polishing the brasswork. It was always the same! He felt the packet of letters still unopened in his pocket. He would read them to-morrow. He would be at Therapia in twenty minutes, and there was no time. Tenterden went into the cabin and lit a cigarette. He came back and threw the match into the water. Yes, there was Therapia, he could see it in front of him, and the site of where the Embassy had been burnt, and the Secretaries' House, and the other house beyond. What a gap the Embassy had left! He was sorry for the gay garish house that he remembered. But the hill behind remained the same, with its archway opening on to the stone pines and the ilexes. There was a summer-house on the top. That was new. He did not remember the summer-house. But it was too much to the right, it was not in the Embassy garden. No, it must belong to the other house.

The engine stopped suddenly, and the sailors threw over the little whitened fenders. A man stood there ready with a shining boat-hook. The little screw churned twice, three times, in the reverse. The boat-hook caught the ring and the fenders flattened against the quay. They let down the indiarubbered steps into the well of the launch. He stepped out on shore Hugh Tenterden had arrived.

(IV.)

They called Eirene next morning with a pencilled note from her mother lying upon her coffee tray. Her mother was going to the islands to-day and would be away for luncheon. She would be too busy to see Eirene before she left.

The launch, "la mouche" she called it, was to call for her at twelve. Eirene crumpled the note slowly in her long, cool fingers: "la mouche" she sneered to herself. "La mouche de Paniotis." A wave of disgust darkened her forehead: how she loathed that man! She had always loathed him, ever since that day six years ago when he had drawn her on his knee and held her struggling arm in his soft, white hand. She had not listened to the words he said to her: she knew only from the look upon his face that they were fat and foul, and sickly. And once he had kissed her by the lobe of the ear, and she had wrenched away her arm and struck at him in his white face with her clenched fist. He had dropped her immediately and stood up confused, angry and foolish. "O, la rosse!" he had exclaimed, patting his face with his silk handkerchief, and Eirene escaped to scrub her neck and hands, sobbing to herself in the bathroom.

Her mother? Paniotis? The connection of the two made her shudder. They were going to the islands to-day, in the shining white launch with the pink curtains and the large Greek flag behind it. They would be away till evening; her mother was too busy to see Eirene before she went. A little chord of pleasure vibrated through her disgust. She would be free, she would avoid the morning interview. It was good to be alone. One could read at luncheon, and one ordered the food for oneself. It was going to be hot to-day; already at that early hour the air quivered above the garden wall. Eirene stretched her limbs luxuriously. She would read Shelley at luncheon: she would lunch early, and go up to the summer-house. She would find Angus: it would be hot and dry and clear, and the cicadas would scream out from the thyme. Eirene swung her feet out of the bed and stretched her long, lithe arms above her. She had forgotten Paniotis. She was happy now, in the expectance of freedom and a long, indulgent day of idleness. She would wear her ear-rings to-day—the large brass ear-rings that the gipsy had given her, and she would knot a scarlet handkerchief close round her hair, with the wide basket hat above it. She would do all the things that mother did not like. Eirene sang to herself as she dressed that morning.

They had laid her luncheon under the magnolia; the flowers were faded now and the metallic leaves crossed and recrossed each other, alone of all that vegetation, impervious to the sun. The book was propped in front of her; it was propped against a bowl of scarlet roses. It was not Shelley. Shelley was too cold for such a day as this: and besides, to-day she could do the things that mother did not like. She finished hurriedly, and taking the figs as they lay there in their basket, she rose to climb the hill. Her left hand held the book, with one finger thrust between the pages. She climbed the steep path slowly murmuring to herself. The lines came back to her disjointedly, and with them other lines that were as good.

> " Des roses," [she murmured,] " des roses encore!
> Je les adore à la souffrance:
> Elles ont la sombre attirance
> Des choses qui donnent la mort."

That was good enough! Or *was* it very good?

Was it as good as what she held there in her hand? She moved her forefinger within the pages, stroking them possessively. It was not as good! There was nothing quite so good, that morning, as what she held within her hand. She quickened her pace and came out suddenly upon the summer-house. She put the figs upon the table; she pulled a chair out into the full fury of the sun. No, there was nothing quite so good, that morning, as what she held within her hand. She read it to herself: she read it aloud to the cicadas, and the sun and sea and the two eagles wheeling there above Buyukdere: she read it reverently:

" Men shall not see bright fire nor hear the sea,
Nor mix their hearts with music, nor behold
Cast forth of heaven, with feet of awful gold
And plumeless wings that make the bright air blind,
Lightning, with thunder for a hound behind
Hunting through fields unfurrowed and unsown,
But in the light and laughter, in the moan
And music, and in grasp of lip and hand
And shudder of water that makes felt on land
The immeasurable tremor of all the sea,
Memories shall mix and metaphors of me.
Like me shall be the shuddering calm of night,
When all the winds of the world for pure delight
Close lips that quiver and fold up wings that ache;
When nightingales are louder for love's sake,
And leaves tremble like lute-strings or like fire;
Like me the one star swooning with desire
Ever at the cold lips of the sleepless moon,
As I at thine; "

Eirene took the little key from behind the door. She went along the little path between the arbutus: even in the half shade there the sand was hot beneath her feet, the scent of the thyme was hot within her senses.

The door opened easily now. She shut it behind her, and stood straight and tremulous in the adjoining garden. He was there of course. He was there in his shirt-sleeves, and the spring behind him shot out of its stone into the marble trough. It shot out in a cool, clear plunge of water; it seemed strange on a day like this that there should be so much water. He saw her and fumbled with the buttons of his shirt; it had been open and she had seen the smooth, brown line of his chest. She sat down beside him. As always, when she came to him, he was resentful; an air of defence. He was so intimate to her; for her there was no such sense of repression.

"Listen, Angus," she said at once. "Listen to what I am going to read to you."

He looked up at her in surprise, in sudden surprise at her glib use of his Christian name. She did not notice it: she was reading to him, reading that flaming passage from the book. She finished reading. Her eyes fixed, as always, upon the line of the Black Sea, rising above the dip of the two capes and beyond them.

He looked at her intently. She knew that he was looking, but she did not meet his eyes. He interrupted her once. "But why do you read me all this? What do you mean by reading me all this nonsense?"

There was a note of petulance in his voice, but she did not heed it. The heat quivered over there above Beicos, and a thin haze hung over the water's edge. She was above it; up there on the hill everything was clear and hot and dry: the eagles soared clear-cut against the blue. She was up above the veils. His coat lay there beside her upon the thyme. She seized the edge of it and clenched it in her hand. He was fixing the links into his shirt-sleeves; he had pulled them down. "Let me help you," she said: the triteness of the phrase brought him back to reality.

Again that wave of irritation against her! He recoiled and stood up suddenly: she looked at his slim figure against the sky. He sat down again and took her hand: one by one his fingers locked in hers. "You are mad to-day, Eirene." But she did not answer: she pressed her fingers into his. "You are mad," he repeated, and his voice dropped to a hiss of anger: "do you hear me? Mad, mad, mad!" His lips were close, his cheek was close to hers. She swung away from him.

"You frighten me, Angus," she panted, "you frighten me."

But he only laughed. He rose and stretched himself luxuriantly. There was silence between them, and the water splashed into the marble. Her mouth was dry, and she crawled to the fountain. She put her mouth to it where it shot out from the rock in a clear stream. He looked at her and dropped beside her on his knees. His mouth came forward and drank of the same water: the water splashed their faces as her lips met his. It splashed upon her hair, upon his hair, upon the bare line of his neck. He drew her away and kissed her searchingly upon the lips. Again and again he kissed her. The veils were falling: the pines were very still on Tchamludja. They were waiting for her, waiting for something to happen. He had laid his hands upon her shoulders: he was pressing her down. He was frightening her: she must get back: she was frightened. She struggled to her feet: he lay there foolishly, his face flushed, a gawky smile upon his face. A hot thin wire of anger stabbed up within her.

"But who are you?" she said, her teeth clenched at him, "who are you? and what have you done to me?"

She stood and looked at him; he seemed suddenly to have become personal, paltry, terribly alien. She gave a low cry of pain, twisting her arms behind her head. "Oh, God!" she said, "Oh, God! What have I given you? What is it that I have given up to you?" She turned and swayed trembling from him down into the sodden shade of the ilexes. For a moment her dress caught the flecked sunshine of the outer trees: the arch of darkness swallowed her retreating figure.

Angus stood there where she had left him. He stood looking over to the Black Sea. A faint puff of cool wind stirred the curls upon his forehead.

"What a fuss!" he murmured, "what a fuss; I merely kissed the girl!" He laughed; a little virile, brutal laugh. He undid his links and rolled the sleeves above his forearm. "I merely kissed the girl." Well, he had done it; that, after all, was satisfactory. She had been frightened when it came to the point; the sensuality of these women was always timid. It lacked sincerity. But he, at least, had been sincere. Yes, he had forced her down and she had been frightened. He had taken her by the shoulders and she had struggled, and he had kissed her brutally. There was some sex in that. He rolled up the other sleeve, holding his arm outwards. Yes, he had been male enough for once, there could be no doubt of that. It had been a scene, of course, but even as a scene it had worked well. She had been angry, and had stood against the sky looking down upon him; he had lain there. He must have looked foolish lying there and looking up at her. That had been the one ungainly moment in the whole episode. Yes, that moment had been ungainly: he ought to have said something at once soothing and passionate: but he had just lain and blinked at her: he blushed at the remembrance. The beginning had been the best part—spontaneous, gay and animal. They had drunk into the same stream of water; that was a good thing to remember. The spontaneity of it! Their lips had come together and the water had splashed upon her hair, just like . . . Angus paused. Of course it was like something—two people drinking together from a spring. It was like something he had read somewhere. In Italy, wasn't it; or in Sicily? No, it had been Corsica, a book by Prosper Mérimée. No, the analogy was closer, it had been a sensual book. Angus hesitated, bewildered. And then he remembered. His cheek flushed in mortification.

"Oh, damn it all," he said, "the end grotesque! And the beginning Maupassant!" He seized his coat and strode in shame and anger down the hill.

(V.)

Aunt Emily closed her book and marked the place with a hairpin. And then she sighed; a duplicate, double-barrelled sort of sigh: there were two notes to that sigh, the first sharp and short enough, the second flat, prolonged and tremulous. Instinctively she repeated the second note, making it even flatter than before. The minor key. Aunt Emily liked the minor key: she funked realities; her little timid eyes would flick away from the realities. They would hop away into her wide, dim world of half-lights and luxuriance. It was the only world in which there was a place for Emily, for the young Emily with the slim figure and the green eyes; the *fatal* Emily of whom she told herself such lurid stories in her bath.

It was not very good, perhaps, for Aunt Emily to read so many novels. There always came a stage about three-quarters through the novel when it became clear that the ending was, after all, to be a happy one. And always at that stage, when love and birth and riches turned valiantly together into the last clear lap towards the happy goal, always she would take out a hairpin, mark the place, and sigh her double-barrelled sigh.

The first note of her sigh that evening had been particularly acute. She had not liked it at all. It had been necessary to repeat the second note twice in order to restore the balance. Aunt Emily sat there, looking down upon the water. Yes—it was more than twenty years ago now. The year her brother married. She had been thirty-two then: her figure had been plump, perhaps, but at least plump in the right places. She had worn her pearls. They had come out on the terrace, her brother and Hugh Tenterden. It was the opening night of the Yacht Club at Prinkipo. She had heard his laugh as he paused a moment in the light of the French windows.

There were Japanese lanterns strung across the terrace, and from the balustrade one looked out across the Marmora to where the lights of the city quivered together by the sea. They had been playing "Venetia," and towards the end of the evening he had called her "little one." He had said it like that, looking down on her: he had said, "Are you tired, little one?" She had stretched out her hand and pulled a rose. She had meant to do something significant with the rose, but she had not had the courage. She had put it in her handkerchief. Aunt Emily sighed as she thought of that rose: it was still in the handkerchief in her drawer upstairs.

Hugh Tenterden! He had come back; she had seen it in the paper that morning. He was important now; but he had always been important. There was "something about him." She remembered having said that once to Eirene. She had been talking about him, and Eirene, in her tiresome way, had said: "Did you love him, Aunt Emily?" How silly of Eirene! Aunt Emily had been quite cross—she had said, "Of course not, dear." And Eirene had gone on: "Was he very good-looking?" It was then that Aunt Emily had said that "there was something about him." She had said: "No, dear, not good-looking. He was tall and he had a big head; and his shoulders were narrow. No, he wasn't good-looking, even then. But there was *something about him.*"

The servant was crossing the path towards her, with a card upon a tray. She looked at it. Her little eyes flicked in confusion. There it was in black and white. "Mr. Hugh Tenterden," and underneath it. "Conseiller d'Ambassade."

"Oh, no," said Aunt Emily, "say I am out." And then quickly: "Oh, yes," said Aunt Emily, "say I am in; and bring the tea." She gathered up her belongings and changed across into the chair where the vines threw a deeper shade. She hid the book behind her. Her little hands twitched nervously at the lace about her neck. He came quickly across the garden: no, he was not good-looking: he was dressed in flannels. He looked thin and taller somehow, but as he came up to her he laughed. Oh, dear! That laugh framed in the lighted window of the Yacht Club. Aunt Emily panted a little as she rose to greet him.

The dominant note in all that followed was the ease and intimacy of it all. *Had* she known him so well as that? Aunt Emily's mind flickered weakly back across the years. She had seen him often, of course, after that first meeting at Prinkipo. He had been best man to her brother. And once there had been a picnic out at the aqueduct, and he had twisted his foot and come back with her in the carriage. But he spoke to her now as to an old friend; a gentle, interested deference. That was the Tenterden charm: the famous Tenterden charm, that and the boyish, infectious laugh. Was it deliberate, or a habit only? Or was it kindliness? Tenterden would have been amused if one had suggested kindliness. But Aunt Emily knew nothing of the Tenterden legend. For her he was always the vaguely sinister figure of the Yacht Club. She was a little disconcerted by his ease and interest. She was a little disappointed. And she poured out the tea, and he took three lumps of sugar. And jam. She was a little disappointed. Her replies to his enquiries became a little sketchy. It was so difficult to think of two things at once. And then there came a sharp rapping at the garden door.

Aunt Emily jumped. Eirene, without her sunshade, appeared across the garden. How tiresome of her! She had no tact, that girl. Aunt Emily valued tact: it was one of the defences.

Eirene did not see Tenterden at first. She did not see him until it was too late; until she had said: "Oh, Aunt Emily, I've had such a dreadful scene . . .!" It was then that she saw him and that she flushed: a glow of scarlet seething up to her ears. Aunt Emily was not good at coping with situations. Tenterden was. He rose at once. He did not ask to be introduced. He said: "Really, I think this is the best view in Therapia, looking down on it like this." And then he said good-bye; a cordial handshake to Aunt Emily: and for Eirene a slight and deferential bow, a little continental, perhaps, but in the circumstances justified. A bow as to some known, but not as yet introduced, ambassadress: a bow which ignored Eirene's breathlessness and confusion: ignored the flustered school-girl in her pose. It came back to her afterwards, that gesture, with penetrating vividness.

Aunt Emily was at her most indirect, her most elusive when they were alone together. She fluttered a moment like a bird caught in a room seeking for escape: and then she found it. Eirene had come to ask her for advice: this must be avoided. For the moment Eirene was confused by what had passed. When she recovered she would tackle Aunt Emily: she must *not* recover

"Bread and butter first, dear," said Aunt Emily sharply, as Eirene's hand strayed to a chocolate cake. "You can have a cake afterwards." That was it; the schoolroom atmosphere. Anything rather than reality.

Eirene remained silent: Aunt Emily had won: she was free now to sprinkle the silence with the usual vacuities. "Mrs. Pearson was lunching with me to-day, Eirene: she wants you to go over and play tennis with them: they have got the Hawkers' house at Candili; and, by the way, Eirene, you remember the other day when . . ."

The evening light was creeping up the hills opposite: the Genoese castle showed its walls pink upon the sky-line. Eirene waited listlessly while her aunt talked. She rose to go. "That was Mr. Tenterden, Eirene, who was here when you came."

"What?" said Eirene, suddenly bewildered, "that bald man—Hugh Tenterden! *Your* Tenterden, Aunt Emily?"

(VI.)

Eirene walked down the hill-side with leaden feet. She was alone; there was none to help her. Aunt Emily was no good at all. Aunt Emily was absolutely no good. She was soft and flabby and afraid. There was no one to rely on, no one except herself. Eirene's head was set defiantly as she reached the quay. Bela Lukacs was sitting at the café drinking vermouth:

"She walks like a queen, that woman," but as she came closer he corrected himself: "That girl there walks like a woman." And Lukacs knew about these things. His little eyes blinked with curiosity. He muttered to himself in Hungarian.

Round the bend Eirene walked, and on under the French Embassy. The Secretaries' house stood between her and her home. She would have to pass it, to pass close to it along the narrow quay, close to those three grated windows on the ground floor where one heard the click of typewriters. It was not to be avoided. Eirene's head was set defiantly as she walked along the quay. Suddenly it stiffened to a quicker defiance. Angus had come out of the garden gate and was walking with bent head quickly in her direction. He had not seen her, he would be close upon her before he looked up. It would be too late for him to escape. She would bow to him coldly; that would be the thing to do. If only she did not blush; she pinched the lobe of her ear to keep from blushing; it made it worse. A sedate, a statuesque but scarlet Eirene was what Angus saw when he looked up. He clapped his hand to his pocket, the words "Oh, I have forgotten my pipe" framed on his lips. No, that would be silly. There was no escape. The thing had to be gone through with; and after all, better now, perhaps, than later.

He walked on, his pace quickening. Eirene had noted the gesture, but had not understood it. A letter, perhaps, was what he had felt for, a letter of apology. He would put it into her hand without a word, fixing her with calm apologetic eyes. He would raise his hat and pass on respectfully. Yes, that would be a good way out of it. Poor Angus! How awkward it must be for him, how very awkward. The scene—rather, the absence of a scene—with her aunt had blurred for her the preceding scene with Angus. She was unhappy now and lonely. She was not angry now. The self-conscious swing of his head, as he came nearer, stirred a fibre of pity, of protection. Poor Angus, he was ashamed! He was looking guilty as he walked along. His head swayed with self-conscious nonchalance. And she must bow to him coldly, that was the only thing to do: the muscles of her neck tautened, ready for the gesture.

He was close to her now: she stepped towards him: she held out both her hands. "I am sorry, Angus—it was silly of me—I was startled. I know that it won't happen again."

He looked at her blankly for a moment, and then his cheek flamed. "Oh, not at all; don't mention it," he stammered. She said: "Look here, Angus, you must meet my mother. We go back to Pera in a week, and you must come and see us."

He did not know what to answer: he looked at her pitiably for a moment, and raised his hat. "Thank you very much," he murmured; "that's very good of you." Again he raised his hat. "I shall miss my boat," he mumbled, and then hurried on. "Thank God!" he thought, as he stepped on to the little pier. "Thank God that Edhem is coming to dinner to-night."

Eirene walked on slowly past the grated window. The sun had set, and as she reached the little point the wind from the Black Sea blew cold upon her. She shivered, and hurried into the house. They were lighting the lamps in the passage. She went to her room. It was dark there and suddenly cold. She shut the window.

How silent it was in the little room without the noise of water! She sat upon the bed. She spoke to herself:

"That was generous of you, Eirene. That was a fine gesture." She spoke aloud like this, and her lips moved; but in her mind the thoughts wheeled and turned like swallows lost upon some dark and threatening sea; pitiably they wheeled and fluttered, seeking for the light, and the black waves battered at them as they dipped; round and round they wheeled in panic flight, chirping in agony at the dark menace of the night. Was there no light, no land? Faster they wheeled, dipping to the waves and up to the dark bluster of the sky. No light? No land? How dark it was, how cold! The night was racing with the scudding stars. The wind of panic howled upon the waves.

"Oh, Angus! My Angus . . . my little Angus!"

Eirene flung herself upon the bed: her face was buried in the pillow.

CHAPTER V.

October

(I.)

ANGUS rapped with his cane upon the blue door in the wall and Hamsa opened. "The Bey has already arrived," he whispered. "I have given him some coffee."

"That is right," said Angus, and he hung his hat upon the nail.

Edhem was lying in a deck-chair with the cigarette smoke in a light brown cloud around him. The little coffee cup was on the floor to his right, and on the other side a pile of Angus's books. His fez, immaculately ironed, was laid upon the little table. Hamsa had been awed and a little shocked by the deliberate way in which the Bey had flung his fez upon the table. It was only in the streets that Edhem wore the national headdress; he would come into a room and place it ostentatiously upon a piece of furniture, and then he would run his fingers through his straight, black hair. It was all very Parisian, very calculated; the blue serge suit, the careful monochrome of tie and sock and handkerchief, the Cartier cigarette case. And the skilful thing about it was that Edhem Bey managed to seem unconscious, or at least almost unconscious, of the effect that he produced. It was very successful.

His sisters in the chattering, giggling Haremlik of the big house at Ortakeui would call him "Monsieur le Marquis," and his old mother would raise her fat little hands and cluck around him, asthmatic and subservient. Only his father would sit there obdurate upon the divan, raising his eyebrows sometimes and jerking back his head: a gesture of Old Turkey, dignified, resigned and sceptical: a click of the tongue, and with it that strange backward motion of the head and eyebrows: a gesture of the Grand Signior; a gesture from the buried past.

Edhem rose languidly as Angus entered. He spoke to him in French, in the clipped staccato French of the Rue de Varennes. There was nothing quite so correct or quite so modern as the French of Edhem Bey. It was at the same time brittle and undulating, classic and futurist, precise and elusive. It was the shibboleth of the small exclusive set which during those ten years in Paris he had so assiduously frequented; a set, gay and brilliant, unkind yet tolerant, narrow and yet receptive. Edhem had been fortunate in the period of his arrival. He had coincided with the transition from lacquer to Persian miniatures: more precisely, he had coincided with Scheherazade. Edhem had been a success. And now that he was home, he was acutely homesick. He read of the doings of his friends in the social columns of the "New York Herald." "Parmi l'assistance on remarquait——" and a squeal of giggling would come from the women's quarters. A whole year before he could return: a whole year! He counted the weeks before his departure. He would not be back till October, 1913. He would take his old rooms in the rue de

Lille, and he would buy two cushions at Martine. The details of his installation gave him great thought, and greater solace. He devised his afternoons and his mornings: he would go to London first to get his clothes. He would return furbished and very welcome. The old life would begin again. . . .

"Parmi l'assistance on remarquait la Princesse Marthe de Beauharnais, le Baron et la Baronne Jean de Maintenon, Mme. Stocks, Edhem Bey, M. Aristide Coquebert—Mme. Wahlfeldt. . . ."

Edhem would compose these menus with the zest of a hungered man. It gave him pleasure: a pleasure intellectual rather than snobbish. And fortunately he was quite confident about it all: he did not know (fortunately he did not know) that in the interval they had discovered Picasso.

Hamsa had done his best, that day, for the dinner, and Angus had supplemented it from the English shop in Pera. There were caviare and vodka, and some sole, and pilaff, and a jam omelette, and a bottle of Léoville. By the time they had finished there were two bottles of Léoville and considerably more vodka. And then deck chairs, and coffee, and Benedictine, and cigarettes. Edhem smoked the yellow-packetted "Maryland" of the boulevards, a pose which irritated even Angus. He was full of information; he had received the "Mercure de France" that morning, and the "Danse de Sophocle." He had brought the latter in his pocket and he read bits aloud. Angus was grateful for the distraction. He was thinking of something else. He was tormented by the picture of a flushed schoolboy stammering upon the quay-side. He visualised himself detachedly as a grotesque.

The vision was peculiarly galling. Edhem was still reading, his hand swaying to the motion of the verse:—

"Je me sens si frivole et le soir est si grave;
Rentrons! Allume tout! J'ai peur!
Le silence est un mur, le souvenir s'y grave,
Et le silence est dans mon cœur.

"Nous n'avons pas la foi de ces amants illustres
Et c'est déjà, sans rêver d'eux,
Sous le soleil du ciel ou sous celui des lustres
Si difficile d'être deux!"

Angus roused himself at the last line. "Yes," he said, "that's true, that part. It's so difficult not to duplicate oneself. It's so difficult to be with another person when the other person's there also. It makes four really. There is what the other person thinks of you, and what you think of them. And for the other person also one's identity is duplicated in the same way. That makes four. It's all very unreal. And then there's a fifth element which adds to the unreality. There's the element of actual relations, the element of what one really is and what she or he really is. And it's so different from the other four. One feels the gap, and one can't bridge it. One widens it. One does not mean to posture, but one finds oneself posturing."

"Ah, I see," said Edhem, "le côté passion cérébrale."

Angus made a gesture of annoyance. "No, it's not that, Edhem. You see, when one is away, it all seems so secure and important and easy. It all seems sincere. One visualises the person; one has all the emotions. And then one meets: the other person is the same; she is gentler, more beautiful, more benign even than one had imagined: one's former picture is but the wraith of the original. And then across the mirror of her beauty one sees oneself: a caricature of oneself floats in between; one's fœtid self, body and hair and limbs and stomach. The horror of one's own familiar self: the little bits of one. And one becomes chilled. A cloud comes over the sun."

"Tiens," Edhem murmured, "le côté Baudelaire."

Angus dismissed the interruption with a petulant snap of his fingers. He leaned forward. "No, Edhem, *please* listen seriously. You call yourself a psychologist. You know how you liked the Barrès books. The whole basis, the whole physical basis, seems wrong from the beginning. The conquering male, the unwilling female. Rape, violence, abduction. The whole business is so primitive, so savage. Why should the thing be so one-sided, why should the whole responsibility fall upon the man? Has a woman no sensations? Why, then, this beastly theory of force and violation and surrender?"

He stood up angrily: he had a childish impulse to burst into tears. He clenched his fists. "I loathe this sex fallacy. I loathe it." He flung himself back in the chair. "I can't cope with it, Edhem," he concluded lamely.

There was a pause. "Mon pauvre ami," said Edhem, "mon pauvre vieux Angus. You see, you have never been in love. You don't understand. One does not analyse the thing when it comes to one. It is not a question of nerves. It's a question of skin. Not your skin, but her skin. You see, you have never been in love. You should come with me to Paris."

Angus looked at him in angered surprise. "But you're wrong, Edhem, you're quite wrong. You see, I am——" He checked himself. "I *have* been in love. I really have: that's what I'm talking about."

Edhem rose impatiently. He was always apt to be bored when people talked at length about themselves. He walked to the table and brusquely clapped his fez upon his sleek black hair. "Eh bien," he said, "next time you fall in love be careful it is not with a virgin. C'est une femme mariée, une veuve plûtot, qui fera ton affaire."

Angus walked with his friend through the little garden, to where the boat was waiting. The two rowers in their white shirts were greasing their rowlocks with a stick out of a little tin pot. There was a lantern in the stern which threw its pattern over the velvet mattress. "It is the last night of summer," said Edhem gaily as he settled down among the cushions.

Angus waited till the sound of the oars had died upon the water. The night was very warm. "The last night of summer," he repeated. He would be sorry to leave Candili. He dreaded the winter in Pera, and the cold wind from the Okmaidan, and the trams clanging through the rain. Winter and summer, spring and autumn. The procession of the years. What would they bring for Angus? What would Angus be at thirty—forty—fifty?

He slammed the garden door behind him and blew out the candle.

(II.)

October came, and with it a gale from the

Black Sea. The little tin tables on the terrace of the Summer Palace rocked and tilted under their pink linen umbrellas. The waiters hurried about, carrying them indoors. They were stored in double rows in the glass veranda: they would not be wanted again that season: already the hotel was emptying. The long road that led across the hills from Therapia to the city was dotted with the ox-wagons carting furniture back from the villas to the town. Mattresses and kitchen chairs; a wide tin basin; a canary still singing in its cage. And behind them the dust rose in columns, swirling above the trees that clothed the valleys.

Down by the water Therapia was being dismantled like a Christmas tree. Shutters were closed upon the gay façades: the little shivering box-trees at the café were taken off in a cart; the deserted, stayless awnings flapped and struggled in the wind. The English launch was bobbing in front of the Secretaries' house. There was Angus in his shirt-sleeves carrying out papers. They were tied in bundles, and some of them were in green canvas boxes. Backwards and forwards he went, handing his charges to the coxswain. A Kurd came out carrying a typewriter; and then two more Kurds struggling with a Chubb safe. The sailors came to the rescue. "'Ere, easy there"—Eirene heard them as she watched from her window in the other house. Angus came back again. He had his coat on this time. He stopped and talked to someone through the window. It was funny to watch him like this, the other Angus, the official Angus. Her little Angus, such a muddler in other things. Oh! so incompetent in other things! Her own Angus!

So busy now and so important, ordering them about like that. And they saluted him. But only she, Eirene, knew what Angus really was. Her heart went out to him. She laughed to herself delightedly.

"Well, that's all," Angus shouted, and jumped into the well of the boat. They pushed off with the boat-hook: with a wide sweep, that brought the white ensign fluttering against the awning, the launch cleared and headed down the Bosphorus. Eirene watched till it had turned the corner at Yenikeui.

"He did not look up," she thought, "he did not look up to the summer-house." She sighed a moment, and then recovered herself. Eirene was buoyant that day after days of leaden unhappiness. She clung to her period of buoyancy. "How like a man!" she concluded, using instinctively the trite and heartworn phrase: that phrase, useful, elastic and condoning: that opiate in the pharmacy of love: that futile, pitiful phrase.

Eirene turned from the window and began to pack her things. She laid them tenderly in the basket trunk. She was feeling very tender that evening. She smoothed their creases almost maternally: she smoothed the crumpled surface of the tissue paper. The box was nearly full: she stood up looking round the room, a finger to her lip. Had she forgotten anything?

Yes! There was the Italian box. The secret? She had almost forgotten it. She paused, surprised at herself, her hand fingering the key at her bosom. She had almost forgotten the secret! She sat suddenly on the bed, amazed that such a thing could be. The secret? Father? They seemed remote to her. None of the old pang and stir at their recollection. They seemed as remote as that Eirene of the long ago; the lonely schoolgirl with the long legs and the flapping tennis shoes. Remote as the June-Eirene; the pre-Angus Eirene. so remote! Remote and alien and unreal. Yes, *unreal*. A fairy story, and it had meant so much. The secret? She laughed at it. How disgusting! Her lips set suddenly to a smile; a hard smile. She took the little key and opened the cabinet. She laid the flap down open upon the table. She put the key in the bottom drawer. She slammed the trunk and fixed the straps. And then she went upstairs, leaving the door open. "I am ready, mother," she said, "I have packed my things."

"You have been quick, my little one," her mother answered: "you have not forgotten anything?"

"No, mother, I have not forgotten anything."

(III.)

Hugh Tenterden opened the despatch-box which had been sent up to him from the Chancery. There were several telegrams in the box. He looked up at the clock. He had been kept late that evening: it was nearly eight already. He glanced at his engagement book. "Tuesday, October 8th." No, he was not dining out that evening. He could dine late at the club without dressing, and meanwhile he could read the telegrams.

He gathered the papers together and tapped their collected edges upon the table till they formed a neater pile. A characteristic gesture. He was humming through his teeth: he was humming the song from "Sadko." He smoothed the topmost paper with his palm and began to read. It was not a long telegram. It was marked "Very urgent," and was dated that afternoon from Cettinje. And as he read it the tune from "Sadko" ended in a long-drawn whistle: and then came the laugh: the laugh which was his comment on most human developments. "Well, I'm damned!" he said, "a week before I expected. Well, that's done it! That's *fairly done* it."

He shuffled the remainder of the file and looked rapidly at the headings of the other telegrams. Berlin, London, Sofia, London, Sofia, Sofia, Vienna, Bucharest, St. Petersburgh, Paris, Paris, Paris, Berlin, Belgrade, St. Petersburg, London, Belgrade, Vienna, Athens, Athens, Bucharest. He began to read them carefully: he read them and he laughed again. The Powers apprehended that there was trouble impending in the Balkans: they feared that unless something were done urgently ("in twenty-four hours," said the telegram from London), there would be war: they suggested mediation: they proposed a "Joint Note" to the Sublime Porte: the wires had been buzzing with suggested formulas. The wires were still buzzing. People were sitting up in lighted offices drafting and decoding: the whole of Europe was suggesting formulas. Tenterden leant back in his chair and looked at the ceiling. He thought of Europe, of London, of the October fog in Downing Street. How well he could see it all! The light in Treasury Passage, the slamming of the side door on the

Horse Guards' Parade. And over there in Paris: the long, waxed corridors of the Quai d'Orsay. And beyond. The smell of anthracite in the Wilhelmstrasse, the stove-pipes in those overheated rooms opposite the Winter Palace. He saw it all. Earnest old men in black coats hurrying up marble staircases: people bending over tables together with pencils in their hands: the buzz of muffled bells, the clicking of a thousand typewriters; and over it all electric light, rows and rows of little white bulbs; vistas of them: the electric light of twenty capitals.

He reached out for the telegram which had been the first on the pile. He put it back with the others in the despatch-box, banging his palm upon the lid while he turned the key. And then he laughed again.

For that morning the King of Montenegro had declared war upon the Turkish Empire.

The dining-room of the Cercle d'Orient was crowded when Tenterden entered, but he found a table in the corner. Some secretaries of the German Embassy rose respectfully as he pushed past their chairs. He nodded at them cheerily: he had always stood out against the continental habit of shaking hands. He propped the "Revue des Deux Mondes" against a decanter: he tilted the chair beside him to show that it was engaged: that, at least, would prevent people from intruding. It was nearly nine. The waiters were already bringing coffee to the other tables: the slim smell of cigars cut through the heavy vapour of the room. Tenterden's blue eyes wandered with a look of interest round the groups of his colleagues. So different in type, yet all with something indefinably in common. It was evident that they did not know as yet: he smiled as he foresaw that babble that would arise when once they knew. The head waiter stood at his side patiently. He took the menu from him: "Has Nouri Pasha been here to-night?" he asked in a low voice.

"No, Mr. Tenterden," the man answered, "I have not seen His Excellency yet."

"So they know at the Porte," mused Tenterden. . . . "Poor people! You must give me some caviare, Paolo," he said aloud, "and an omelette and some chicken, and half a bottle of Pommard—no, I shall have some champagne: a bottle of Krug, Paolo, for myself." He laid his hand upon the tilted chair beside him. . . . "And this seat, you understand, Paolo, is engaged."

"I understand, Mr. Tenterden; c'est entendu."

"Poor Nouri," thought Tenterden, "he will be tired when he comes. The champagne will do him good."

It was half-past nine. A page-boy came in and gave a note to one of the Secretaries at the German table. He glanced at it and pushed back his chair. "Come," he said sharply, "we must go back at once." The words rang out like a military command.

The other four rose quickly, with a look of surprise: they filed from the room. "Ah! it begins," thought Tenterden; "it begins like this. But it is the end that matters. Good God! Where will be the end?"

For a moment the room swam before him in a haze of smoke: he felt small, individual, and helpless: he felt buffeted, confused, and afraid.

Yes, Hugh Tenterden afraid. The shapes of Europe danced symbolically before his eyes, a Europe wreathed in fire. And up there in the western corner the fretted jig-saw outline of the two Islands, isolated, puny, and detached.

"England!" he murmured slowly, "what can I . . ." but he did not complete the phrase: the reaction was too quick for that. He poured out the champagne. The balance, the perfect Tenterden balance, was restored. He was thinking; thinking in the jargon of his trade. "They will get the worst of it: almost at once they will get the worst of it. I must make that clear in my telegrams. They will talk in Downing Street of 'localisation.' Good enough. The 'conflict must be localised,' —that's how they will minute my telegrams. But the real work will have to be done here. It is here that matters. Hopeless to talk of localisation once Ferdinand's at Chichli. No, it's internationalisation we want. 'The crisis must be internationalised.' That's the business: that's the formula." He laughed to himself: he felt confident again. "Thank God!" he said, "thank God the Ambassador had to have that operation. They can scarcely send another one in time. They will have to give me six weeks. It will be over by then. My show," he murmured, "my show at last."

A man came hurriedly into the room, a tall, pale man with a stoop. His scant auburn hair contrasted strangely with the scarlet of his fez. He dropped into the nearest chair and unfolded the napkin. He looked up and saw Tenterden. He rose at once and came across to him, carrying the napkin in his hand. Tenterden pushed back the chair which he had tilted against the cloth. "I was expecting you," he said, and he poured the champagne into a tumbler.

Nouri drank it off without a word, and leant back in his chair. He looked exhausted; his hollow eyes blazed as if with fever. He looked at Tenterden, and a wan smile creased at the corner of his red moustache. He pointed to the champagne: "So you have had the news," he said; "it was thoughtful of you."

"Yes, I have had the news," said Tenterden. "We can talk about it later."

Nouri Pasha pushed back his plate: "It was a mean trick," he began, "a 'coup de bourse.' It will bring the others in before to-morrow. It will take us a month to get the redifs up from Anatolia. A month at least—anything may happen in a month. They are confident, of course, at the Seraskerat. They are always confident, these soldiers. They call it *morale*." He laid his hand on Tenterden's arm. "Tell me, Tenterden. You are a friend of twenty years. Tell me what can you do for us?"

Tenterden leant back, and for once there was no laughter in his face. "Nothing," he answered brutally; and then he repeated it: "Nothing."

Nouri Pasha poured out some more champagne.

(IV.)

Aunt Emily was a modest, and, in fact, a diffident person. She had few pretensions. She would say: "People must take me as they find me." She would say this with a thin note of defiance. She would say: "Of course, I'm only your aunt, my dear, and I know you think me a foolish old woman." She would say this knowing nothing of the sort, she would say it with a thin note of anger. And when Eirene answered in her level monotone: "Of course not, Aunt Emily," she would bunch her little round shoulders in ruffled irritation.

There was one point, however, on which Aunt Emily prided herself with flaming arrogance. It was the bazaars. Nobody knew exactly how it came that Aunt Emily had adopted so fierce a personal attitude towards the bazaars. The moment she entered those rambling blue arcades she became a different person: she became seismic. The doves would flutter anxiously to the roof, the merchants in their shops, seeing her short round figure in the offing, would hide their choicest wares and tremble. She knew no Turkish; her Greek was very rudimentary. Her methods of bargaining were physical, therefore, rather than oral. She would hold her little crocodile purse in her hand, and plump down two medjidiehs. She would seize the nearest available object, a butter jar, a strip of Persian embroidery, and thrust them into her wide string bag. And then she would snort at the astonished shopkeeper and stamp from the shop. Sometimes the man would call after her from his door. "They have no manners, these people," Aunt Emily would say; "they are mostly Jews."

Her shopping took upon itself the flurry as well as the excitement of all predatory raids; when she got home she would take stock of the booty; it was only then that she would be forced to realise that her loot, however decorative, was not, perhaps, essential. "It will be sure to come in handy one day," she would say. She always said that. No one gave more Christmas presents than Aunt Emily: there was no more munificent donor to the annual sale of the Dorcas Society.

On occasions her methods had led to trouble. She had tried her system on the bazaars at Smyrna. Ever afterwards, if Smyrna were mentioned, "That horrid place," Aunt Emily would say. "Nothing but Greeks." She hated Smyrna. And then there was that unpleasant story of the ham at Harrod's Stores. Aunt Emily had just arrived in London after an absence of several years. It was a most unpleasant story.

She met Hugh Tenterden in the Grande Rue de Pera. He greeted her with his accustomed cordiality. He wanted some bookcases made for his room: he could not trust Giuseppe to specify the heights required. He was particular about these things. Aunt Emily radiated with power and inside knowledge: her little fluttering eyes became fixed as those of an eagle. It was absurd to buy things in Pera; they cheated one abominably. It was better, far better, to go to Stamboul. But one must "know the ropes." Now she knew, she "happened to know" of a little man in the bazaars. . . . The expedition was arranged for Sunday. "Directly after church," said Aunt Emily. "I will drive you down," laughed Tenterden. And Sunday saw them travelling across the bridge in Tenterden's victoria.

The carriage stopped at the wide archway of the bazaars. Aunt Emily led the way, a little awed by Tenterden. But once within the hushed murmur of those blue arcades the old corsair spirit returned to her. The carpenter and

Tenterden's bookshelves were both forgotten. A crowded half-hour, and the little string bag was full to bursting. They went up through the outer bazaar, the bazaar where the jewellers worked, to the square of Bayazid. The square in front of the War Office was filled with ox-wagons. "Oh, dear," said Aunt Emily, "I suppose there really is going to be this war they're all talking about."

"It began," said Tenterden, "a week ago."

"How dreadful," said Aunt Emily. "Thank goodness it's so far away!"

Tenterden laughed. "Oh, it's near enough. Quite near enough. You see, it moves, Miss Davenant, it moves. It moves south. It is moving now," and he made a vague gesture towards the north. "They are all in it: Greece, Serbia, Bulgaria; all of them. And it moves very quickly indeed, Miss Davenant. Too quickly."

"Fancy that, now!" said Aunt Emily.

They had reached the Suleimanieh. The October sun blazed luminous and mellowed upon the wide terrace of the mosque. Tenterden paused a moment, looking out upon the view. Upon the Golden Horn, and the ships in the basin and the white façade of Dolmah Baghtche by the water. He smiled grimly. "The doomed city," he murmured. Aunt Emily heard the remark and was puzzled. She had always called it "domed" herself. "The city of domes and minarets," that was what she called it sometimes. But Tenterden must be right. He was always right. Aunt Emily put on that flat tone which she reserved for the æsthetics. "Look, Mr. Tenterden—oh, look! the colour of those dooms against the sea!"

He did not hear her. He was still looking down upon the city. "Just think of it," he murmured, "six hundred years! Six hundred busy, wasted years! And then in twenty days. . . ."

She blinked up at him, incomprehension and subservience flickering in her eyes.

"Yes," he concluded, "it is coming nearer, much too near."

They found the carriage waiting for them by the tomb of Roxelane.

(V.)

Eirene's little room in the Pera house stood at the corner. There were two windows which gave on the untidy open space down which the trams screamed, turning the corner from the Petits Champs. The third window was more important. It had a view. One looked out over the scarred and battered cypresses of a disused cemetery, out over the little roofs of Kassim Pasha, a glinting strip of the Golden Horn, and then the dark ridge of Stamboul and the two minarets of Sultan Selim, slim as pencils against the western sky. At sunset the outline of this window would be thrown across the room, a rose-red oblong of light upon the wall opposite, receding gradually from the bottom upwards. Eirene would watch it disappearing, and when only the brown wall was left she would rise and look out on the silhouette of Stamboul fretted against the flaming sky. That would happen in November, the month of sunsets. But afterwards there would be black clouds streaming across from the Okmaidan: and at night the house would shake to the howl of the north wind, and the heavy rain-drops would be dashed upon the panes. December, January, February; in March they would be selling narcissus in the streets, and little tight tulips, and in April would come the Judas trees. Eirene sighed. How long, it seemed, till May! She looked at the books and the great white stove. She would read a great deal that winter. She straightened a little picture on the wall. She must be going downstairs now. It was time for tea.

It was in the Pera house, in the long drawing-room with the painted ceiling and the parquet floor that Eirene's mother felt herself most at home. She was not quite at her ease out there in Therapia, in the old mouldy house above the waters. Her face powder would clod and coagulate in its little cardboard boxes. Pera was different: there was electric light, and the parquet, and the trellis with the vines, the parrots and the two monkeys painted on the ceiling. The room was filled with little chairs and tables: there were photographs in silver frames, and some embroideries from the bazaars, and endless cushions. It was not, perhaps, a very successful room: Eirene's mother, except in regard to her clothes, was not a woman of exacting taste. There was a pink brocade screen in one corner, and behind it an ornamental palm. There were three carved chairs against the wall in Spanish walnut: these had cushions on them cut into the shape of sunflowers.

Her mother was not alone when Eirene entered. She was sitting on the sofa with her doeskin gloves on, puffing at a cigarette in a long, diamond-studded holder. She was in one of her siren moods: Eirene could see that from the doorway. She was leaning back among the cushions, looking frail and interested and luxurious. She was exercising her charm. She was talking in English, with the little tripping accent which had been found so fascinating. She was saying: "How very interesting! How wonderful it must be for you to see history being made, from inside. To see it being made before your very eyes. I envy you, Mr. Field. I have only gossip to go on; and you know what Pera gossip is."

Eirene walked quickly into the room, and Angus rose awkwardly to greet her.

"How late you are, Eirene," said her mother. "Mr. Field has been telling me such wonderful things about the War. He has been very indiscreet. But we won't give him away, will we, Eirene?"

Eirene felt a stir of irritation. She did not like that "we." After all, Angus was her discovery. Mother always bagged things, and monopolised them. Angus was her discovery. It seemed so strange to see him there. Eirene went to the tea-table and occupied herself for a moment: tea and lemon, no sugar. How silly to see Angus there, and in his best clothes. He looked smug in his best clothes, and he was obviously completely taken in by mother. Eirene brought her cup across to where they were sitting: with her foot she pushed and manœuvred a stool into its place: she sat down and put the cup upon the parquet beside her. She was very composed. A little smile played at the corners of her mother's mouth. Eirene listened to the conversation. Angus was making a fool of himself. Angus was being made a fool of. That was quite evident. He was talking about his writings now. He was saying that he wrote poems in prose. He would not have dared to say that to any other public. And her mother was leading him on. Her mother was saying things like "And what a great deal you must find to write about now." She was saying: "You really must put down everything you hear. After all, we are living in stirring times. You have a literary gift: you are modern, but I can see that you have the real literary gift. It is your duty to record what is passing. Now promise me! I shall keep you to your promise. You must come and read some of your things to me. I do not pretend to be a blue-stocking like my little daughter here, but I am not wholly illiterate: I know what I like."

Eirene sipped her tea in silence. Was this Angus? This fatuous-faced young man in the blue serge suit? Angus? He was being funny now: he was being "nimble-minded." And her mother was laughing, a graceful, inward, musical laugh: hard and deliberate as the diamonds that trembled on her little ears. "Oh, Mr. Field," she tinkled, "quel faiseur de paradoxes!"

The little china clock struck six. Eirene was out of it. Yes, there was no doubt, she was out of it sitting there upon her stool. It was her rôle, of course, to be detached: it had become a habit with her to be conversationally lethargic. A habit born of shyness to some extent, but still more of indolence. She would keep in her hand the drab pennies of ordinary conversation and dole them out with a sleepy gesture when it became necessary; she would hand them out abstractedly as she gave pennies to the toll-men on the bridge. She would say: "Is it long since you have been in Constantinople?" and she would not listen for the answer. She would say: "Yes, of course, it looks very beautiful from the sea when one first arrives. But it's a different story when once one has landed. The mud, you know, and the *smells!*"

Eirene would say these things quite unscrupulously. They served well enough for the occasion, and then there was always her mother there to prattle for her. But what was worse, she said them with a too transparent lack of conviction: it was all too perfunctory. This annoyed people: they thought her conceited. Poor, humble Eirene! It disconcerted people: they never knew how to take her. "That strange, solemn girl," they would say; or "that poor girl may be *very* clever, but she has no sense of humour." Eirene felt that she was unpopular. It distressed her. She would envy, sometimes, her mother's faculty of forming a conversational centre. But then her mother was silly. Surely her mother was very, very silly? And *mean;* yes, it was mean of her to make a fool of Angus.

Eirene spoke to him: her voice broke in upon the tinkle of their talk. "Mr. Angus," she said, "we are going to the Sweet Waters to-morrow. Will you come with us? The Sultan is coming in his State barge. It will be interesting."

Angus noted the tone of dismissal. He rose, and shook hands with her mother. He arranged with her the details of to-morrow's expedition. They were to pick him up at the Embassy after luncheon: they would drive to the Sweet Waters and watch the people from the carriage. He became self-conscious again as he said good-bye to Eirene. His head swayed self-consciously as he walked towards the door. It was raining when he left the house: he turned up the collar of his aquascutum. "What a pleasant woman," he thought, "such charm! So slim, and pretty, and refined. So easy to talk to. It was good, that what I said about one's being able to see Olympus. I can work that in somewhere. I hope it will be fine to-morrow: good copy."

He turned up the narrow street, the Tepé Bachi, the street at the top of the hill. The pavement glittered in the rain. "How sulky Eirene was!" He walked over the wide gravelled forecourt of the Embassy. "I wish," he thought, as he shook out his dripping aquascutum in the archway, "that Eirene had a little more bounce. That she were a little more resilient. She cramps one's style, sitting there and looking at one. How different she is from her mother! The father must have been a heavy cove."

And in the warm and lighted room under the painted vine leaves, Eirene's mother was laughing, as she lit another cigarette. "How secretive of you, my little one. Mais il est très bien, ton ami, très presentable. And you never told me he was so beautiful. Why, it's the young Apollo come to earth."

The young Apollo!—Eirene did not flame to the suggestion. She felt dispirited. The young Apollo! In a blue serge suit, making conversation. She rose and went up to her room.

(VI.)

The wind changed to the south the next morning and swept the sky to the clear, warm blue of late October. Angus sat opposite to them on the little seat of the victoria. He had a camera with him in a black case, and his fingers played incessantly with the lock. They talked together, he and her mother: her mother's tone had altered. Eirene noted the alteration. There was a note of badinage. It marked a stage: Eirene recognised the stage. Her mother would smile across at Angus: a gay, distinguished little smile. There was nothing wrong about the quality of the smile: it was its duration that was so significant. It lasted just a second longer than was warranted by the cause which had provoked it. Only a second longer, but enough to leave a faint vibration in the air; —the faintest fœtid breath in the air of innuendo. Had Angus noticed it? How bad for Angus! He *must* have noticed it; he was expanding like a flower to the sun. Eirene felt like a dark rain-cloud lowering in the west: she felt sinister towards Angus. She felt revengeful: how she longed to dissolve in rain; a cataract of tears upon their gaiety. How they would run and scamper! How cross her mother would be: her hat! The colour in her cheeks! Eirene lolled, silent and menacing as a rain-cloud in a windless June.

They had reached the hill-top from where the road cuts down into the valley of Sweet Waters. The meadows on each side of the river were dotted with figures walking on the bank: a parasol: a man with a white handkerchief under his fez: a group of Turkish women in magenta: bright, isolated colours against the green. The carriages were lined up along the road under the hill.

"We can get down," her mother said, "and walk across the meadow. It is early yet." They crossed the meadow, Eirene trailing a few steps behind them. After all, one had one's pride.

The people were thicker along the bank. They were waiting for the Sultan in his great barge. The little boats had crowded to one side, leaving the fairway open. The Sultan would be rowed up to the kiosque under the trees. He would have tea there, and then he would drive home. It had all been in the papers that morning. There was a man selling ices and lemonade. He rang a brass bell. Nobody took any notice. The crowd was mainly European. Angus and Eirene's mother were making fun of the women's clothes. What a pointless thing to do! Surely it was very pointless to laugh at other people's clothes? There was an old woman selling nuts and sugar-sticks upon a trestle. She was cooking something in a pot on a brazier: the smell of vanilla mingled with the smell of the trampled grass. Eirene smiled grimly: yes, it was just like that: she murmured the words to herself: it was just like that.

"Je me souviens d'un soir aux Eaux-Douces d'Asie,
  Soir si trainant, si mou,
Que déja, comme un chaud serpent, la Poésie
S'enroulait à mon cou.

"Une barque passa, pleine de friandises,
  O parfums balancés!
Des marchands nous tendaient des pâtes de cerises
  Et des cédrats glacés.

"Une vielle faisait cuire des aubergines
  Sur l'herbe, sous un toit,
Le ciel du soir etait plus beau qu'on n'imagine,
  J'avais pitié de moi."

"J'avais pitié de moi." The crowd was getting thicker. They were lining the banks. Some of them had brought camp stools. There was a sudden stir of interest and a glint of scarlet and gold in the fairway. It was not the Sultan: it was the Embassy caique, the six-oared caique which was only used on State occasions. Tenterden was there, and some London women. Angus took off his hat self-consciously as they passed. They had not seen him. The garish boat passed into the shadow of the plane trees by the kiosque: she recognised Tenterden's laugh above the murmuring of the crowd. They moved on behind the thin line of people on the shores. Eirene loitered a moment by the sweet-stall. The crowd closed tightly along the bank. Some Frenchmen up there were taking off their hats. The Sultan was coming. The crowd was silent and respectful. A woman waved a pink handkerchief. Eirene could hear the splash of the oars as the boat passed: she loitered by the sweet-stall. The Sultan's band was up there in the kiosque, the famous Ertogrul band. A burst of music greeted his arrival. The crowd stood there looking at the boats as they passed up the river. She could not see Angus or her mother: they had gone on ahead somewhere. One had one's pride. The smell of the vanilla, the smell of trampled grass, the shadows lengthening on the brown, bare hills. "J'avais pitié de moi!" Was the rain-cloud going to burst? Eirene straightened her head in defiance. She was punching holes in the grass with her parasol: one made four holes all round and put one in the middle: that made a quincunx. And then one began again.

"So you were bored by the procession?" The

voice was close to her. She turned round suddenly: it was Mr. Tenterden: the man who had bowed to her that evening at Therapia. It was to her he was speaking: he had raised his hat.

Eirene smiled at him: a smile that caught her unawares. She had smiled so candidly across to him. A smile of relief: a smile of liking at his buoyant voice and eyes: a smile of liking. She did not answer his question, she had nothing to say. She stood there a little embarrassed now at her first smile: her head drooped a little: her cool hands were holding the parasol, thrusting it into the turf. He came and stood beside her silently. They looked at the crowd. It was melting away now: people were streaming back across the meadow. They stood in silence. And then their eyes met and they smiled again.

"The smell of vanilla," said Eirene: it was on her mind. "I must be getting back," said Tenterden: it was on his. "I must find my motor."

"Ah, there you are, Eirene," called her mother. "We had lost you."

Tenterden did not wait. "I must find my motor," he said again and left her, with his buoyant smile. She bowed to him, a little awkwardly.

"Who was that stranger, Eirene?" said her mother, "who was that man you were standing with?"

"It was Mr. Tenterden, mother, of the Embassy."

"Oh, the famous Tenterden! The breaker of hearts. You were not being very polite to him, Eirene. Tu manquais d'amabilité."

Eirene did not answer. Her mother was less

talkative on the way home. "My head is aching again. The sun and the crowd."

They were almost silent as the carriage rattled through Chichli. Angus, upon his little seat, appeared preoccupied.

(VII.)

The sound of her mother's voice came up the staircase a little stridently. She was calling for Eirene. She was standing there in evening dress on the landing by the drawing-room, and she was calling for Eirene. The light sparkled on the sequins of her dress and upon the diamonds, with their spurt of osprey feathers, in her hair. Eirene paused upon the staircase, dazed into poignant admiration. How slim she was! How radiant! Those long gloves, the line of the pearls that hung so straight and gracefully. Eirene felt a twinge of the old fear come back to her. She paused upon the steps, descending slowly and with apprehension. How drab she felt beside that radiant figure. It wasn't fair; it wasn't fair that the old fear should come back so suddenly. A schoolgirl; that's what she was, a schoolgirl who had been naughty. She felt the violet ink-stains again upon her thumb.

Her mother was speaking while she buttoned her gloves. "I am dining with the Antoniadis to-night, Eirene. They asked you to come in afterwards, but you look so tired, my little one. Perhaps you had better go to bed early. You have been looking tired these days, ever since we went to the Sweet Waters."

"No, I am not tired, mother, but I shall not

come to the Antoniadis." There was a sullen note in her voice.

Her mother's shoulders twitched in irritation. "Well, as you like, little one. As you like. It will be a dull party, I expect. Only Ion Paniotis and that young Apollo from the Embassy. I promised to take him there in the carriage." She glanced at the clock. "It is a long drive, but I have still time."

She paused and looked at her daughter. Eirene was leaning against the double door of the drawing-room, her face impassive. That maddening, imperturbable calm of Eirene's: obtuse, superior, maddening. Her mother's voice rasped in irritation.

"Oh, by the way, Eirene, I have been meaning to speak to you. It was foolish of you to stand there alone with that Mr. Tenterden at the Sweet Waters: and you know his reputation; or, at least, you should know it. I do not wish you to be conspicuous. You must be careful. You are not a child, and we know so few of the right people. Your father was so peculiar. We know so few people. And you will have to marry some day. It is foolish to advertise yourself with people you cannot marry. You make yourself cheap, little one. And Hugh Tenterden, of all people! Why, he has had Queens and Grand Duchesses to choose from. Do you think he would look at you, Eirene?" Her voice was rising in anger at her daughter's indifference. "You, who never take trouble with anyone, but just go about like a damp hen."

Eirene was leaning back against the doorway, her open palms pressed hard against the panels. She was not looking at her mother. She was looking out beyond to where the pine trees at Tchamludja were moaning in the darkness. She did not know that she was speaking aloud. She did not know that in her dreary voice she had murmured the name of Paniotis. She was awakened by her mother's startled exclamation. She looked across at her and saw the little face twitching suddenly as from a lash. She saw the little jewelled fingers clutch on the slim row of the pearls. Only then did she realise that she had said the name. Slowly and deliberately she leaned forward and nodded at her mother, solemn, menacing. "Yes, Paniotis, mother. You forget that I saw it: you forget that evening at Therapia. I saw it all."

With a strange, flurried little rush her mother stumbled towards her, the twitching fingers seized upon the silk of her daughter's jacket. Eirene recoiled against the door, her open palms pressed tight upon the panels.

"So you lied, did you, innocence; so you lied to me about it? And you have been spying upon your mother, with your sullen, sulky eyes? You have been spying, have you? Spying? Spying!" At each word her mother's voice rose a key, at each word she tugged and twitched at Eirene's clothes.

They stood there pressed together, panting, her mother looking up at Eirene, her features drawn and tense: Eirene's eyes were fixed dreamy and immovable upon the wall beyond.

"I could kill you, Eirene, when you look like that. I could kill you, do you hear? Kill you! Kill you! Kill you! It is the look your father had, your fool of a father. He knew that it maddened me. Are you deaf, Eirene? Do you hear me? Your fool of a father: your red-faced fool of an English father!"

Slowly Eirene raised her palms from the door behind her. Slowly she laid them on her mother's naked shoulders. She looked down at the fierce, flushed face panting up into her own. She noted the quick flash of fear that crept across the startled eyes. She laughed aloud, and her wide, strong hands stole upwards, slowly, very slowly, to her mother's throat. She held them there, watching the panic strain and twitch across those painted features. And then she dropped them to her side. "Go, mother," she said, her eyes narrowing down to that taut visage: "Go, mother, or I shall strangle you."

The little jewelled fingers flicked back to the pearls. For a moment her mother hesitated. She stepped back and picked up a comb which had fallen on the carpet. Her voice was low and trembling. "You are unstrung, Eirene, you must go to your room. You must stop there till I send for you."

But Eirene remained motionless, her palms pressing again upon the panels. A faint smile parted her lips, showing a line of set teeth. Her mother was picking up the sequins on the carpet. There was a sudden ringing at the bell.

"That must be Mr. Field," said Eirene.

CHAPTER VI.

November

(I.)

EIRENE woke the next morning with the leaden feeling that something had happened; something terrible. She rubbed her eyes, and then with a stab it came to her: it came to her as the probing stab of a sword. "How absurd!" she said: "how beastly!" She was awake now. She sat up and smoothed the hair away from her forehead. And then her life, the circumstances of it, the drab, intricate circumstances of it, the sombre hopelessness of it crashed down upon her. It came suddenly, in a descending darkness as at the turn of a switch. "My poor Eirene," she said, "poor Meirene." She said that to save time: to save her face. She was frightened. She pushed the spectre of her life away from her; but it came back, it swept back in a reflux and overwhelmed her. It swept back and sent her head burying deep into her hands. The agony of it! Physical agony: she bit her lip so as not to call aloud. She had defiled herself: she had defiled the real Eirene. She had lost control: control was the real Eirene: control and balance. Oh! she had been unbalanced before, sometimes, terribly unbalanced! She knew that. But it had been by herself; it had been in secret. This time it had appeared in front of mother: it had happened *to* mother, *with* mother. Eirene had demeaned herself. She swayed with mortification.

And Angus? What did Angus matter? Romance? Love? That was a schoolroom business. Or something worse. The dry hill-top, the smell of thyme, the water splashing in its trough. How filthy! Eirene tried to feel that it had been filthy. And then there was Angus! He had been so busy, so important, in his shirt-sleeves upon the quay. He had hurried backwards and forwards with his papers. So important! The coxswain had saluted him. Little Angus! The sun had flashed upon his curls. And then the launch had swung out and up to Pera. That had been the end.

No, it wasn't mother's fault exactly. Mother was like that. Eirene knew the way she would hold her cigarette, the little diamonds upon the slim black holder, the long doe-skin gloves: she would hold her cigarette away from her, and the dark eyes would narrow at the smoke. It was an effective method: it was significant: significant for Eirene: she had so often seen it employed before. And little Angus. Her lithe, strong Angus? Her big Angus? Surely he was worth it for anyone? Eirene smiled bitterly. It was not mother's fault. She had shown taste. No, it was not mother's fault: mother was like that, she could not help it. But Angus! He had made society conversation. He had sat that day looking self-conscious upon the seat opposite. He had made up to mother. Eirene was feeling angry again. He had *wanted* to make up to mother. To that extent he was diminished. Diminished! She sucked the breath in through her teeth; the stab to her heart: a little, tortured fish there inside her. Diminished? She could improve all that. She was wiser, cleverer than Angus. It would be something to improve, that side of him, the silly side. Eirene smiled again, gently this time, tenderly. She would put stakes round him; little, gentle bamboo stakes, like those the gardener at Therapia would put round the clump of purple lilies. Angus would not notice the little stakes. She would protect him from himself. Eirene yearned to protect him. She understood Angus: she was quite sure now that she understood him. Her little Angus! It was not mother's fault. He was a toy to mother, a beautiful, rare toy. Mother did not realise how silly Angus was. How could she? He belonged to Eirene. It was only Eirene who knew how silly Angus was.

She sat up and smoothed her hair again. She must make it up with mother: she would have to apologise. Her heart sank at the absurd embarrassment of it all. But she would have to make it up: that was the fair thing to do. And she must be calm and confident with Angus. She must pretend that she had noticed nothing. That also was the thing to do: calm and confident.

She rose and went to the dressing-table. How late it was! She had not slept last night, and sleep had only come to her in the late morning. It was half-past ten. The coffee on her little tray was cold. She drank it down in one draught, and shivered. How the window rattled! She went across to it and felt the bolt. It had never rattled like that before. It rattled at intervals, as if someone had pushed it gently with a bolster. How strange it was! She looked down at the cypresses. No, there was no wind that morning

—no wind that morning, and yet a gale of despair howled through her empty heart. She put her hands to her face, a hand on each cool cheek. She held her face there close to the mirror. "How beautiful you are, Meirene!" She said this to herself—oh, God! What was the future to be? Was there nothing, nothing that remained to her of good? She rocked herself upon the little stool. She would have to go downstairs. To face it all: this morning and the long day, and the next long day. The perspective of the months in front of her, a dark, dripping perspective, leading nowhere, like the gallery of a mine. She rocked upon her little stool.

Again the window rattled. Eirene went to it and pulled at the sash. There was a strange, muffled thudding coming across from behind Stamboul. Down in Kassim Pasha there were figures standing on the roofs: looking to the north. The people in the streets below were standing there in little, anxious groups. What had happened? Everyone was looking the same way: white faces turned towards the west. It was very strange, that thumping there beyond the city walls.

She did not understand. She dressed hurriedly and went down to the drawing-room. Her mother was there with Paniotis. They were sitting on the sofa together. Paniotis came across to her with little, shambling steps: he had been crying. Eirene looked at him in amazement: he fumbled for her hand. He spoke in Greek to her.

"Eirene," he said, "you are so sensible, people listen to you. People do what you say. You must help me with the Embassy."

She looked from him to her mother in blank astonishment. "I do not understand," she said.

Her mother came across to them. There was a look in her face that Eirene had not seen before. The little, mobile face was set in firmness, in dignity even, and she spoke oddly: she spoke slowly and with a solemn face. "No, Ion," she said, "No, Eirene would not understand. You see, she has never seen a man so frightened."

He looked at them. He hesitated an instant, and then he shambled from the room.

Her mother trembled for a moment, and then the little back became rigid again and proud. She sat upon the sofa. Eirene came and knelt beside her. She put her arm upon her little shoulders. It seemed natural to do this now—the first instinctive gesture of protection. "What is it, mother? Tell Eirene."

Her mother was sobbing, sobbing broken-heartedly into the cushion. "The Army has been beaten," she sobbed. "The Bulgars are advancing: they will be at the gates to-morrow. He is afraid of massacres. Ion is afraid."

And as she said it the large windows shook and trembled at the sound of the guns.

(II.)

Hugh Tenterden blotted the telegram which he had written and placed it carefully in the despatch-box. He stretched out for a red label and wrote across it "Very urgent" in blue pencil. And then he rang the bell. "Take this," he said, "and tell the gentlemen that it must go at once. It is very urgent. There will be nothing more to-night." He pulled down the roll-top to his desk and pushed in the flap. And then he locked it. "It was the only thing to do," he said. He went to the window and drew aside the red silk curtains. He pulled up the French latch and the double windows swung open: the cold night wind from Thrace burst in upon the room. The row of pictures swayed out from the wall. The guns were silent. For the first time that day the wind was empty of the soft thud of the guns. Tenterden closed the windows and drew back the curtains. "Good!" he said, "there will be time enough." He took his hat and coat from the table, and then he paused. "Or does it mean that it is over already?"

He laughed, a little nervously. He had done all he could. There was no more to-night. He laughed again, but the frown remained there, an unwonted line between his eyebrows: a pensive, serious Tenterden. He braced himself as he reached the Cercle d'Orient; it was the buoyant, everyday Tenterden who entered the hot and crowded room. They made way for him: they were standing in excited groups, voluble and nervous. There was a momentary hush as he came into the room. They eyed him curiously: they did not stare at him, they were too polite for that. But when he looked up from his table he would find them glancing in his direction, noting his look and gesture. Yes, he must not show them what he felt. He sat at his table with "La Vie Parisienne" propped opposite to him on the decanter. It was well to bring a note of flippancy into so tense an atmosphere. This time to-morrow he would know better: they would all know. How much did they know already?

He strained his ears. They were talking of Baba Eski. But that was weeks ago—or, rather, days ago. That was quite out of the picture. The Army of the West? The papers of that morning had been discreet upon the subject. . . .

"Nous croyons savoir," had said the Journal de Constantinople, "we have reason to believe that the Army of the West is continuing its triumphant progress." But the Cercle d'Orient, at least, must know of Koumanovo: must know that the Army of the West had ceased to be an army. And Salonica? "No Ottoman Patriot," had written the Tanin, "will lend his ears to the tendencious rumours which our enemies are spreading in regard to Salonica." But, surely, the Cercle d'Orient knew about Salonica? And the Army of the East? Kirk-Kilisse, and Lule Burgas? A strategical retirement? But, surely, the Cercle d'Orient knew that it was more? The whole city to-day had learnt abruptly that it was more than that. The most apt of communiqués could not explain away the menace of the guns, the thunder of the guns so close, so close beyond the bare ridge of the hill. Tenterden raised the paper closer to his eyes. Far other visions danced across his brain. A defeated army, a wild, retreating army, falling back in panic and starvation to the great city which they were about to lose for ever. In little groups they would come along the road from San Stefano: and some of them from the East, from Dercos: in little groups they would come, slouching along without their officers. The Government would have left by then. They would have left in the night, to-night perhaps, for Broussa. And all the time the guns would come nearer. A fire would begin down there in Stamboul. And then another. The minarets would topple in the flames. Why should they let the Christians desecrate their shrines? The Christians? The rich, inert population of the town, scattered, unorganised, afraid: sheep for the slaughter. To-night, perhaps, it would begin. To-night? To-morrow? If only he could have till Sunday: only three days, and then it would be easier. Only a fortnight's war, and then this thundering at the gates! But he had warned them at home. That, at least, was a consolation.

The responsibility! Tenterden's brain reeled: he picked up the "Vie Parisienne" and forced a smile to play upon his lips. There were drops of perspiration on his forehead: he wiped them off. The colony? The English colony? That girl there—Davenant's daughter—whom he had met at the Sweet Waters. That calm girl, with the gentle voice. Well, she would manage. She was serene and competent. Yes, she would manage well enough. But the others, the governesses and the futile people! He had done all he could. The rest must be left to chance—to the Tenterden luck. But those poor, frightened people! He prayed that they did not know, as yet, what cause there was for panic. Perhaps they would not know till Sunday. And by Sunday morning, perhaps. . . . he counted the hours upon his fingers: yes, at the earliest by Sunday morning. To-day was Friday. Thirty-six hours. And every hour along those mudded roads the groups of tired, desperate men were streaming back, back on the quailing, helpless city.

It was with sudden relief that Tenterden looked

up to find Nouri standing beside him. "So you are still here," he said to him. "I feared you might be off to Broussa."

Nouri sat down abruptly; he put his hand on Tenterden's arm: "Cher ami, je vous prie," he said in a low voice, "ne plaisantez pas." The room was eyeing them, watching their expressions.

"We shall hold them," murmured Nouri, "we shall hold them at Chataldja. They have advanced too quickly; there must be a pause. It is their cavalry we are afraid of. We have no idea where it is. We have lost touch with it. There is great disorganisation. Their cavalry may be quite near to us to-night." He smiled despairingly and shrugged his shoulders. "It may at this moment be in the town. Can you do nothing? A word at Sofia? Two days' delay, and we are safe. And you know, if they come on, you know what will happen here: you know what will happen," he paused for an instant, "*when we are gone!*"

"I know," said Tenterden gravely. "I have made arrangements." It was best to say that. Nouri would think that there were no arrangements he could have made.

A man came in and handed a note to Nouri Pasha. He crumpled it in his hand. "Better news," he said; "they have located the cavalry. It is re-forming at Chorlu. We have time. If you can do something, we have plenty of time."

Tenterden's laugh rang out across the room. "At Chorlu? I, too, then shall have time."

Tenterden had laughed: Nouri Pasha had received a note, and Tenterden had laughed gaily. The news spread round the club and out into the trembling town beyond. It reached the German Embassy. "But he is always laughing," they said; "he laughs at everything."

It reached the Austrian Embassy. Bela Lukacs was sitting in the corner smoking his cigar. He got up quickly from his chair. "That is true," he said, "he always laughs. But, none the less, I shall go upstairs. I must tell the Ambassador."

(III.)

A day of suspense, that second day of November; a day of suspended anxiety. In the Greek and Jewish quarter, at the Phanar, and down in Galata, the poorer aliens herded together like sheep at an approaching thunderstorm. It needed but a spark to light the panic: already, down by the bridge, the tyre of a motor lorry had burst with a sudden report, and had been followed by the rattle of closing shutters. The story of it had spread like wildfire through the crowded streets: a soldier had fired his rifle in the air: they had tried to arrest a man on the bridge, and he had shot the gendarmes: an attack had been made on the Director of the Ottoman Bank: they had shot at him as he drove past in his carriage: there had been an attack on the Bank itself. The Armenians shuddered: that was the way the massacres had begun in 1895. It would be the same thing again. There would be Kurds to hit them on the head with hammers: the corpses would be piled up in a line along the parapet of the bridge. The Powers would do nothing. They had done nothing in '95. They had done nothing last time at Adana. It would begin again. The Armenians sat herded together rocking in agony. And the day wore on. And still the guns were silent at Chataldja. What did it mean? The silence frightened them more than the previous bombardment. It was more sinister than the dull thudding of the guns: one did not know what had happened: one did not know where "they" were. Already strange men from Anatolia had been seen lurking in the town. The Government were leaving for Broussa: the Sultan's yacht had kept up steam. One could see it there in front of Dolmah Baghche, and as one looked the paint and gilding quivered in the heat of the funnels. The Powers were doing nothing. The great Powers of the world with fleets and soldiers. Once again they would leave the Christians of Constantinople to the slaughter. And the Ambassadors would, in their turn, go off in their yachts. They would go across to the Gulf of Ismid, and stay there fishing, while the smoke of murder hung over the abandoned city.

It was thus that they were whispering furtively in the crowded alleys of Galata. And up in Pera their richer compatriots were murmuring the same. And the launch of Paniotis, without its flag, was heading with full steam for Prinkipo. Paniotis sat moodily in the little cabin. He was drinking Benedictine: he was thinking how much he loathed the English.

(IV.)

It was different for Eirene: different for Angus. For her, the turmoil in her heart left little respite for the thought of other things. For him, there was a new excitement in the air: there was an atmosphere of zest. Eirene sat in her little room, and the wet autumn evening descended slowly upon the four brown walls. She sat there motionless, and the white porcelain stove glimmered in the growing darkness. She was piecing the whole thing together: she was trying to be reasonable and detached. She forced herself to think of her life, of the present confusion, as a tangible object, an object which she could hold in front of her in her hands. She would turn it this way and that, scrutinising its every facet, finding there a flaw and here a flaw: perhaps she would find the secret of its incompetency, the measure of its confusion. She tried to think consecutively: she kept on repeating the headings of her theme: "Eirene, Angus, mother." But no thought would fix itself under these headings, only a dark cloud of pain which weighed upon her faculties. She tried the other method. She said: "No, Eirene, you must start from the beginning; you must tell yourself the whole story from the start." But where did it begin? The roots of it pressed down, down right into herself, right down into the child Eirene, the child who had stood there at Haidar Pasha when they buried her father. She said: "I suppose, Eirene, that you are in love with this man Angus." But *was* she in love with him? She scarcely knew him; how little did she know him when she came to think of it? For who was Angus? He was beautiful of course, but his hands were limp and clammy. How disloyal of her to think that! And then he was not a man, not a real man like father had been. Or like Mr. Tenterden. Eirene smiled in spite of herself. Mr. Tenterden, what did he think of Angus? But Angus appealed to her. He had been so cross, so childishly cross, when she had laughed at his writing. And how bad it had been! Dear Angus! And then he had been taken in by mother. It wasn't mother's fault—she was like that. But Angus should have been a little more dignified about it. He had been flat and smug, and bumptious: he had said little, brilliant things: the little things that Eirene could not think of, and which, for that reason, annoyed her all the more. She was not attracted to the nimble-minded. To her it seemed a mere gambol faculty: it rang false. "Yes, that's what it is," she repeated: "he's very pretty, Angus, but he is not very real."

And Angus, working there up at the Embassy, was beginning to feel impatient. It was not fair to be kept in like this when so much was going on in the town. It was not fair, when he would be so welcome in many lit drawing-rooms. He would know the news: they would ask him when he came into the room: there would be a chaos of enquiry: even the important people would stop talking and would listen to him. He would be greeted as if he really were a member of the Embassy. Not a mere archivist for once! He would be discreet, of course: he would not give anything away: but it was unfair to keep him there when the whole town was throbbing with excitement. He glanced at the clock. It was nearly six. He would go in five minutes. Where should he go? He knew well enough: he would go and see Eirene's mother. She might be feeling anxious: it would help her if he went round.

Angus hurried along the Tepé Bashi and down the street of the little fields. It was raining drearily. He could see the lights in the drawing-room. They had not closed the shutters, and he could see the big, pink shades. He rang the bell.

"Yes, Madame was in: but they did not know if she would be receiving anyone." "Tell her it is I," said Angus, "Mr. Field, of the British Embassy."

The answer was not long in coming back. "Madame regrets that she is unable to receive Mr. Field."

Angus walked back slowly under the rain. He had better look in again at the Embassy; there might be some more work to do.

There was.

(V.)

Tenterden was having tea that evening in the German Embassy. The long red room was crowded with people: they had come there from curiosity partly, and some of them because they, also, were afraid. It all seemed safer in that huge, white barrack.

Tenterden was standing in the window talking to Bela Lukacs. The Point of the Seraglio and the sea beyond shimmered gloomily in the drizzle of the autumn evening. The clouds hid the Bithynian mountains, and the Marmora spread grey and cold in the failing twilight.

Lukacs had been to the front. He had been taken to the front by Abdullah Pasha. He had been at Kirk-Killisse, and Lule Burgas. He had witnessed the retreat. He was not very convincing. "The technical services," he was saying, "are beyond reproach; the men also: also the officers. The morale is excellent."

Tenterden smiled at him: "Then to what, my dear Bela," he asked, "do you attribute this—this comparative absence of victory?"

Lukacs grunted and shrugged his shoulders. "They were not prepared," he said; "the others were. It was the first rush that did it. But, mark you, it was not a rout; there was no panic: it was a retreat; had the roads been in better condition it would have been an orderly retreat. As it was——" He spread out his fat hands sideways.

"And you think," enquired Tenterden in his level voice, "you think that they can hold them at Chataldja?"

"It is a question of days, Mr. Tenterden, a question of hours. I do not know. It is no use my saying more to you than that I do not know."

There was a pause, and Lukacs continued, a note of aggressiveness rising in his voice. "Ah! you diplomatists," he said, "you do not know the meaning, you do not know the facts, of war. Why should you? It is not your business. With you there arises so seldom the unaccountable, so seldom the unforeseen, the very urgent. I know you! I have no prejudice. You are all the same. Benign and well-intentioned, intellectual and industrious. Ah, yes! You have all the qualities. But you have little sense of time, Mr. Tenterden; you move courteously and prudently, but you have no sense of time. You have no sense of action. Your business is a negative one; you are there to *prevent*. Oh, I do not say that you do not know your business. You have prevented many things, even the reforms in Macedonia. But what have you done, I ask you? What have you constructed? Oh, you are negative people, you diplomatists. And you have no sense of time. You sit around the cauldron noting the bubbles. There is not a bubble which escapes your attention. But when it boils over you all start backwards in astonishment, in pained astonishment: you do not think of putting out the fire." He waved his hand at the city below them. "To-morrow," he continued, "we may have the Bulgars in Stamboul. Who is to get them out, Mr. Tenterden? What is to be the end? Tell me that, Mr. Tenterden; you who are so clever at preventing things; tell me, can you find the cure? To-morrow, may be, Tsar Ferdinand will ride through the Golden Gate. He will not find the Sultan here. He will not find the Government. They will have gone three hours before he enters. And during those three hours? A lot may happen in three hours, Mr. Tenterden. You should have thought of that."

"I *have* thought of it," said Tenterden abruptly.

"Yes, but too late, my dear friend. You diplomatists have no sense of time. What will *you*, alone, be able to do in those three hours? Answer me that, Mr. Tenterden, answer me that."

Tenterden's eyes had fixed suddenly upon the line of sea beyond Stamboul. His gaze had stiffened into a sudden alertness. Was it an illusion of the fading twilight? He pulled out his watch. A quarter to five. Scarcely possible: and yet she was the fastest of our cruisers. The very fastest. Oh, God! if it were true!

Lukacs had not noticed Tenterden's sudden rigidity: he had his back to the window: he was chuckling to himself and murmuring: "Answer me that, Mr. Tenterden, answer me that."

Tenterden looked again: there could be no doubt about it: it could be nothing else: he sighed, the deep sigh of sleepless nights. He put his hand on Lukacs' rounded shoulder: the temptation was a strong one. He could have swung the man round: he could have pointed to those four grey funnels, to the spurt of foam about her bows: he could have said: "That, Lukacs Bela, that is my answer."

He did none of these things. He led Lukacs back into the room. "Come," he laughed, "come, let us have some tea." He spoke a moment to his hostess. "The winter has come early," he said.

The sound of a gun crashed suddenly against the windows. And then another. Lukacs put a trembling cup upon the table.

Tenterden's voice broke in upon the silence: "There is no need," he said, "to be alarmed. It is a British cruiser. She is saluting the Turkish flag."

(VI.)

The mosque of Little St. Sophia lies on the seaward side of the seven hills, where the ridge of Stamboul slopes gently to the Marmora. Lonely but secure it stands, a small oasis in a world of devastation. Above the little wall that bounds its precincts rise pomegranates and a single fig tree. Around are ruins.

To the north, climbing the hill-side, runs a dishevelled tract of recent destruction: the wake of some Stamboul fire, a thousand wooden houses levelled in one evening to the ground. And they have left it thus: the Administration, the Municipality, the Ministry of the Interior. It was a *fait accompli*, this scab upon the hill-side, and they accepted it. It remained. The rubble has been piled on each side of the gaping, grass-grown streets. A drab Pompeii: a wall, may be, still standing here; a tottering chimney-stack; the bones of a brass bedstead among the nettles; some blackened wall-paper peeling beside a rusted grate. It had remained like that: it would remain like that so long as the crescent pointed to the sky.

To the south, fringing the soft lip of the Marmora, another ruin; the frail façade of a palace on the shore. Three marble arches opening to the sea: the carved brackets of a fallen balcony, the waves below splashing on heavy capitals half-buried in the sand. And through the arches the wide level of the Marmora, blue as a lapis pavement, stretching across to the sharp shore-line of Bithynia: and beyond, the soft sweep of the mountains, twenty miles away: the snows of Olympus hanging in the sky. The Palace of the Bucoleon, the Palace of Hormisdas, that balcony where fourteen hundred years ago Theodora had dreamt of lust and love and Empire; a pavilion, merely, to the vanished palaces upon the hill, a pavilion, delicate and imperial, built out into the waves. Ruin had come and touched it with a gentle dignity. The Turk had come, and fouled it with the squalid finger of the East. Some chickens pecked upon the trampled grass: a shanty had been built against a buttress, roofed with petroleum tins: the waves that splashed among the columns were garbaged with orange peel and straw: the place smelt like a latrine. Only the colour of the sea, the purple colour of the sea against the marble, to speak for Theodora!

The little Mosque of St. Sophia, the Mosque of Little St. Sophia, lies between these two devastations, between the Palace of Justinian and the ruined hovels of a later age. Justinian himself had built it and had given it its name. "St. Sergius and St. Bacchus" he had called it, but now it is known to the Turks as Little St. Sophia. Isolated it stands, with its old narthex and the later Turkish portico. Within, the Greek inscription still runs, white on blue, around the frieze. "Byzantin" the old Hodja will say, pointing to it, "byzantin": it is his only word of French. He will shamble about the church in his loose slippers, smiling at the visitors. He has made a little garden in the courtyard. In summer there are petroleum tins there bursting with mignonette, and roses in a wide oil jar. But that afternoon it was November: the Hodja was preparing already for the spring. He was rubbing the soft soil between his hands, making a seed-bed in an old biscuit-box. Beside him there was a little dry pile of seeds in a magenta handkerchief: he had not noticed Eirene when she entered. She had for long been sitting on the steps of the portico before he noticed her: he looked up and smiled. "Byzantin," he said, pointing at the inner narthex: and then he stooped again to his work.

Eirene was reading; she had brought a book with her. She had walked there early across from Pera. It was a long walk, but she knew that she would be quiet here and warm, that in the sheltered garden, under the portico, she would catch the full, faint glow of the November sun.

It had been raining all the week: the clear sky of Sunday had lured her across Stamboul to the warm southern slope among the ruins. Eirene yearned for the sun again: the sun warm upon the stones, and some book to act as sedative. How calm it was in the little garden! There were some dried pomegranates still hanging on the trees. Oh, what a dreary interval till May! What days, what nights, and always the trams screaming round the corner! Poor Eirene!

The door in the gateway creaked upon its hinges. It was Tenterden who entered. He, too, had come there in the search of quiet: the little, deserted Mosque that he remembered seemed even stiller now that the great fire had robbed it of its quarter.

He saw Eirene sitting there, and his tongue clicked in irritation. He had not recognised her: he was annoyed merely that he was not to be alone. He also had wanted to sit upon those steps in the sun. It was provoking. There was nowhere else to go: nowhere else where it would be warm and peaceful. Eirene raised her head and smiled at him: he recognised her. He experienced a faint stirring of relief. "Thank goodness," he thought, "at least it's no one tiresome!"

He sat down beside her on the lower step. She smiled slowly at him. "You were annoyed at finding me here, and I looked on you as an intruder."

He laughed: he did not deny it. Eirene continued in her level voice: "I come here often," she said, "it is so quiet. And so pathetic, in a way, with all these ruins. And then I like the sea: I like, more than anything, this view of the sea above the wall there, and the mountains beyond. It is different from the usual view, with Stamboul always in the foreground. One looks away from it." She paused. "You see, I have always lived in Constantinople. I am tired of the outline of Stamboul. It's so Turkish."

He did not speak for a moment. He sat there silently looking at the sea: and then, abruptly, "I knew your father," he said, "twenty years ago, when I came here as a boy. We yachted once together over there; we went further, we went out beyond the Straits, to Thasos and to Samothrace, and we visited the Plain of Troy." He was silent for a little space. "It was twenty years ago," he added; "I had just come of age."

He had turned round and was looking at Eirene as he spoke. "Tell me about it," she answered quietly, but Tenterden resumed his silence, looking out across the sea, looking back across the busy intervening years. Yes! he had been young then; it had been before all places and all people had come to mean the same. He had possessed youth then and glorious vanity, and the zest of the spray that broke under their bows. The sparkle of the spray, as the wind filled the mizzen, and beyond, the outline of pink islands and the thought of quiet havens mysteriously under and among the hills. Imbros and Samothrace, Tenedos and Mitylene! They had meant something to him then. That had been before Paris and Rome, and those six years at Petersburg! And now? Success and middle age! A reputation! A habit of success: it would be difficult for him, at this stage, to lose that habit. And then one night they had been becalmed off Samos: there had been a fire burning on the hillside; they had read the Iliad. It had been fun then to read the Iliad. They had read the part where the sailors are becalmed at night-time and see the fire blazing upon the hill. And one of the crew had sung sleepily in the bows.

Yes! He had been young then, and now he was only successful. The end was clear and evident: the end was inevitable; the last lap was already opening before him. Success, and more success: a scarlet ribbon across his shirt-front; and then retirement, and the little home in Kent. Alone this time: his mother would be dead by then. He would be alone there, on November evenings. He would sip his port alone, and think back, back upon the Ægean, and the crisp sound of the spray upon the bows. He would think back on the Ægean: it would not soothe him to think back upon the rest, upon the afterwards.

And Henry Davenant? The companion of those days. Florid, exuberant, and sensual: how came it that he could have fathered such a daughter: so calm a daughter: so statuesque a daughter? A marble Demeter, with the grave and level eyes; the mother of Persephone; the quiet orderer of the home.

It pleased him to remain silent. It pleased him that she should not agitate for talk. It was a new experience, deliberately to prolong the silence. How long, he wondered, could it be prolonged? Eirene did not break upon the stillness. In the end it was Tenterden himself who rose: "Come," he said, "I must be going back. You will let me drive you to your home. And one day, but not to-day, we shall talk about your father. He was a great friend of mine. We had a yacht together, once, in the Ægean."

November

(VII.)

Angus locked the big safe in the Chancery and put away the keys. He had been busy that day: the messenger had come in from London with the bag. Angus had been obliged to dine near the Embassy and to come back afterwards. It was past eleven o'clock. He was feeling exhausted and dispirited. And he was feeling bored. More cruisers had arrived. The situation had been "internationalised." The Turks had asked for an armistice: the Bulgars had been held up at Chataldja. It was the end, the excitement was over. Life was very flat.

And now he must go home to his hotel: the porter would be asleep and he would have to wake him up. Or perhaps he could get out by the side door. But then he would be challenged by the sentry. No, it was better to wake up the porter. He had his pass with him: it would not matter if he met a patrol. All those restrictions had lost their meaning, now that there was to be an armistice.

He walked down the dark and deserted streets, and reached his door without interruption. There was a light up there in his rooms. He had not been back there since the early afternoon. Why should there be a light? He climbed up the dingy hotel staircase, and pushed open the door of his sitting-room. A man in khaki was asleep upon the sofa. Angus drew away for a moment into the doorway: and then, on tiptoe, he crept back into the room. It was Edhem, a dishevelled Edhem with a two-days' beard.

Angus put his hand upon his shoulder, and Edhem started up with a sudden cry in Turkish.

"Edhem," said Angus reassuringly, "What is the matter, Edhem? It is I."

Edhem sat down again upon the sofa: he leaned forward with his hands between his knees: his slim, white hands with the lapis ring. And they were trembling. He did not speak for a moment: and then he asked: "Can you keep me here to-night, Angus? May I sleep here on this sofa?"

There was no answer for a moment: Angus was puzzled by the strange sound of Edhem's voice, as if it had cracked: he was too puzzled for the moment to answer, and Edhem rose and scrambled towards him.

"Oh, Angus!" he quavered, "you *must* keep me here to-night. You do not understand. You simply must. I am in danger." His words ended in a sob, and his hand fluttered at the case of his revolver.

"Of course," said Angus, "of course you may stay here, Edhem. Sit down again and tell me what has happened. And do you want anything? I have some biscuits here and some whiskey."

Edhem sank again upon the sofa and closed his eyes. Angus brought him a glass and the decanter. He poured it out. He went into the next room and fetched a pillow and an eider-down. He was very puzzled. He spread the cover over Edhem's shaking limbs and made him lie upon the pillow. He sat on the sofa beside him and put a hand upon his shoulder. "Now tell me, Edhem, what has happened?"

"I have deserted from the army. I have run away. They will shoot me if they find me."

"Deserted, Edhem? But you had done so well. Sefir Bey told me when he came back with despatches. I met him at the club. He had seen you at Kirk Kilisse. He said you had been splendid: you had galloped about, and you had lost your temper and shouted at them in French, and beaten them with your sword. He said that Abdullah Pasha had spoken very warmly of you. He said you were a hero."

"Oh, that was long ago," said Edhem, "that was during the fighting. That was different. I did not mind the fighting. That was different. It was afterwards that it happened, at San Stefano." He shuddered, and reached out again for the whiskey.

"San Stefano?" echoed Angus. "*That* San Stefano over there? Quite close?" and he nodded towards Stamboul.

Edhem was lying back upon the sofa and his eyes were closed. Slowly he began in a dull monotone, as a man speaks in a fever:

"They sent me down there from headquarters. There was a block upon the railway: the reserves were not arriving. I was to go down and investigate: I was to come back and report. They gave me a motor car. And I have deserted." He paused, and drank again with parched, pale lips. "There is a camp there. They have concentrated there the division which broke at Lule Bourgas. The division is to be re-formed there. Re-formed at San Stefano!" He laughed in a high falsetto: he clutched at Angus's arm. "It is a camp by the sea. By the salt, thirsty sea, Angus: there is a little strip of beach between the tents and the sea. I went there. I did not understand at first. The men were kneeling on the beach, or squatting: there were thousands of them: and some were lying on their faces: there were marks of cart-wheels upon the sand. And other marks." Edhem tautened in a spasm of disgust. "You do not understand, Angus. You have not seen it. And the sound of it all! I did not know, at first, that it was cholera. The men were kneeling there: and squatting: they were being sick, Angus, sick upon the sand: they were vomiting all over the sand, and other things as well, Angus. They were crouching half-naked, and the sand was black with it: and the stench, Angus! Thousands of them, twisted and grotesque. They cried to me for water: they looked at me with yellow, glassy eyes, and cried for water. There was no water there: only the sand and the sea. And I saw a man crawl down to the sea: his trousers had slipped to his knees: I could see his shirt, his spattered shirt, and his bare thighs: he stooped to the sea as it came in and he drank it. The others watched him enviously, but they were too weak to move. And then the cart came, and they turned some of the men over on their faces with a pole and piled them into the cart. I did not realise at first that they were dead. An arm stuck out of the cart with stiff fingers: it was then that I realised it. I ran away, Angus; yes, I ran back to the Commandant. I told him what I had seen. He shrugged his shoulders. He said: 'but, Lieutenant, you forget: they are the division that broke at Lule Bourgas.' And he laughed, Angus: and I struck him in the face. We were in his office. I struck him and I ran to my motor. I got out at Yedi Kouleh, and I sent back the motor. And then I walked here: it was dark: I got through somehow. But I shall be shot." And he shuddered again.

Angus stood there for a moment in silence. And

then he reached for his hat. "You will be safe here for to-night, Edhem. I am going out. I am going at once to see Mr. Tenterden. He will know what we can do."

CHAPTER VII.

January

(I.)

TENTERDEN at his most official: Hugh Tenterden, in a way, at his best. Angus, in the short distance that separated his hotel from the Embassy had realised, had, in fact, come to relish, the dramatic possibilities of the situation. He, Angus, was about to play a rôle: he was about to be the central, nay, the directing figure, in a human drama. He was harbouring a deserter: he was coming round at midnight to give information to his chief: he would ring at the great door of the Embassy, and Marco would open it sleepily. "I must see Mr. Tenterden at once, Marco: it is urgent." And then he would be taken upstairs, and Tenterden . . . but by then Angus had reached the gate of the Embassy garden.

They peered at him with a lantern before they opened it: he hurried past them flinging his name behind him: the gravel crunched under his important, impatient footsteps. He reached the front door, and Marco opened it. He hurried up the marble staircase. He reached Tenterden's door. He knocked at it and then opened. He stood in the doorway pale and a little breathless.

Tenterden looked up from his table. He was writing by the light of a green lamp. He looked across at Angus, and his quill pen was suspended for a moment above the silver inkstand.

"Come in, Field," he said. "What's the matter?"

"Sir," panted Angus, "something has happened. Something about which I must have your instructions."

The pen had dipped into the ink and was now scratching and squeaking again upon the paper. Angus modified his phrase. "Your advice, sir," he concluded. It was provoking that he should be out of breath. It would have been better to have walked slowly. Tenterden would think him nervous, hysterical, expansive. He must give the impression of strength and reserve. But that was difficult when one was out of breath.

"Sit down, Field," Tenterden answered, "sit down and help yourself to a drink. I must just finish this, if you don't mind."

Angus sat down. Angus did not like Hugh Tenterden. He did not like him in the least. But he sat down, a little breathless still. And, what was more, he remained silent. The quill pen scratched upon the paper. "Do you use a quill, Field?" asked Tenterden, after a few minutes, in the detached voice appropriate to a split thought; "I hate them. But then I hate other nibs worse. I've got a filthy fist, that's what it is: I never could write legibly," and the quill scratched on. There was a further silence. "Field, tell me," said Tenterden, "you'll know." He was fiddling with the pen upon the blotting-paper. "You'll know. How do you spell 'embarrassed'? You see, I have used 'confused' already. I have said 'His Highness appeared confused.' Now I want to say 'His Highness seemed embarrassed to find a suitable reply'; or ought it to be 'in finding'? The F.O. notice these things, you know. One can't be too careful. And I don't know how to spell it, Field. You will."

Angus did.

The quill scratched on again in the silence. "I saw the Grand Vizier to-day," said Tenterden as he wrote; "I'm drafting a telegram about it. Poor old man, he talked about photographs. About a photograph that had been taken of him at Port Said when the King was on his way to India. He had been photographed in a group there: they had sat the old man next to the Queen, and the King had stood behind him. He showed me the photograph. He seemed to think it made a difference. He seemed to think that it was an excuse for not giving up Adrianople." Tenterden paused. "Poor people," he concluded, "but they will have to give up the beastly place. It's not use hoping for peace until they agree to that."

Angus sat there in the chair. He was thinking of Edhem. Edhem would be getting anxious. And the story was yet to be told: how inconsiderate of Tenterden to keep him waiting like this. How typical! The typical diplomatist! it was a pose, of course. This pose of impassivity. And the quill went on scratching. How it squeaked! It gave Angus goose-flesh. He had sat far back in the chair at first, and now he found himself poised upon the edge. That was the worst of Tenterden. Angus rose and mixed himself a drink: it was a noisy drink: deliberately he made a noise over it. He allowed the syphon to howl out a dirge like a fog-horn: and then he went back and flung himself into the ultimate recesses of the chair. He felt for his cigarette-case. "You'll find the cigarettes upon the table there," murmured Tenterden without looking up from his writing. So he *was* aware of his presence! The clock and the quill kept pace in the silence. It was half-past twelve.

"There!" said Tenterden at last. "There! I've finished." He stood up with the sheets of foolscap covered with his Elizabethan writing He gave them to Angus. "Look here," he said, "ask them to get this off very first thing to-morrow morning. It's too late to-night. They'll have gone to bed."

There was a note of dismissal in his action and the words which accompanied it. Almost, so nearly almost, Angus had taken the telegram and withdrawn. And then he remembered Edhem. Tenterden remembered also and simultaneously. "Oh, I'm so sorry," he said; "you came to tell me something. Sit down: let's have it."

He sank down into the armchair there by the grate. "Go on," he said, "fire ahead!"

Angus fired, and ahead. Tenterden was picking absently at his thumbnail. Angus came to the realistic part: he made it very realistic. There were little pauses as the words were wrung from him in spurts: half medical his terms were, and half slang. And still Tenterden picked absently at his thumbnail. The story died out rather lamely.

Tenterden got up, stretched himself, and yawned. "Christ!" he said, "it's nearly one!"

Angus got up too.

"Well, Field," said Tenterden, "I'll go into

this. I'll speak to Nouri about it. Something must be done. But I must have information first. I do not trust your Edhem Bey: he's scarcely a Turk, that man. I can't trust him. No, I'll send the little doctor over to-morrow in my car. How cross it will make them!" Tenterden laughed.

"And what am I, sir, to do with Edhem?" asked Angus, a trifle petulantly.

"Who? What?" answered Tenterden. "Oh, I know nothing of Edhem Bey. We can't have members of the staff harbouring deserters. I *prefer* to know nothing. You understand, Field? You have not mentioned Edhem to me."

"But, sir," said Angus, and his voice quavered, "he is there in my rooms. He is on my sofa."

Tenterden laughed. "Well, that's not my business. It's yours. Use your intelligence. Good-night, Field." He went back to his desk, and chose a piece of paper from the rack in front of him.

Angus went rebellious, but crestfallen, to the door. "Oh, Field," Tenterden called after him. "You know Sidgwick, of the 'Imogene'? Well, go and see him to-morrow morning. You can tell him about your visitor. Don't mention me. A most resourceful man is Sidgwick. And you will remember," Tenterden looked up, and his eyes were very peremptory, "You will remember that the Embassy wish to know nothing of your Edhem. Nothing whatsoever."

Angus shut the door carefully behind him. The footman was asleep on a leather sofa at the top of the stairs.

In the warm, silent room which he had left the quill was scratching again upon the paper.

Tenterden rang the bell. He had to ring twice before the man answered.

"Wake someone up," he said, "and tell them to take this at once to Doctor Williams. He must have it before morning. And the car will be wanted by nine o'clock."

(II.)

The launch of Ion Paniotis was heading across from Prinkipo, its awnings dripping in the rain. Paniotis sat in the cabin writing a letter, a letter to Mrs. Davenant. It was a skilful letter: Paniotis leant his head back and quizzed it through narrowed eyelids as one scrutinises a work of art. It *was* a work of art. It spoke of overwork, of nervous exhaustion: no one could have worked as he had worked during the past year without paying for it in nerve power. It spoke of what the doctor at Prinkipo had said: it repeated the analogy he had used of the nerve cells being emptied, like the accumulators of an electric engine. It was a mere chance that his collapse had not been more complete than it was. He had been on the verge of a stroke. He was coming back to Pera to settle up his affairs: and then, perhaps—he underlined the "perhaps"—he would go to Biarritz. It depended. It depended upon Mrs. Davenant. Now that peace was inevitable and impending, it was necessary for him to keep his finger on the pulse. He would lose fortunes if he absented himself at such a moment. But it was impossible for him to remain in Constantinople if his Zoe were to be unkind to him: he would go to Biarritz, and the millions that he,

Paniotis, could have made must be made by someone else. It depended on Zoe. She must send him a note at once by the bearer.

The launch was approaching the quay at Galata. Paniotis folded the letter and closed it with a wafer which he took from his pocket-book. And then slowly he screwed on the cap of his fountain-pen, smiling to himself. "We shall see," he murmured, "we shall see."

Eirene was sitting in the drawing-room with her mother, when they brought the note. "It is from Ion," Mrs. Davenant murmured, and she opened it with hesitating fingers. She smoothed it out upon her knee. "Yes, it is from Ion." She read it slowly, and then she folded it again. "Poor Ion," she said; "he has been very ill. He has been seriously ill. He has had a crisis of the nerves. He is going to Biarritz. He wants to see me."

Eirene sat there without speaking, her head bent above her work. A silence descended on the room. "I must answer this," her mother said at last; "he requires an answer by the bearer. His man is waiting for my answer." She spoke nervously: there was a note of querulous impatience in her voice. Eirene was used to that. The little foot, she realised, would be tapping upon the parquet. But there was something more. There was a new inflection in her mother's voice, a little, thin note of something new that vibrated through her querulousness. A note of loneliness? No, it was more than that: of despair? Less definite. Of apology? Yes, that was nearer; it was almost a note of apology. Her mother had dismissed Paniotis: she was going now to take him back. She was ashamed of what she was going to do. She deserved to be ashamed. Eirene's head was bent obdurately over her sewing. Mrs. Davenant moved hurriedly to the writing-table. She opened the brass blotter with those crisp, irritable movements that Eirene knew so well. The top of the brass inkstand was flicked open with a jerk. Apology? Why, already her mother was angry with her. Whatever mood that new inflection had denoted it was gone by now. Eirene, once more, was getting on her mother's nerves. It always came back to that. *Always.* Eirene rose, and taking her work with her, passed in silence from the room.

It was warm up there, with the big stove and the brown walls. Eirene locked the door and moved to the bookcase. She put out a finger and pulled a volume from the row: she drew her chair up close to the stove. And then she began to read. But she did not read for long. Out of the gathering darkness came the thoughts, the nagging, buzzing thoughts which clustered round her solitude, the black, familiar thoughts that clouded her faculties. They would buzz out at her from every angle: some would come quickly at her with dart and stab: others would wheel, and poise, and settle. They seemed so numerous at first: distinct, detached, and numerous. Dark all of them, but with a different darkness: some grey, some black, some shimmering with a deadly blue. And they would settle, and penetrate, and poison. The poison would sink into her heart, turning everything into a drab monotone. And then it would be only one thought that crowded in her soul: a blunt, dull thought: a thought of iron that weighed her heart and brain. No stab or rending now. Only this weight, this dull, dull weight upon her soul. If she could only take it from her: it was there so definitely: it was so palpable: so hostile and so palpable. She could almost feel its iron outline with her hands. It filled her heart: it filled her brain. Why could she not tear it out and throw it from her? She was so weak, so helpless.

She lay back in her chair, her lips half parted, her head rolling from side to side upon the cushions. She and the weight alone together in the dark. Angus! Angus!

There was no other appeal. No appeal from this dull pain, but to the cause of the pain. No one to tell it to. "My poor Eirene," she murmured. "Poor Meirene!" She was so helpless and alone! There was only Angus: the whole world of life, the whole, aching world of life was Angus. She had passed him yesterday in the street. He had seen her coming. She had no doubt that he had seen her. And he had turned aside. He had looked self-conscious, and he had turned off to gaze into a shop window. There was no appeal from Angus. And *to* Angus there was no appeal.

It was getting dark there in the room. Eirene rose and went to the dressing-table. Yes, it was the weight of it which was so unendurable: the actual, physical weight: the enemy within one, and no escape. No one to share the weight. No one to help or insist. Yes, if only someone would say definite things to her: would say, "Do this, Eirene, it will help you." But who was there to say this? Who? Mother? Mother did not understand. Mother never understood anything. Eirene got on mother's nerves. How strange mother had been just now! What a strange note that had been in her voice. There had been a note of apology. *Was* it a note of apology? It was unlike mother: it had startled Eirene, it had been so odd: a diffident note, a plaintive note, a note of appeal. Eirene paused suddenly and looked at her own reflection in the glass. Appeal? Yes, that was it. It had been a note of appeal. Mother had wanted to escape. She had wanted Eirene to say something definite: to share the responsibility: to lift the weight, if only for a moment to lift the weight. And Eirene had been selfish and had not understood. Poor mother! Poor, helpless mother! Oh, she had appealed for help, and Eirene had been too selfish to understand.

She rose quickly and unlocked the door. She ran down the staircase and burst into the drawing-room. Paniotis was kneeling by the sofa, and he was crying again. And mother was crying, too. She was dabbing her eyes with a little handkerchief.

Eirene stood there in the doorway. Her voice fell like a bell upon the room. "Oh, I'm so glad, mother!" she said. "Oh, Mr. Paniotis, I'm so glad!"

They looked at her foolishly. She smiled at them in understanding, and she closed the door.

(III.)

Tenterden's limousine splashed and rattled along the road back from San Stefano, and inside it, upon the grey cushions, rattled Dr. Williams, returning from his visit of inspection

On the left, an endless trail of ox-wagons, lumbering up to the lines: a block from time to time at a bridge or crossing, and there, on the right hand, the sudden sound of the sea sighing upon the sand. Over it all, rain and low clouds: and the large windows of the limousine flecked and striped with spurts of liquid mud.

Dr. Williams sat back upon the cushions with both arms extended stiff to each side of him: by this means the bumps were rendered for the most part vertical, and indeed, his little tousled, tonsured head jerked up and down in front of the back window till it flicked like some pallid heliograph. Up and down he bumped upon the cushions, and on his face was fixed a frown of perplexity. For Dr. Williams was a man of dual functions: he was doctor to His Majesty's Embassy, and he was British Delegate upon the Constantinople Board of Health. In general, these two functions of his were not irreconcilable: they fused, they overlapped, they gave him a little extra salary, but they did not clash. To-day they were clashing horribly. Dr. Williams was seriously perplexed by the way they clashed. He had been out there to San Stefano: he had seen the little camp by the beach: it was bad, of course: his medical conscience had revolted against the inefficiency of it all; and behind it his human conscience had been outraged by the callousness of it. He had been very rude to the Commandant. He had come into the office with his untidy little head, and his glassy, myopic eyes, and he had put his face quite close to the Commandant's, in order to see him. He had told the Commandant what he thought of the little camp there by the beach. The Commandant had been polite: he had suggested with politeness that it was not Dr. Williams' business to enquire into the sanitary administration of the Ottoman Army. That was where the Commandant made a mistake. It made Dr. Williams angry, and it was a mistake. In the first place, it *was* Dr. Williams' business, the business of that half of Dr. Williams which sat on the Constantinople Board of Health. San Stefano was well within the province of that efficient body. In the second place, there was Nouri Pasha. Nouri could be told: Nouri *would* be told: Nouri would not in the least approve of the little camp by the beach, and that would be the end of the Commandant. Dr. Williams told him this. He explained it to him in the terse, clipped, telegraphic language which, from deep and fervent reading of Kipling, had become the essence of Dr. Williams' style. It fitted well, this style of his, with Turkish: it fitted the present occasion even better. The Commandant was evidently uneasy. The Commandant had not realised, apparently, that the thing would spread. He was alarmed by what Dr. Williams told him. Dr. Williams had seen his chance and taken it: he pressed his advantage home. He had been perfectly practical: the little camp there, by the beach, had better remain where it was. There was no hope for what was left of them. They must put a cordon round the camp, and they must give those who remained there water and some opium. That was the first thing. But for the rest, something definite, something drastic must be done at once: there must be no more bell-tents upon the beach. The Commandant must requisition buildings: he must requisition that Greek school, and as many houses near it as could be obtained. And then the whole quarter must be isolated.

"Yellow flags: sentries: begin at once, before any cases come down. See? Back to-morrow to make sure that you have done it." Yes, that was the first thing, the first thing to do. And he had done it. He had frightened the Commandant. And for the rest, it was a question of organisation. "Organisation." Dr. Williams repeated the word: he liked it: it was British, and imperial, and virile. It would give him his chance: it *was* his chance. His chance had come this time: he would show them, he would show them what "organisation" meant in English. The scheme of the thing began to shape itself as he bumped upon the cushions: the headings of the scheme: the professional requirements: the little technicalities: he must write it out on paper: they must try those saline injections: the work must be done as thoroughly as possible: the British Medical Journal: he must try and induce Herrenfals to come down from Vienna: but only when it had been started, only when the organisation was working, working under him, Augustine Williams. He must have full powers: only with full powers could something be accomplished. "Organisation": he felt his will tautening for the ordeal: his chance, his chance at last.

The motor had stopped at a level-crossing: the rain pattered on the roof, and with it came the sound of the sea heaving upon the sand. Yes, he must have full powers. But how?

It was then that the frown of perplexity had settled between the glassy, myopic eyes of Dr. Williams. How? As himself he was only Dr. Williams, of the British Embassy: he vaccinated the housemaids: he treated the staff. As such he had no right to interfere, no right to organise. The power which had enabled him to frighten the Commandant resided in the other half of Dr. Williams, the half that was British Delegate on the Constantinople Board of Health. The Board of Health? His colleagues? Duclaux, and Wertheim, and that little prig Benedetti. *They* wouldn't understand the position. They would talk about "the Board." Why should the Board not intervene, corporately, and internationally? A cholera settlement; surely that was the Province of the Board, international and corporate, not merely of one Augustine Williams, physician to the British Embassy? The Board? Organisation? He would have to tell the Board. He would *have* to tell them: that was only honest: it was his duty. And then they would grab the thing and squabble over it. Dr. Williams bobbed despairingly upon the cushions of the limousine: his chance was fading from him. "Damn!" he muttered between the jerks. "Functional duality. Bad business. God and Mammon."

The car had slowed down to pass the level-crossing by the Seven Towers: they had entered the city: they were clattering now through Stamboul. They reached the Embassy.

Tenterden was serious about it from the first: he did not laugh: he listened seriously. And halfway through he rang the bell and told the motor to wait. He would be wanting it in a few minutes. Dr. Williams was drawing to the end of his report.

"Well, sir, that's all. I must call a meeting

of the Board: it's their business, you know. Not competent, but inevitable."

"Inevitable?" said Tenterden. "But why? Nothing's inevitable. We want this thing done quickly and thoroughly. The Board's all right for other things. This must be done with and through the Turks. It's the only way. I'll collar Nouri about it. You'd better come with me. You'd better resign from your Board. We'll lend you to the Turks, Williams. That's it. I'll stand the racket. You get on with them. They like you. No, we can't have a Board messing about. Come, we'll go now. There is no time to lose."

(IV.)

Angus was sitting in the large over-heated café of the Grande Rue de Pera. It was late, but he sat on there, unwilling to return to his rooms. He was drinking Benedictine: it was his third Benedictine that evening. He was angry and disquieted. Angry with Tenterden chiefly: very angry with Tenterden. How cynical the man had been! He had laughed at him. He had not helped him in the least about Edhem; he had, in fact, refused to help him. And what was Angus to do? It was intolerable that Tenterden should have refused even to hear of Edhem: it made it impossible for Angus to secure his consent, or his support. After all, there must be some way, some means of getting rid of Edhem. In the end he would have devised a plan. And then he could have gone to Tenterden, calm and collected, and he could have said:

"I propose, sir, to do this or that. Do you approve?" Then afterwards, if there was a row, Tenterden would have shared the responsibility. But now Angus had been forbidden even to mention the subject: he had been told to "use his own intelligence." Tenterden had laughed as he said it. Never had there been anything so selfish or so brutal. It was the public school system. That beastly Eton system. Tenterden was still the bully of the Sixth Form. He hated Tenterden. The lines of a bitter, but anonymous, article against Tenterden framed themselves moodily in his mind. He called the waiter and ordered another Benedictine. It was nearly midnight. He wanted to go home. But Edhem would be sitting up for him. Edhem would start up anxiously when he came into the room. "Well?" he would say. And Angus would have nothing to answer: perhaps Edhem would break down again like he had broken down last night. No! Edhem had no right to compromise Angus in this way: people might know already! There were spies everywhere. That fat man at the table, Angus seemed to recognise him. Why was he staring curiously like that? There was certainly an odd, knowing leer in his little eyes. Who was the man? Angus called the waiter and asked him. "It is Monsieur Lukacs," the man replied. Angus remembered.

If Edhem had been really afraid, things might have been easier. But Edhem wasn't afraid; at least, not afraid for himself. It was that which made it all so difficult. Edhem wanted to do something revengeful and dramatic: he was ashamed and remorseful. He was angry. He sat there all day drinking whiskey and abusing the

Turks. "The swine," he would murmur, "les saligauds." He would shake his fist in the air: "I shall get even with them," he would threaten. It was an intolerable attitude for him to adopt. Almost as intolerable as the blatant, vulgar cruelty of Tenterden. It made it so difficult. A panic-stricken Edhem would, perhaps, have been manageable. Angus would have lent him a suit of clothes and a hat, and driven with him down to the "Imogene." And then they could have climbed down the other side into the blue boat and so on board the "Messageries." Sidgwick would have arranged all that. But Edhem would not hear of it. "Moi je ne suis pas mufle à ce point là . . ." he had said, and there had been a faint but unpleasant implication that he, Angus, might, in similar circumstances, have been just that sort of mufle. And then Edhem was not grateful: he did not realise—he refused to realise—the position in which he had placed Angus. He took it all for granted: he was surly and saturnine and sinister. He was unshaven. Even his voice had altered: it had become the voice of an apache. And the whiskey—there had been a whole bottle of it yesterday—only made him worse. Oh, it was intolerable, intolerable that such a thing should have happened to Angus. He looked back at the old, quiet, ordered days with an angry yearning: if he could get back to them! This was an adventure, he supposed. Copy! Never, never would he wish for an adventure again. And Tenterden had laughed at him as if he were a child, a school fag. Angus called for another Benedictine.

Lukacs rose from his corner and came across to Angus' table There was an ingratiating smile on his face. "I think," he said, "that we have met at Therapia. Your face is very familiar to me." And then he clicked his heels. "Lukacs Bela," he said, and bowed jerkily.

"My name is Field," said Angus, looking up at him.

There was a pause: "I may sit at your table for a little? That is so?" said Lukacs, drawing up a chair. "It is late, and I must be going. But your face was familiar and we can talk for a little while." Angus managed to smile at him politely: he was angry with Tenterden and Edhem; he was not angry with this fat little man. And it was better than being alone.

"You are of the Embassy, are you not?" said Lukacs. "I have seen you going in to the house at Therapia. It is pleasant up there. I do not like this city. I shall go away when peace is signed. You think that there will be peace?"

"Well, it depends on Adrianople—doesn't it?" said Angus.

"You are right, my young friend. Yes, the present Government will surrender Adrianople. They will reply, when is it? On Thursday. To-morrow there is to be a Grand Council. And the day after, they will reply. They will agree to Adrianople. I have it on the best authority that they will agree."

"And then?" said Angus.

"And then," chuckled Lukacs, "then there will be peace, and I can go back to Szolnok."

Angus felt he must say something. He said: "Well, there's many a slip—you know our proverb."

The little eyes of Lukacs blinked suddenly: he leaned quickly closer to Angus.

"So you also have heard something?" he asked in a whisper. "Tell me; this is a chance meeting, but it is only such meetings that are of value; tell me what you have heard, and I, Lukacs Bela, will tell you what I know." He hesitated. "Waiter!" he called, "two more Benedictines."

Angus was startled. What was it that he had said to provoke such sudden intentness on the part of Lukacs? "Many a slip?" So Lukacs suspected something was peeping underneath. And Angus had just made the remark to bridge a silence. No, he had not been indiscreet. Even Tenterden could not say that he had been indiscreet: and perhaps this little man really did know something. Tenterden would be impressed: Angus must keep the thing going. He leant back and smiled at the Hungarian, a knowing smile. "Well, in this country, at this time, one never knows. A change of Government. . . ."

That was good enough for the moment, but there must be more if Tenterden was to be impressed. Angus toyed with his glass. "I have," he said "a Turkish officer now staying with me: an officer of some distinction. I think he must be a deserter. His manner is very curious. Yes. I feel sure he has deserted. It is very awkward for me. He has not said anything, nothing definite, but . . ."

Yes, that had done it. The interest glowed in those little eyes. Angus must keep it up.

"Tell me," whispered Lukacs, "tell me the name of this young officer. He is young, is he not? But not so very young. He is a small man? Am I right? He has a little moustache?"

Angus was beginning to get uneasy. They

were getting on dangerous ground. He had no conception of what Lukacs was after.

"I am not," he said sententiously, "at liberty to disclose the name of my visitor."

"Ah, so!" said Lukacs, "but I, perhaps, can guess the name. Does it, by chance, begin with the letter E?"

Angus looked frankly startled. Lukacs chuckled. He leant closer. "You see, I have my sources, too. I know, I happen to know, my young friend, that two days ago Enver Bey arrived secretly from Tripoli and is hiding somewhere in the town."

He flung himself back in the chair, gurgling to himself as he watched for Angus' discomfiture. A blank look of bewilderment stole over Angus' face, and as he marked it Lukacs, in his turn, looked puzzled, confused, and angry.

"Enver Bey?" repeated Angus blankly. "Enver? No, the name of my friend is Edhem."

The Hungarian clicked his tongue in annoyance. He banged a coin on to the marble table. "Good-night, my young friend," he said; "you have had the privilege of making a fool of Lukacs Bela."

Angus walked home in anxious bewilderment. It was a pity to have told that little man about Edhem: especially as it had made him angry. A great pity. But Angus had been taken by surprise. Oh, how he hated adventures! They took it out of one: one lost control. It made one feel exhausted. He climbed the stairs dejectedly, dragging one foot after the other. Edhem would be waiting there for him. He would jump up eagerly and say, "Eh bien?" It was better to forestall that.

Angus opened the door dramatically, and stood there with his hat on. "There is news to-night," he said; "the Government are going to accept the conditions about Adrianople. They are to accept them on Thursday. And Enver Bey has arrived secretly from Tripoli, and is in hiding."

Edhem leaped from the sofa and ran across to Angus. "Enver? Here in Constantinople? Are you sure?"

"Yes," said Angus. "I am sure. But I don't know where."

And then Edhem did a singular thing. He laughed in a high falsetto: he flung his hands into the air. And then he collected himself: "Some hot water quick, Angus. I must shave. I must go out at once. I must leave you."

Angus stood there, after he had gone, in the middle of the room: dazed and sleepy.

"Enver Bey? Who the deuce is Enver?" he murmured.

(V.)

Eirene stood there in her little room, eyeing her books in sullen slumbering indignation. How wrong they had been! All of them! They wrote of little else but love, and yet they had been wrong. Completely wrong. They had been worse than wrong. They had been misleading. They had deceived. All her life they had spoken to her of these things: they had lied to her. They had lied to that helpless, solitary schoolgirl with the long legs and the tennis shoes. An easy victim! And they had lied consistently. Not always in the same way:

they had adopted different methods for the lie. Some of them had draped this love business in the hangings of romance: others had touched it gently with the butterfly colours of fancy: sometimes the flame, sometimes the adventure. But never this; no hint of this. No hint of the enemy. This dumb, relentless enemy: this dull, drab enemy within her heart. This cold and palpable weight, that hung upon her soul and clogged her faculties. Not pain exactly, not always pain: a stab sometimes that made her catch her breath: but that was not important; that came from the other things, the sneaking companions of her enemy, from jealousy and pride. These she despised even as they hurt her. She did not despise the enemy. She was afraid of him. He was so silent, so elusive, and yet so palpable: always there: there ready for her at every hour: there all the night: there beside her after the trams had stopped, when only the clock could be heard striking in the dull light before the dawn. It was making her ill: her brain reeled with the longing to escape. To escape if only for a moment: a short respite. An hour's respite from this persecution. How intolerable that it should have wrought its filthy nest within her soul! It wasn't Angus. No, she could think quite calmly now about Angus; about his clammy hands, and the smug look on his face when he spoke to mother. Oh! it wasn't Angus: Angus was an illusion: No! It was the enemy. He had built his nest within her heart: he brooded there: he sat there huddled within her, nurturing doubt, and jealousy, and sorrow. There was no escape. She was enclosed in it and she enclosed it. Even if she could pluck it out, she would find it around her:

a steel prison outside her in the place of the leaden weight within. There was no escape.

She moved towards the bookcase: they had deceived her. There he was! That man Shakespeare! "On such a night as this!" He was as bad as any of them! He, too, had told the lie. She laughed bitterly and pulled out a volume at random. She read:

> "My love is as a fever longing still
> For that which longer nurseth the disease:
> Feeding on that which doth preserve the ill,
> The uncertain, sickly appetite to please.
> My reason, the physician. . . ."

Eirene sat down hurriedly upon the chair.

> "And frantic mad with evermore unrest,"

she read on:

> "For I have sworn thee fair, and thought thee bright,
> Who art as black as hell, as dark as night."

She turned the page: it was uncut: all the last pages of the book had been left uncut. The middle pages were scored and underlined. She remembered now: she had thought the later sonnets dull. Was it the same with all of the other books? Had they, too, given the message to deaf ears. Was it she, Eirene, then, who had been the fool? Was it the fault of the schoolgirl with the long legs? Eirene looked back resentfully at herself. How badly she had brought herself up! She had tricked herself into a habit of mind: a sickly, glutinous habit of mind. She had shirked the unpleasant things: she had shirked the things which did not pander to her own illusions! It was worse than that old business of the secret. That had only been morbid: this had been cowardly; it had left its brand upon her. She had funked the realities, like Aunt Emily. She was paying for it now! The wide curve of her mouth twisted into a smile of anguish. She had deserved it and she was paying for it: well! she would bear her punishment without a whimper. They should not see: Angus should not see. Even the enemy might be deluded. Eirene set her head defiantly, and unlocked the door.

(VI.)

Aunt Emily was sitting by the little open fire in her drawing-room when Eirene entered. She had been obstinate about that fire when she had first come from Moda and taken the flat in the Rue Hammam. They had warned her that it would smoke. It did smoke. They had warned her that it would give no heat. Here again they had shown foresight. But Aunt Emily had been obstinate: she would sit shivering beside it, her eyes bloodshot from the smoke. "It is so cheerful," she would say blandly, "to see an open grate. Even in summer it is nice to have a fire on the hearth." Only in the very coldest weather, when the snow covered the roofs below her, would Aunt Emily permit herself, even to herself, any disloyalty towards the fire: then there would be a brazier behind the screen, a surreptitious brazier. And once she had tried an oil stove: but it had behaved badly and allowed a smell to permeate from behind the screen; Aunt Emily had been found out: so ever after that she stuck to the brazier.

That evening there was no brazier: there was also no coal because of the war. Aunt Emily was burning wood in her open grate. She had a shawl round her shoulders and a furtive hot-water bottle on her lap.

Eirene, as usual, was tactless. "Oh, what a smoke!" she said, "and how cold it is in here. Really, Aunt Emily, you should have a proper stove: they warm the room beautifully. And they're no trouble at all."

"*I* don't find it cold in the least," snapped Aunt Emily. "You young people are so luxurious nowadays. I don't hold at all with all these foreign heating appliances. That's what gives you all that washed-out look. Oh! I'm sorry, dear," she added hastily, and tapped Eirene's knee in apology

Aunt Emily had scored: she felt better. She sat back in her chair. "No," she concluded, "give me a nice cheerful blaze to look at, like at home." Aunt Emily leant forward for the bellows. "Let me do it," said Eirene, and knelt down beside the fireplace. The bellows had been bought ten years ago at Interlaken: they were carved, as is the friendly Swiss way, with two chamois and an edelweiss. As bellows they had from the first been a failure, and with the passage of years this failure had become marked: they did not bellow now at all, they wheezed; and that backwards at one through their pink but scrannel lungs. "Better blow," said Aunt Emily.

Eirene put down the bellows and blew with her face close into the smouldering fire. A shower of white ashes shot up from the grate and settled slowly down upon the hearthrug, upon Aunt Emily, and upon Eirene's raven hair. Eirene laughed and blew again. Aunt Emily sat there coughing slightly, hesitating between indignation with Eirene and loyalty towards the fire. Eirene knelt and blew again until a thin flame shot up among the smoking logs.

"It's alight!" she said, turning in surprise to Aunt Emily.

"Of course it's alight, dear. What do you suppose? And what a mess you are making! There's ash all over the place: your hair's quite white!"

Eirene laughed and went on blowing the harder; the glow of her smooth cheeks quickened with the glow of the expanding fire. Aunt Emily fidgetted. How tiresome Eirene was! She always rubbed one up the wrong way. "Oh, please stop, Eirene!"

But Eirene went on. What was the matter with the girl? She was generally so obedient. "Eirene, did you hear me?"

But Eirene went on blowing, and the fine white ash of the olive wood hung like dust in a sunbeam about the room.

It was thus that Tenterden found them. He came in suddenly on the heels of the servant. He stood at the doorway.

"Ah, I see," he said, "an old-fashioned English grate! What the French call 'le confort Anglais.' It's magnificent, Miss Davenant. Magnificent! But, I beg you, get a stove."

Eirene looked up from the fire. "Oh, Mr. Tenterden," she said ruefully, "Mr. Tenterden, now you've said it, too!"

She turned and looked up at him: she laughed. Her face glowed like some burnished russet fruit, her hair was grey and powdered with the ash. The smoke had brought the tears into her eyes, her heavy-lidded, gentle eyes. And she laughed, kneeling there she turned round and laughed up to him: a calm and gentle laugh, the laugh as of a placid river sliding among the fields: the fields in summer; English meadows. Cowslip and daisy, dappled by the shadow of the elms; wisdom and youth and gentleness, and more than that! Yes, she was more than that! She had bent down again, dismayed at his close scrutiny. The line of her neck, the poise of it! The little, virginal nape of it, the firm womanly swing of the back: and the arm, the stretch of those long, firm fingers on the rug! No, he would not sacrifice his scrutiny. He would be mannerless; he would be rude. He would stand there staring down at her, until his mood—this sudden tremulous mood, this keen ecstatic mood—had passed. He was too old, to-day, to sacrifice this sudden penetrating mood: this precious vivifying mood! This warm pang, suddenly, at the sight of a girl by the fire with ashes in her hair. How grotesque! Instinctively his reason interfered. But for once the balance would not swing back to the level; for once the scale had hit the beam. And Tenterden, the real Tenterden, was glad. He could have cried aloud in triumph: it was youth that had come back to him, a sudden stab of youth! Oh, let him savour it! Let him not flinch from it! Let him be glad!

He spoke to her: "Oh, Miss Eirene, do turn round again. Just like you did before."

She turned and looked at him surprised.

Cinderella? A child again: a fallow deer. Ruth amid the alien corn? The emotion was becoming blurred: he cut it off with a snap. "Oh, Miss Eirene," he laughed, "go and brush your hair. Go to your aunt's bedroom, and brush your hair: it's white all over."

She rose, smiling. "May I, Aunt Emily?"

"Of course, dear," and the little lady hurriedly recovered the hot-water bottle which had slipped to the floor. How deft was Tenterden at redeeming situations! How deftly was that situation, the sudden startled gap which had followed his entry, redeemed! Soldered together so that even in retrospect those few minutes, those tremulous broken minutes when he had stood and stared at Eirene, were mended beyond recollection. It had not happened. It was really too improbable to have happened. Aunt Emily nursed her hot-water bottle, and her little fluttering pulses slowed down to equanimity.

They were talking easily when Eirene returned: the glow had left her cheeks: the smooth pale line of them under the smooth dark hair. The carriage of her head! Oh, Tenterden noticed now! Even as he spoke to her aunt he noticed.

"And the little doctor," he was saying, "is in the seventh heaven. A raging epidemic all to himself. He is making things buzz, I can tell you."

"Buzz!" echoed Aunt Emily at her most polite.

"The cholera, you know, out at San Stefano. The conditions are appalling. The whole organisation has broken down. It is spreading rapidly: three to five hundred cases a day. The Turks lost their heads: I don't blame them, poor people. And the little doctor has been at it three days now, and three nights, too, and already something has been done. He burst in upon me yesterday. He was extremely rude. He wanted me to send telegrams to the London Press. I refused. He became angry: he called me 'my dear man.' That from the little doctor! He wanted me to order all unoccupied British subjects to go up to San Stefano at once to help him. He has got some already. He has got an American and a little Dutchman, and an English tourist. He works them like coolies. They'll all break down in a week. Oh, he's in the seventh heaven!"

Eirene was listening to him intently: there was a frown on her forehead and her lips were parted.

"He's requisitioned a whole quarter at San Stefano, and has bagged two thousand mattresses from the Red Crescent Society. He took them away in motor lorries. Oh! he's dynamic, I can tell you. His eyes burn like Savonarola's. He jerks about the room muttering: 'Augean stables. Florence Nightingale. Outrage on humanity.' He tried to take one of my staff from me this morning. Young Field. You know, the little overdressed clerk who looks after the papers. I put my foot down there. He called me 'my dear man' again. But the little doctor collared Bridges all right: you know, the young engineer on the harbour works. He packed him off in a motor within the hour. He even tried to collar Miss Wrightson." Tenterden laughed.

Eirene startled them: she stood up suddenly. She looked down at her aunt; she looked at her in silence for a moment, and then quite quietly she said: "I am very ready to go to San Stefano. I should like to go there. It is the best thing I can do. How soon can I start, Mr. Tenterden?"

Tenterden rose slowly from his chair: their eyes met: she met his eyes calmly, confidently: she did not waver. Nor did he.

"You can start to-day," he said; "you can have my motor. Yes, you had better start to-day."

She bent down and kissed her trembling aunt upon the forehead: she did not say good-bye to Tenterden. She walked to the door and left them, without another word.

Aunt Emily sat there fluttering. She was out of it: completely out of it. "It is your fault," she sobbed. "Eirene thinks of such silly things: how could you let her think of such silly things: and what will her mother say: what on earth will Zoe say about it?"

Tenterden glanced at her sternly. And then he looked at the door through which Eirene had just passed.

"Her mother," he said deliberately, "does not count. She does not count in the least."

(VII.)

It was Thursday, the 23rd of January. Tenterden was waiting for the reply of the Turkish Government to the joint note of the Powers. The Cabinet was meeting that afternoon to sign the document: it had been passed already by the Grand Council of yesterday. They had agreed to give up Adrianople: there would be peace.

Tenterden felt relieved. The strain of the last two months had begun to tell upon him. There would be peace now, and the negotiations would begin seriously in London. And in April his chief would return. Tenterden could take his leave. Kent first: he felt himself looking forward to it, the line of the Weald, the daffodils in the orchard. He would not be bored this time! No, he would not go to Paris this time! Why go to Paris? The old round of gallantry: the satiety of it all! He felt tired at the very thought of it. He would go to Kent, to the Weald. His mother's primulas, and the wild garden down there by the brook. And in May there would be the orchards, and the tulips in the old Venetian well-head. Health, and sanity, and calm! That was what he wanted. How much he wanted it! To get away from the soft shambling of the East to something clear and delicate and bracing! Home! It stirred a chord within his heart! How strange that he should think of it; in this way; now. Yes, he would go to Kent first: he would stay in Kent. He would stay there all the time. Not London, certainly. The least possible of London. But Kent, and the flat outline of the Weald. He would be alone with his mother. How pleased, how surprised she would be! And over there, in Paris, they would be saying: "What has happened to Hugh Tenterden? He has not come this spring." He would not come: no, not this spring, nor the next. No, all that was over. He smiled grimly to himself. "Il faut quitter le Louvre," he murmured, "avant qu'on crie 'On ferme.'" Yes, it was closing time. He was glad of it. After all, there was home, and work. He was very glad. He sighed, and passed his hand across his forehead.

He looked at his watch: four o'clock. The

reply would be in soon. He went down to the Chancery. "I am going out into the garden," he said; "you will find me there when the reply comes."

He walked to the edge of the garden and looked down over the low wall upon Stamboul. How cold and sinister it seemed, so drab and squalid under the dark sky. The Palace of Porphyrogenitus glimmered there on the right, and the twin minarets of Sultan Selim stood out like two black chimneys against the scudding clouds. How inappropriate! How crudely inappropriate! Appropriate only in the glaring sun of June. His eye wandered along the ridge noting the houses and the minarets, colourless as lead: it fixed for a moment on the tower of the War Office, the tower of the Seraskerat: the flag at its summit blew out straight in the north wind, and as he looked it fluttered suddenly to the base. That was strange; they had pulled down the flag at the War Office. Now they were pulling it up again: he saw its little square rising in tight jerks against the skyline: and then it stopped. It stopped halfway. The flag was at half-mast. That was very strange! He turned quickly to go back into the house. There was the sound of someone running on the gravel pathway. "Yes," he called impatiently. "Yes, what is it? What has happened?"

"The Government has fallen. They burst into the room where the Cabinet were sitting, and they have shot the Commander-in-Chief. They shot him dead at the door. The Committee have come back, and Enver is the Minister of War!"

Tenterden swung round and looked back upon Stamboul.

"War!" he said, "war again! There will be war again. Worse this time than before. War and pestilence. . . .

"And it was I who sent Eirene to San Stefano."

CHAPTER VIII.

February

(I.)

ANGUS was lying that evening on the sofa in his bedroom feeling irritable. It was the end of a bad week: an absolutely rotten week. It had all begun on the Monday; things had happened together; in a sequence. They had gone from bad to worse.

It had begun by his intending to tell Tenterden of what Lukacs Bela had blurted out in the café. He had left the Chancery mysteriously and gone slowly upstairs. He had climbed the staircase slowly, in order to rehearse how he was going to say it. It was better to be prepared. Tenterden had a way of making one forget what one meant to say; or, rather, of making one say it with the wrong intonation. And then it was important not to arrive out of breath: the last time he had panted when he got there, and it had ruined the effect. This time he would be calm, resolute, and reserved: a little hostile even: dutiful, of course, but a little hostile. Official. That was the intonation.

He arrived at the door and opened it: Tenterden looked vexed at the interruption: he was not alone. The Russian Ambassador was leaning over his chair, and they were reading a paper together. The Ambassador was tapping the paper with a ringed forefinger. He was saying: "Mais non, mon cher, mais non, *mais* non!"

Angus shut the door hastily and went downstairs. He had better put the thing in writing. He could write it down and send it up in a box, with a red label. He wished he had thought of this from the start: he felt disconcerted already: he had been thrown out of his stride. He wrote a draft and typed it out. It was calm and curt; it merely said that he had heard from a reliable source that Enver Bey had arrived from Tripoli and was in hiding somewhere in the town. "I cannot," he concluded, "disclose the name of my informant, but I can assure you that he was a man who is likely to know." He underlined the "*know*." And then he added a paragraph. "This information is, I venture to think, not without importance." He crossed out the "importance" and added "significance." And then he typed it again, very neatly, and put it in a box. He rang the bell.

"Take this," he said, "at once to Mr. Tenterden. It is very urgent."

The two attachés in the room looked up in surprise. It was not the business of an archivist to send messages upstairs. Angus noted their surprise: he was not displeased by it. Shortly after that the box came back. Angus opened it: his own paper was inside: he took it out: scrawled across the top in Tenterden's writing were the words: "Thanks: it was in the paper this morning."

Angus blushed.

That was the first thing which had irritated Angus: the second thing was even worse. It had happened on Tuesday. Tenterden had sent for him: he was upstairs in his study with the little doctor. The latter was pacing about the room impatient and excited. Tenterden wore his "amused" expression: Angus hated that look upon his face.

"Look here, Field," said Tenterden, "the doctor wants to take you from us; he wants you to help him up at San Stefano. He says that any ass can look after our papers for us while you are away."

"San Stefano, sir?" queried Angus, perplexed.

"Yes—the cholera camp. There is cholera in the army. The doctor has started an isolation camp. He wants assistants: he wants you."

Angus did not like the little doctor either. They had never, somehow, hit it off together. He did not in the least want to go to San Stefano with the little doctor. He hesitated.

"But I'd be no use there, sir. None whatever. I know nothing about cholera. And I'm just reorganising the archives. No one else could possibly find their way in them until I get them straight again."

Tenterden laughed. "There, doctor, you see! You must apply elsewhere for recruits. The others are worked off their heads as it is. There can be no question of them."

The doctor snorted; Angus left them. It was not till he had got downstairs that it dawned upon him. They would think he had been afraid. Afraid, he, of going to San Stefano! How monstrous! He had refused simply because the little doctor bored him. And now they would think he had been afraid. He must put that right at once: it was easy to put that right. He bounded up the staircase. He paused at the first landing. Cholera? The word had a sinister ring about it. An isolation camp? Cholera? An unpleasant job, of course. He climbed the second fight more slowly. It would be a mistake to arrive out of breath. Cholera? An ugly job it would be: a filthy job: a degrading, infectious job! How like the little doctor! How like Tenterden! His feet fell softly on the pile carpet outside Tenterden's room. He could hear their voices within: the angry, excited voice of Dr. Williams: the laugh of Tenterden. He paused. Slowly he walked back along the carpet and down the staircase. He shut his door with a bang.

"Well!" he exclaimed, "if they think me a coward, they're welcome to it. One day they'll realise their mistake."

The third thing had happened that morning. He had met Tenterden in the passage. "Oh, by the way, Field," he had said, "what on earth induced you to tell Lukacs about your visitor?" Angus had stood there speechless, looking at him: he had become scarlet, his tongue had refused absolutely to function.

Tenterden glanced at him curiously for a moment. "Well, we're all indiscreet at intervals," he said; "try and make your intervals as long as possible." He had said this and hurried upstairs. And Angus had not replied: he had stood there, his cheeks burning. How patronising Tenterden had been! Oh, it was intolerable!

That was the third thing that was depressing Angus that evening. And there was a fourth. He did not admit to himself that there was a fourth; but there was; it sat there on his knee in the shape of a bound copy of the "Golden

Journey to Samarkand." He had been reading it to restore his equanimity. After all, there were always books and writing. He possessed "the second string." That was more, far more, than Tenterden possessed. And so he had picked up the "Golden Journey," and the "Golden Journey" had got upon his nerves.

"Death," he read—

> " . . . . Death has no repose
> Warmer and deeper than that Orient sand
> Which hides the beauty and bright faith of those
> Who made the golden journey to Samarkand."

"Beauty and bright faith?" he had murmured grudgingly. "And the last line doesn't scan. Why didn't he call it the 'golden *road* to Samarkand?' It would have scanned then all right. Poor Flecker! He writes prettily, but he has got no ear for metre: he writes very prettily. . . ."

Angus read on. He read "Yasmin." And then closed the book with a snap. That was the fourth thing which was depressing him.

No, his life was not going well. He was being buffeted. Ever since Edhem had come to him he had been buffeted. He wanted a rest, he was overworked. He might go to Broussa: a week at Broussa would put him right. He would ask for leave to-morrow. Oh, damn! He couldn't ask for leave after what he had told Tenterden about the archives. Yes, circumstances were deliberately conspiring against him: that proved it; he flung the "Golden Journey" across the floor: everything conspired.

It was since his return to Pera that things had gone wrong: Therapia had been all right. . . .

Yes, it had been warm and coloured at Therapia——

Therapia? Eirene? She, at least, had been easy. He was surprised, when he looked back on it, how easy, how friendly, she had been. In a way, she stimulated. Eirene! He had cooled off of late: she was so disconcerting, with her quiet, superior ways: she had no sense of humour. She did not contribute; one had to do it all oneself. How much easier her mother was: her mother met one halfway—more than halfway. Angus felt his cheeks reddening.

Yes, he must pull himself together. He was becoming a failure. There was no doubt as to that. There must be a change: a radical change. An immediate change! A change which would be drastic and permanent.

He rose and dressed for dinner. He was dining in the ward-room of the "Weymouth." It was a noisy, cheery dinner.

Angus walked back alone up the steps that led from Tophané. The rain had stopped, and the stars shone clear and cold above the cypresses. Yes, there must be a change: he could manage that: it was merely a matter of concentration. He could manage that, but how?

He turned out of the Rue Hammam into the main street of Pera. It was then that he decided to concentrate on marrying Eirene.

But Eirene that night was not in Pera: she was lying sleepless in a bare, white room at San Stefano: she was lying there with the rough corner of the sheet between her teeth. From time to time her limbs twitched with panic in the little bed. She was afraid of sleep.

February

It was the end of her first day at San Stefano.

(II.)

A month passed: a sodden, sullen, hopeless month. Three weeks, now, since the guns had begun again to rumble at Chataldja. It was the end of February. People were getting used to it: a gloomy apathy had descended upon the town: people were getting used to the north wind blowing daily across the Okmaidan, weighted with rain, and the distant grumble of the guns. It was war: they had come to expect it. The cold and squalor of it; the mud in the streets; this monochrome of rain, and fear, and hopelessness.

The Powers had washed their hands of the whole business: the Conference in London had broken down: and Adrianople was invested: any day now it would fall. And then, once more, would come the turn of Chataldja: then again would come the menace to the capital. But for the moment it was only rain and cold, and the distant grumble of the guns. An intermittent, desultory grumble; perfunctory as yet, but one day they would wake up to hear it turn into a sudden snarl as in November: that would mean that Adrianople had fallen. That would mean that the Bulgars were once again battering at the gates. They shivered over their braziers and waited in despair. And the rain poured upon the grey, sodden city. It was very cold.

Lukacs Bela was sitting gloomily at his accustomed table at Tokatlian. He had ordered luncheon for two, he had ordered champagne. He was waiting for someone, for Major Edhem Bey, aide-de-camp to the Commander -in -Chief. His fat little fingers drummed upon the marble table. Edhem was late. Lukacs took his hands off the table while the head waiter laid the cloth. He spoke to him in German: "Ernest," he said, "tell me, how long is this to continue?"

"You know better than I do, Herr Lukacs. That is, if you mean the war."

"I do *not* know, Ernest," said Lukacs petulantly. "I have no idea. It is very provoking."

"Yes," answered Ernest, busy straightening a knife upon the cloth, "yes, it is very provoking. You have said it, Herr Lukacs. But in this cursed country . . ." And he began to speak of Bucharest, and Paris, and the Carlton in London. Ernest had no power of concentration: Lukacs was glad when the arrival of Edhem put an end to his reminiscences.

"You are late," said Lukacs: he was in a bad temper.

"Yes, I was kept at the Ministry," Edhem answered: "c'est la guerre."

"Edhem," said Lukacs, "tell me, how long is this to continue?"

"You know better than I do, Monsieur; that is, if you mean the war."

Lukacs snapped his fingers irritably. "The champagne, at once, Ernest," he called. And they began their luncheon.

Lukacs thawed progressively as the meal developed: the heavy pouches under his eyelids straightened gradually: the little eyes became glassy and bright again. By the end he was rather enjoying himself. "And so," he was saying, "you foresaw what has happened? You had your information? And you came down here and joined Enver on the 19th—four days before."

"Yes," Edhem answered, and he smiled complacently. "Yes, I had my information. I made an excuse, of course. I said that I must inspect the base at San Stefano. There was some hitch upon the line. They gave me a car. I *did* go to San Stefano. I reported to the Commandant. And then I drove on to Yedikoulé, and sent the car back to headquarters. I entered Stamboul on foot. That was the risky part. I was safe once I had found Enver."

Lukacs poured out the remains of the champagne. "And then, the first night," he remarked casually, "the first night you stayed with young Field, your English friend?"

Edhem started. How much did Lukacs know? How much? He hesitated. "Yes," he answered. "I slept a night—three nights it was—with Angus Field. Until I could discover Enver, you understand?"

"I understand," said Lukacs. His eyes glinted maliciously. Well! it was worth trying. "And did you," he asked, "explain to Enver that you had deserted—and why? Did you explain why, Edhem Bey?" He glanced up at his companion as he put the question: he noted the quiver of the slim nostril: the sudden pallor of his cheek. It had been an arrow shot at a venture, but it had found its mark. That, at least, was something gained: something to the good: something to go on. Lukacs was enjoying himself.

Edhem toyed for a moment with his glass. His

fingers were trembling, he put his hand hurriedly below the table.

"I explained," he said, "of course, that I had left headquarters. That I had come down to Constantinople to join him for political reasons." Edhem paused, "For patriotic reasons," he added. "Enver understood. I have known him, you see, for years. I knew him when I was a boy, and he was attaché in Berlin."

"Of course," said Lukacs absently, "Enver would understand. He would quite understand the circumstances. He would not appreciate, so readily, perhaps, *other* circumstances": he dropped his voice and leaned close to Edhem: "if there had been, let us suppose, other circumstances which caused you to come, so suddenly, to Constantinople."

Edhem was sitting back upon the leather settee: "It is very hot in here," he murmured, "so close to the stove."

Lukacs ignored the interjection: he leaned over to his companion: "I am your friend," he whispered; "it is my duty to warn you. You have enemies; it is impossible that in your present privileged position you should not have enemies. It would be unfortunate, very unfortunate, if any of your enemies were to know . . ."—he hesitated a moment, his little eyes bright with friendliness, —"were to know," he concluded, "what *I* know." Lukacs sank back in his seat. "But then, fortunately," he concluded, "I am your friend. Your secret is safe, quite safe, you understand, with me."

So much for the first act. Lukacs was pleased, more than pleased, with the results of the first act. He called for Benedictine, and proceeded luxuriantly, and at his ease, to embark upon the second act.

"It is interesting," he began, "to talk with a person of your peculiar qualifications. You are a Turk, a good Turk, a patriotic Turk. But you are also a European, a good European. One can say things to you which one would hesitate to say to other men. You see the thing in its right proportion. You understand."

Edhem swallowed his Benedictine at a gulp. "What is it you want, Lukacs Bela?" he asked in a low voice.

Lukacs laughed, a reassuring laugh. He patted Edhem on the arm. "I want nothing, my dear friend; you are my guest. Let us discuss the situation. We can discuss it as two good Europeans. We can discuss it with a sense of realities. You have lost the war: you will lose territory: you will lose Adrianople. But you have gained experience. You can write off your loss and begin again. You have gained great experience: it will be valuable to you for the next war. It will be of no value for what remains of this war. It is too late now, you have lost too much. You will only lose more if you continue. What you require is peace. Immediate peace; immediate preparation for the future. It is very important for all of us that you should make peace."

Edhem was on the defensive. "But how?" he murmured.

"In a week, perhaps in two weeks," continued Lukacs, "Adrianople will fall. It is inevitable: they will then bring up their heavy guns to Chataldja. You must not let them do that. You must make peace when Adrianople falls."

"But supposing," said Edhem, "supposing Adrianople is relieved?"

Lukacs rubbed his hands together under the table. At last they were getting to the point. He took a sip of Benedictine and swilled it round his mouth. And then he leant forward upon the table.

"If I," he began, "if I were a good Turk, a patriotic Turk, and at the same time a good European, I should argue this way. I should argue that the Powers will not allow Serbia an access to the Adriatic: I should argue that Serbia would be diverted thereby to the south-east, to Macedonia: and I should base my policy on the effect this will have upon the Balkan League, on the effect it will have upon Bulgaria. I should regard peace, even a humiliating peace, as but a move in the game: a step backwards to aid me in the final leap. Yes, I should make peace at once, and await developments. For there *must* be developments: you can count on that. And if I were a good Turk, a patriotic Turk, a far-seeing Turk, I should say to myself: 'For the moment,' I should say, 'there is only one thing of importance. Adrianople must *not* be relieved: the sooner Adrianople falls, the better.' That is what I should say," concluded Lukacs Bela.

Edhem sat far back upon the leather cushions: he did not speak. He sat there with his eyes half closed, and his nostrils quivered.

Lukacs leant forward again: he spoke in a low voice: "Yes, I should feel it a sacred duty to prevent the relief of Adrianople. I should not mince matters. I should argue thus. I should say: 'An expedition is being prepared; a relief expedition, to land somewhere behind the enemy:

somewhere on the coast of the Marmora. As a *surprise*, it may succeed. It may be able to join up with the Gallipoli army: it may be able to take the enemy in the rear: to relieve Adrianople. But only if it comes as a surprise.' You see my meaning? As a clear-sighted, patriotic Turk, I should prevent this thing, this surprise. Oh, it would be an easy thing to do; if one knew: if one happened to know. A very easy thing. One could lean forward, as I am leaning now, and one could take this dinner-card. And with a pencil —with this pencil—one could write on the back of the card. One would only have to write the name of the place and a date. It would be quite easy to do. That is, if one knew; if one happened to know. It would be quite safe": Lukacs hesitated significantly: "it would be quite safe," he continued, "far safer than other possible forms of indiscretion."

Edhem leant forward suddenly. He was very pale. He took the card from Lukacs, he took the little silver pencil from his hand. "Charkeui," he wrote, and underneath it he wrote a date. He handed back the card to Lukacs.

Lukacs called for the bill and paid. "You are coming?" he said, as he buttoned his fur coat.

"No," said Edhem between his teeth, "No! I shall stay here. Foutez-moi le camp."

(III.)

The little doctor lay back in the armchair and puffed at a cigar. "They like it," he was saying, "they lap it up like milk. It *means* something to them. Organisation. They can't create it for themselves, poor blighters! God has not granted that. But they lap it up when one gives it to them. They're white men, you see: sahibs. One has only to treat them like white men and they respond."

The doctor was unusually fluent. He had come in that morning from San Stefano, and Tenterden had allowed him to have a bath upstairs. A real hot-water bath from Doultons with Scrubbs' Ammonia in it. And a clean shirt. And luncheon: luncheon that he could eat for once in security. For the first time in four weeks he could use a fork or knife without first having to pass them through a spirit lamp.

He had been silent at first and ejaculatory: "Cases dropped to forty a day," he mumbled over the omelette; "thing's petering out," he added with the chicken. But by the time coffee came he had begun to talk about it. Of organisation, and how it was being lapped up. And then they had moved into Tenterden's study, and the doctor had become fluent, electrical even.

Tenterden listened to him. There was a light in his eyes, a light of admiration, a little light of envy. He got up and went to the mantelpiece. He looked down from his great height upon the little doctor. "Great God! man," he said, "I envy you. I envy you all you've done."

The doctor looked up at him confused. "Oh, I! Sir!" (He put in the "sir.") "Oh, it's my job, you see. Hobby, if you like. But the others! They get more than they bargained for. There was that poet chap. He turned green at first. But he kept laughing all the time. Laughed at the top note. Like this." The doctor imitated. "He crocked up in the end. They would all have crocked up if it had gone on." The doctor puffed at his cigar. "It was hell, of course," he added, "slimy, stinking, belching hell!"

How strange that he had not mentioned her! He had spoken of the others. He had not spoken of Eirene. Time and again the enquiry had framed on Tenterden's lips. A casual inquiry: "And Miss Davenant, how did she stand it?" Something like that. It had framed upon his lips, but it had not passed them. Something had checked it. A feeling of restraint: an odd feeling: not a very reasonable feeling. A feeling to be examined later: Tenterden put it away for subsequent examination. But the doctor? It was odd that the doctor had not mentioned her. It was odd that he, too, should feel the restraint. It was an irritating pose for the doctor to adopt. A tiresome little man. A brave little man, but tiresome. Tenterden looked down at him with an inward stirring of hostility. It was absurd this beating about the bush: it was cowardly. It was unbalanced.

The doctor had started talking again: he was giving a word picture of the average mentality of the Anatolian peasant. Tenterden interrupted almost sharply: he took the plunge.

"And Miss Davenant?" he said.

The doctor winced: Tenterden had been watching him, and he winced. "Oh, she's crocked, too," he said, "heart strain: I don't wonder either. I brought her in with me this morning. Left her at her home. No more San Stefano for her!"

"And Bridges?" Tenterden enquired hastily. He did not listen to what the doctor said or thought of Bridges. He was thinking of Eirene. It was ridiculous that he, Tenterden, should be shy of mentioning the girl. The thing had got on his nerves: he was unbalanced on the subject. How often in the last four weeks had he revived the problem, the problem of how far he had been responsible. He might have stopped her, of course: authoritatively. He might have forbidden the doctor to employ her. He could easily have done that: the doctor was his subordinate. But he had sent her out, yes, *sent* her deliberately; and why? Because of a whim, an emotion: an emotion or a lapse of thought, they came to the same thing. He had thought her like Demeter! She had looked like Demeter, serene and impervious. And he had sent her down to Erebus! And he had not dared to call her back. And now he was afraid to mention her. Yes, the thing had got upon his nerves: he was unbalanced on the subject. He must readjust the balance. He cleared his throat.

"Miss Davenant," he interrupted. "She is not, I hope, seriously ill?"

"Oh, no," the doctor answered, "I do not think so. Strain, you know. Anxiety. Fear, if you like. She had the guts to own that she was afraid. And then the physical exertion. No joke for a girl, even a girl like her, scrubbing latrines."

Tenterden leant against the mantelpiece.

"She worked too hard," the doctor added. "Said she would run away if she stopped work for a minute. She didn't stop. Yesterday she fainted." The doctor hesitated. "She cried a little. I tried to comfort her. She is such a gentle girl, you know, Tenterden, like a child.

She made me promise that I would take her back. I *did* promise; she was crying, you see. And you must get me out of it. Can't break promises."

Tenterden was still silent: he leant against the mantelpiece.

"She can't do cholera again, anyhow. All that chlorodyne tells on the heart. But, and I would have told you this anyhow, the Turks want me to run a field hospital for them at Chataldja. Cholera's nearly over now: San Stefano can look after itself. She might come there, when she's well. Say a fortnight. Tell me, Tenterden, can I take the job? May I?"

"*You* may take the job," said Tenterden, "but I'll be damned if you can take Miss Davenant. I'll see you damned first," and his fist crashed upon the mantelpiece.

(IV.)

It was a week later: they were alone together, Eirene and Tenterden.

"No," said Eirene, "I can't think of it as yet. I prefer not to think of it. You mustn't ask me. It was not the horror: I shall get over that: one took that for granted after the first moment. It became one's work, it became interesting almost. It isn't that which haunts me. It is my own fear."

She looked at him: there were black lines still under her eyes. "Tell me," she said, "have you ever been afraid?"

"Yes," he answered, "once I was afraid. It was in Russia. I shall tell you about it one day. I was afraid for two hours. I tried to sit down. I know what it is; one catches one's breath."

"Two hours?" she smiled at him; the lines

darkened underneath her eyes: her lips were tautened. She closed her eyes and lay back upon the cushions. They were sitting together on the wide terrace of the Embassy. It was the first week in March. He had sent his motor for her, and they had carried her out there: the sun was warm again upon the wall. He had arranged it for her: this sheltered corner. The rugs, the cushions, the table with the flowers on it: the books. It had amused him to arrange it for her. Giuseppe had helped. Giuseppe had been sympathetic: he had gone up by himself and gathered violets, a great glass bowl of them.

"How nice of you!" she had said, "how thoughtful!"

"It was Giuseppe," he had answered.

How pale, how wan she looked sitting there in the chair. And she proposed to begin nursing again on Friday! No, that was not possible: he must prevent it. But it was no use arguing now. She would only smile at him vaguely. "You don't understand," she had said already. "It will not be the same this time. It will not be—it will not be—that horrible disease. It will be things one can see and touch and help. I am not afraid when I can see."

No, it would only disturb her to revive the argument. It was so peaceful there under the wall: a kind of spring, of summer almost. The birds there in the ilexes.

"Look," he said, "those grey blades there in the grass. The daffodils are coming up. I planted hundreds of them last autumn, a whole case full which my mother sent from Kent."

"Kent? Oh, tell me, speak to me, please, of England."

He laughed at this. "Oh, but I'm so bad at telling things. I always was a duffer at that. And then Kent, you know—Kent—it's not a thing you can describe exactly: not in words it isn't: you'd feel it if you knew. *You'd* feel it more than most people. It's sort of soft, and hard, and clear, and dim. It lies there by the sea."

His eyes were half-closed as he leant forward in his chair, and with his hands he made unconsciously a slow, soothing movement as from right to left: something at once flat, and soft, and strenuous: something at once melting and sturdy. And then he began. He told her of the downs; the clear, clean sweep of them against the sky; the sharp, white edge of them upon the sea; the soft feel of them beneath the foot: the wind upon one's face: the wind upon the grasses: the little coppices that nestled in their hollows. And of the Weald he told her: the Weald of Kent, the look of it from One Tree Hill, the red-brown roofs among the oaks, the quilted pattern of the fields: the flash of water there to mark the Medway, the Romney marshes melting to the sea. And of the sequence of the months he told her. The misted, purple woods of winter, the smell of fallen leaves, the stirring of the sap. The catkins quivering in the lanes: primroses, and then the sudden splash of bluebells. He spoke of cleanly and of gentle things, of apple blossom, and the lush grass in the meadows, of hawthorn and of little cottage gardens: Sweet William, hollyhock, and columbine, and the soft scent of the garland rose. "Pembury, Goudhurst, Biddenden," the names came glibly to his tongue; and he told her of the smooth-flanked cows, and of the sound of the reaping. And then he spoke of Chiddingstone and his home: the toolshed where he had carpentered as a boy: and the woods of Penshurst, and the orchard sloping to the brook. "But I am boring you," he said. She did not answer him. "But I am boring you?" he asked again.

"You give me health," she answered: "you take me away from here: from this place of terror and decay. You have given me health."

There was a flush upon her cheek. He welcomed it tenderly. He looked at her with kind and humorous eyes. "It is like you, you know, my Kent: gentle, and calm, and dignified, and hard sometimes, and so obstinate. But sane, and wise, and mellow. You are all those things."

"Sane?" she echoed. "I—sane and wise? Oh, no! not yet. I want to be: I will be. But not here: I must escape from here." She smiled and looked at him. "And you will help me, Mr. Tenterden? You will not mind my going to the front?"

Tenterden laughed buoyantly: what weeks it was since he had laughed like that! "Oh, you're a woman after all, Demeter!"

Eirene frowned like a puzzled child. "What was that name you called me? *Demeter?* But how funnily you pronounce it!" And they laughed together.

(V.)

It was Tuesday, the second Tuesday in March, the day on which the British Relief Fund distributed quilts and blankets to the refugees from Thrace. Ever since November the refugees had been pouring in, a limping trail, shambling through the Western gate, the Edirne Kapoussi, the gate of Adrianople. Some thousands had been shipped by now to Anatolia, to Smyrna, to Cæsarea, and beyond. But thousands more remained, herded in barracks, and in requisitioned school-houses, or camping under the damp colonnades of the deserted khans. A mottled, idle crowd: a buzzing crowd of gypsies: sly children whimpering with outstretched hands: little hands whose nails were dyed with henna; back they would scuttle to their mothers, the penny grasped within their dirty palms.

The Administration had organised the care and relief of these infectious thousands: they had been forced by the Board of Health to take immediate steps. The city had been divided into sectors, and each sector had been allotted either to the Administration itself or to some of the various foreign Committees of Relief. The British Fund possessed the largest sector, running down to the water's edge, to Sali Bazaar with the little café rotting on its piles. And twice a month, on every other Tuesday, came the appropriate day for distribution. There was bread to give them, and flour, and cones of sugar in blue paper; but, above all, coarse blankets and the flowered quilts of the bazaars.

A Committee had been appointed from the British colony. The Chaplain acted as Chairman; there was a Secretary from the Embassy, and a Banker, and Aunt Emily, and Miss Wrightson and two others. Aunt Emily had from the first proved an element of disorder in the Committee. She had begun badly from the first. She had called them "refuges" at the opening meeting, and had been corrected.

"Refug*ees*, dear Miss Davenant." It had

been Miss Wrightson who had made the correction. That had put Aunt Emily against the Committee from the start. She would arrive at the meetings like an angry starling, seeking what she might devour. She had pecked, timidly perhaps, but persistently, at every suggestion. There was always being a minority of one, a ruffled, rumpled minority of Aunt Emily.

"Of course, I don't expect you to agree with me, but I *do* think . . ." That was how she would preface her proposals. Defiantly. They would *not* agree. The Chaplain was assiduous in throwing oil, but the waters remained troubled. And at the last meeting there had been a storm: it had been about the blankets. It was Aunt Emily who had bought the blankets, and there had been a storm; a storm which, in the acute circumstances of the case, to an unbiassed mind, was justified. Aunt Emily's mind was not, however, unbiassed: not about the bazaars it wasn't, not about Aunt Emily. "Very well," she said, "very well: I shall resign from the Committee." Her eyes flicked from one to the other. A painful silence. Miss Wrightson was drawing a little row of squares and crosses upon the blotting-paper. The clock ticked ominously.

"We should be sorry," began the Chaplain, "*very* sorry to lose the help of one who has given such substantial, such rational assistance to us in our work. We should be very sorry. I trust, Miss Davenant, that you will reconsider your decision. It would be a blow to the Committee, at this juncture, to lose one whose name has been honoured, if I may say so, sanctified, by the sacrifice and nobility of our modern Florence Nightingale."

That had done it: dragging Eirene in like that. Aunt Emily had not meant exactly to resign. She had not meant to resign in the very least. She had delivered her ultimatum, that was all. And it had been accepted: the Chaplain's tone had been valedictory. He had said good-bye: he had called it "her decision"; politely he had said it, but, still, good-bye. Undoubtedly he had said good-bye. Well, Aunt Emily would show them that she was not one of those women who said things idly like that, without meaning them. She would go. And at once. She went; she made a little murmuring speech, which had begun with "Of course I know," and then had broken down a little, and hopped on to something vague about "no difference, no difference *at all*, I hope, in our personal relations." Miss Wrightson had begun her second row of squares and crosses. Aunt Emily, with stiff shoulders and murder in her heart, had left the room. She did not slam the door: that would have been undignified: she shut it sharply. And when she had got home to her smoky little drawing-room she had cried.

All this had taken place the week before The Chaplain spoke to Tenterden about it: he had laughed. "Better have the niece on the Committee," he had said. "Keep her busy. She's well enough for that now. Keep her away from the front."

And Eirene had accepted with reservations. A mental reservation only: she had not owned to the Chaplain that, eventually, she meant to bolt. Only the doctor knew that. He had looked guilty. "Oh, my word!" he had said. She could rely on the doctor. Poor little doctor!

The distribution took place in the yard of the Embassy stables. There was a long line of tables at one door, and a Sergeant of the Marines at the other. The refugees filled the open space beyond. The Embassy Cavasses, in their scarlet uniforms, arranged them in some sort of order, and the Sergeant of the Marines released them with a jerk. In little twos and threes he would release them into the stable yard, and they would hesitate for a moment, blinking at the sudden open space, like a bull loosed from the torril. Then they would see the line of weighted tables at the other end, and shamble across smiling shyly: and the ladies behind the tables would smile back at them and hand them their apportioned dole. They would be conducted firmly and quickly to the outer door: there was no chance of getting in again to the back of the waiting queue; no chance of hiding one's loaf and blanket in the bushes and repeating that exciting and so profitable round. The hand of organisation had seen to that. One was taken out into the street, and the gate was close behind one: there was nothing to do but to go home to the barracks with one's blanket.

Aunt Emily had shone particularly at these scenes of distribution. Unlike Miss Wrightson, she had not spoken Turkish to the refugees. That would have been a pose. No, she had said useful things to them in English. "You must break it up first," she would say, handing out a loaf of sugar. And sometimes she would say: "Wash your face before you come again. You understand? Like this," and she would make a fierce circular movement with her hands round her face. A child had cried last time she did it: it had looked at her for a moment in amazement, and then had burst into tears. A wail of fear and misery had marked its passage to the outer gate. "Poor wee thing," Miss Wrightson had murmured at the next table, "you frightened her, Miss Davenant."

But that day Aunt Emily was absent from the table. She had resigned. Eirene sat there in her place. She was feeling tired and dispirited: it was a futile job. It was not the real thing. The real thing was waiting for her. She was better now. She stood up to convince herself that she was feeling stronger. There was a stir at the further doorway. "Stand back there, you," the Sergeant shouted, and then he saluted stiffly.

Tenterden walked quickly into the yard. Miss Wrightson bridled. He walked straight across to Eirene. "You will lunch with me to-day," he said, "after the show is over." He spoke abruptly to her, almost angrily.

"Thank you," she answered. He raised his hat vaguely to the other tables and strode out again.

Miss Wrightson at the next table was speaking to Eirene. "How cross Mr. Tenterden seems this morning! He's generally so cheery and so polite. And how he chaffs one! But I like a bit of chaff."

"I expect he's tired," said Eirene.

(VI.)

Her mother knocked before she came into the room, a little, nervous rap upon the door. Eirene looked up in surprise; it was so seldom that her mother came upstairs, and to knock at the door! That was not the usual thing for mother to do; usually mother stood in the landing at the bottom of the stairs and called up to her: "Eirene, viens ici," she would call stridently; her voice, so melodious in the lower notes, became strident when it reached a higher key.

"Eirene," she said, "I want to speak to you. I thought it better not to tell you in my letters, and then you came home ill. You are well now? You feel stronger, do you not?"

"Oh, I am quite strong now."

Her mother held a fringe in her left hand: she was in her dressing-gown: she was combing the fringe, holding it down and away from her. She kept her head bent; she did not look at Eirene while she was speaking.

"It is about Ion," she began. "You know that he went, after all, to Biarritz?"

"I know, mother. It was his health."

"Yes, it was his health. And the cholera. And then the war began again. He went away without seeing me. It was Antoniadis who told me he had gone away. It was just after you had left, Eirene; when you had arrived at that dirty place," a note of the old irritation quavered in her voice, "your mad escapade, little one."

Eirene smiled. "Well, mother?" she said. There was no tremor in her voice.

"It was a week after Antoniadis had told me. Ion wrote to me from Biarritz. One day I shall show you the letter: it was a beautiful letter. 'Le cœur,' he wrote, 'n'a pas de rides.' He asked me—you will think it absurd, Eirene, your old mother—he asked me if I would marry him, at once. He wanted me to come to Biarritz and to marry him. You were not there, Eirene. I did not know what to do. I sent him a telegram, in which I said I had received his letter and was writing. And then I wrote to him: I said that you were away. I did not tell him where you were; he would not have understood. I merely said that you were away, and that I couldn't answer till you returned. I promised to answer in a month: he will expect my answer to-morrow."

Eirene leant forward in her chair. Her face was motionless. She looked at her mother with her level eyes. "Well, mother?" she said again.

"You see, you are so independent now. You do not need me. You have changed so, Eirene, in the last few months. You do not need me; you are so independent now." Again the note of anger rasped in her tone: she combed the fringe vigorously. "You do not need me." The inflexion changed: a sudden drooping of the wing. "You do not need me, little one. You are grown up now. And I am lonely I am so sick of the old life. I am getting older, Eirene. See, little one, there are lines about my eyes, here and here. And look at my neck, my little round neck; these hollows here. I am getting older; it is time I settled down."

"You are younger than I, mother; younger in your heart."

Her mother looked at her, the comb suspended in her hand. It was true, that; yes, it was quite true: it had always been true. Eirene said things sometimes that one had never realised. She was a clever girl.

"Qu'est-ce-que tu me racontes là?" her mother laughed. She was pleased: it was her gay boudoir laugh. She had never used that laugh before with Eirene. She was *pleased*. Eirene smiled tenderly. Mother was like that.

"And then," her mother continued, "there is the financial side, the question of money. I detest that side," she held up the fringe and comb simultaneously in her little fists: she clenched them. "Dieu!" she exclaimed, "si je le déteste!"

Eirene smiled again at so much violence. It was familiar to her, that sudden petulance with money: it used to assail her mother when she was doing the house-books—that is, before Eirene took them over. "Dieu!" her mother would say, her little clenched fists raised above the table. "Dieu merci! Quelle scie!" Yes, she was not a worldly woman: there was always that in her favour.

The voice went on, a little plaintive now: "And when you marry, the money goes to you. All of it, all except twenty thousand francs for me. How can I dress on that? I ask you, Eirene? And Ion is so rich—so rich and generous And more than that." Her mother's eyes widened as she said it, like those of an astonished child.

"Come here, mother," said Eirene, "come and sit here beside me on the sofa."

Her mother came across: a little shyly: a little awkwardly; she sat beside her daughter on the sofa.

Eirene put her arm around her shoulder: how pretty mother was! Poor, helpless, little mother!

"But tell me," Eirene said, "do you love the man?" It did not seem impossible, that question, now: it did not seem grotesque. She asked it firmly now, and gently: there was a serene compassion in her tone.

"Love him?" her mother's forehead wrinkled in perplexity. "At my age, Eirene? A man of his age? What an idea! Love him? Like I loved the others, your father and the others? Like I loved Valentin? But what an idea, Eirene!"

"But I don't mean that, mother, I didn't mean that. There is a difference, you see, between being in love and loving. There is a great difference. It is the latter that counts: that really counts, that always counts."

"You mean *like*, I suppose? Yes, I like him. I am very fond of him. I cannot be without him. He is a friend to me, you see. He looks after the house, and the servants, and all that." The little hand waved vaguely in a gesture "And he is so reliable and gentle. And his health is bad. I would look after him: he has to take sachets before his meals, and he forgets them. Yes, he is a friend. The best friend I have had."

Eirene stroked her mother on the shoulder. "Then when," she asked, "do you leave for Biarritz?"

"Oh, not till June," her mother answered hastily. "You see, he is doing a cure. But I must answer his letter." She fumbled in her dressing-gown. "I have written a telegram—will this do?" And she produced a sheet of paper, so neatly written, so carefully written.

Eirene smiled as she read it. "Yes," she said, "it will do splendidly. It will do him good."

(VII.)

"There!" said Aunt Emily, as she stuck down

the little flap of gilt paper, "there! and I hope it holds."

She was sitting at her work-table in the window, and beside her were scissors and some gold, shiny paper, and a big bottle of glue. Aunt Emily had been in a bad temper that morning; she was in a better temper now: but the ice was still on the thin side. That morning she had bought a Persian miniature in the bazaars. It was a beautiful miniature, mounted between two sheets of glass, both back and front. The picture side showed a young man with black hair and a hawk, sitting under an almond tree, and when one turned it round there were the most beautiful calligraphs in red and gold upon the back. The man in the shop had laid particular stress upon the calligraphs.

"Authentique," he had said, "parole d'honneur."

And Aunt Emily had got the miniature; or, rather, she had taken it, very cheap. It was to be a birthday present for Eirene. Eirene was fond of those sort of things, she "thought she knew about them." Aunt Emily had snorted when she remembered that. At first she had been pleased, very pleased, with her purchase. She had held it in her hand driving back, and it had rained. That had been the beginning of the trouble. The miniature had got wet and the tape that held the two panes of glass together had become sticky, and impendingly unstuck. Aunt Emily had not minded that part: she had remembered some thick, gold paper in a drawer at home; she would pull off the tape and stick the two glasses together again, neatly and luxuriantly edged in gold. No, it was only *after* she had pulled off the tape that Aunt Emily had begun to mind. The two sheets of glass, as was to be foreseen, had opened out separate from each other. But so also had the miniature. That was the trouble; and there was worse to come. After all, the fact that there were two miniatures instead of one, did not mean necessarily that either was a *fake*. Aunt Emily winced at the word: it was a word which she relished only when applied to the purchases of others; to the purchases of that wide and fallible category of beings who did not "know the ropes." No, the fact that the miniature, her miniature, split in halves, did not imply at all inevitably that it, or either, was a fake. For the moment, therefore, she was comforted; but suddenly her eye had caught on something, puzzling at first, but which, on scrutiny, had developed into a proof, a damned and damning proof, of a marked intention on the part of the miniaturist to deceive. It was a little, triangular strip of torn printed matter. She read it carefully.

"German," said Aunt Emily, "a bit of a German newspaper. I was always told that these fakes came from Munich." She clenched her little fists. That man! That man Ahronian! She would get even with him: she would take the miniatures back that very afternoon. She would show him the Munich paper in its entrails. He would have to return her money. It was a disgrace, the way they treated one in the bazaars. A perfect disgrace. That very afternoon she would go up there and see Ahronian.

Aunt Emily bridled. She bridled the whole way through her luncheon. But she did not go that afternoon to see Ahronian. Instead of that she went upstairs to fetch the gold paper in its drawer, and the glue. "After all," she reflected, "it was only for Eirene." Eirene "thought she knew." Aunt Emily chuckled as she stuck the two pieces of glass together. "There!" she said, "there! and I hope it holds." She was feeling better now, but the ice was thin. The ice was still thin when Miss Wrightson was announced.

Aunt Emily did not like Miss Wrightson: but she had asked her to tea. Miss Wrightson had come up to her at the jumble sale, and had talked to her about the war, and Aunt Emily had lost her head. She made it a principle to ignore the war: she called it "politics." "Oh, don't talk politics to me. I don't understand them," Aunt Emily would say as the guns thundered at Chataldja. But Miss Wrightson had gone on about it: she had gone on volubly in her high-school English, and Aunt Emily had blinked for a moment or two, and had lost her head and asked Miss Wrightson to tea. And now the mortgage was foreclosing. It was not a good moment for it to have foreclosed: the ice was very thin that afternoon. And Miss Wrightson had sticking-out teeth and tried to toady Aunt Emily.

The interview went badly from the outset. Aunt Emily had hidden the miniature under a piece of Rhodian embroidery. Miss Wrightson had made a bee-line for that piece of embroidery. "How clever you are, dear Miss Davenant, at picking things up in the bazaars!"

Aunt Emily might have been gratified by this had not Miss Wrightson, at the same time, picked up the piece of embroidery. Not only the miniature, but the snips of the gold paper and the pot of glue were exposed. It was thus Aunt Emily herself who began hurriedly to talk about the war. The discussion had unrolled itself in a crescendo of disquiet, the word "rape" had occurred at least five times: Aunt Emily was by then seriously perturbed.

"Oh, please, *please*," she said at last, "don't let's talk politics."

Miss Wrightson was checked in her stride: there was a pause.

"By the way——" began Miss Wrightson.

"By the way, what?" enquired Aunt Emily a little sharply.

"By the way, your niece."

"Eirene?"

"Miss Eirene Davenant."

"Eirene, my niece, is a most remarkable girl. I always say so. She has a good heart, I suppose, but she is peculiar. I admit that Eirene is most peculiar. Nursing dirty men like that. Maudlin, *I* call it."

Miss Wrightson welcomed the opening: she did not seize at it or rush at it: she approached it with relish, it is true, but cautiously Her entry was hesitating: it was demure.

"How right," she began; "you are," she continued; "you always are," she underlined, "Miss Davenant," she concluded.

And then she began. It was not a very long story. There was not much point in the story until one came to the end. Eirene had been seen, on several occasions lately, in a victoria: alone: with a man. So far, so good. Aunt Emily's eyes had flicked backwards and forwards between Miss Wrightson and the naked miniature. She was thinking:

"Can I get up now and put it away in a drawer?" She was not giving any undue attention to the story. And then came the bomb-shell part. Miss Wrightson's back had stiffened; her lips had stiffened: even the little daisies in her hat had stiffened. "Alone," she repeated, "alone, in a victoria, with a man. And who was the man? It was Mr. Tenterden." The curtain descended with a crash.

At first, of course, Aunt Emily had merely winced. That was the first thing she would have done. The eyes flicked away there into the corner. That was the second thing. And then the ice broke: it broke suddenly as if a meteor had fallen upon it.

"How dare you . . . !" gobbled Aunt Emily. "It is not your business . . .," she panted. "It is not *my* business," she corrected, "to spy upon my niece." There was a pause: Aunt Emily sat there fluttering with indignation, and then deliberately, quite deliberately, she rang the bell. "Miss Wrightson," she said, "is not staying to tea." Aunt Emily had scored. She was alone.

She put the piece of embroidery back over the miniature: she smoothed the top and tugged down the edges. Eirene? Hugh? Not angry now, Aunt Emily. Only a rising tide, a glutinous and rising tide of sentiment: vicarious, perhaps, but doubly glutinous. Eirene? Hugh? Was it possible? *Could* it be possible? Eirene had said: "What! Hugh Tenterden? That bald man?" He was older than her: Aunt Emily counted on her fingers: he was forty-two. And her sister-in-law? Zoe? Zoe's reputation? Eirene's mother? And then Eirene herself was so peculiar, she had such peculiar ideas. One could never tell where one was with Eirene. Aunt Emily was becoming angry again. She checked herself. But Hugh? The violins of romance played their soft music in her ears: it made her cry a little, but inside her the little, rumpled, selfish heart was beating happily. Yes, she had always meant to leave her money to Eirene! And meanwhile she could assist. A present function, and for the future some hope of continuance; some hold for Aunt Emily upon the future. "I shall make a settlement," she blubbered happily, "and when I am old, they will ask me, they will *have* to ask me to stay."

A new interest: a new hope: already it was more than a hope: it was a certainty—a secret certainly, which Aunt Emily, good, kind Aunt Emily, rich Aunt Emily, generous, noble Emily, alone had apprehended, and alone would manage.

Eirene? Her brother's daughter. She had loved her brother. He was the only person she had ever loved.

She went to the table and took up the miniatures. The gold paper was still in the adhesive stage. She peeled it off and laid the two panes of glass upon the table. And then she took the two halves of the miniature, and slowly, with her dimpled fingers, she tore them into little pieces.

(VIII.)

It was late that evening when Angus came to see Eirene. She was lying on the sofa in her room. She smiled at him as he entered. "How nice of you," she said, "to come and see me. I am better now. I shall be well on Friday."

She was thinking: "How beautiful he is! It is strange that I did not notice it before. Not until mother told me. She was right: a Greek god! A young Apollo! An Apollo with short legs. Yes, his legs are too short."

She was thinking: "I hope he won't shake hands when he goes. I'd better be holding some flowers. I can wave them at him."

She was thinking: "I wish mother would come: she is so good at making conversation."

She was thinking: "He is second-rate, of course. But that I always realised."

She was thinking: "I expect Mr. Tenterden will come this evening: he was prevented yesterday."

She was thinking: "How long ago it all seems!"

Angus was sitting on the chair beside her. He was not really nervous. He knew exactly what he meant to say: he had rehearsed it all so carefully. It was to begin tentatively, but firmly. It was to begin: "I have been thinking things over, Eirene; about you and me, I mean." It was to begin that way. Then it was to go on for a stage or two in a boyish vein: "You see, I've been feeling pretty glum lately . . ." That sort of thing for a phrase or two. And then would come the deeper vibration, the diapason of the male. He would lean forward, his hands would clench together in front of him: "You see, Eirene, you are beautiful to me as the sun, and gentle as the moon." Yes, he had thought it out: "broken anapæsts," he had said. That was the metre.

It went well enough, the declaration, till it came to the anapæsts. They woke Eirene from her reverie. They woke her with a start.

February

"Oh, Angus!" she said, "what *are* you talking about? Are you asking me to marry you?"

"Yes," said Angus.

"Well, I won't," said Eirene, "*so there!*"

CHAPTER IX.

March

(I.)

THE yacht throbbed slowly through the oily swell that met it from the Gulf of Ismid. For three days now the south wind had blown across to Constantinople, and that Thursday, the 20th of March, was hot as a day in June. The almond trees in the Embassy garden had burst into full blossom, the gay blossoms of the daffodils danced against the emerald grass.

Tenterden closed his despatch-box with a bang, he must get away from it all for a whole day: a whole day somewhere else. They could start early and be back by midnight. They would go to Yalova. He had written a note to Eirene, he had written a note to Aunt Emily, he had written a note to the Captain of the "Imogene." He had telegraphed to the Director of the Casino at Yalova. And by ten o'clock the next morning the little, crowded steamer plying from the Princes Islands to the city had seen the slim yacht of the Embassy, with its large white ensign, heading across, past Halki, past Antigoni, past Bulwer's Island, to the distant mountain outline of Bithynia.

It was hot there on deck under the awning: a

little patch of sun showed white and dazzling upon the planks: the tar between them became soft and sticky: a polygon of sun upon the deck, the shadow of a rope diagonally across it, the square shadow of the awning; a polygon that swayed and swung and shifted with the pitching of the ship. Aunt Emily did not like that polygon. She refused to look at it. She kept her eyes, intent for once, upon a white farmhouse on the distant mountains. She had read somewhere that this was the thing to do. "One should endeavour," she had read, "to concentrate the gaze upon some stationary object on the shore." Aunt Emily was endeavouring: she concentrated. Every now and then, at regular intervals, at intervals disturbingly regular, the edge of the awning would cut down slowly between her and the little, white farmhouse and then up again. For a few seconds her stationary object would be hid from view: and then it would reappear again slowly, with disturbing slowness. Aunt Emily looked round hurriedly for some other object equally stationary, but less liable to these rhythmic eclipses: there was none to be seen. At least, not without moving. Aunt Emily did not feel inclined to move. It was so delightful there sitting on deck. A smell of cooking puffed at her at times from the galley. Yes, the paper had said that one must keep the gaze fixed upon some stationary object. It had gone further. There had been supplementary recommendations. Something about lying on one's stomach on a hard, flat surface. The deck was indicated as the surface, but the attitude! What would the sailors think? And it would be so difficult to explain to Eirene. Lumbago? No, Eirene would not believe in lumbago; not suddenly, like that, she wouldn't.

By the time they had passed Prinkipo Aunt Emily had recalled the remainder of the prescription. There was something about keeping a weight upon one's chest: Aunt Emily and her purple dressing-case had for some time now been locked in a tight embrace. And then one should blindfold one eye. The blue veil swung rakishly across her sallow cheek. "The glare," she said, "the glare from the sea. So bad for the eyes."

And, above all, one must remain on deck. "One is all right," she would say, "so long as one remains on deck. But if one goes below . . ."

Tenterden and Eirene were walking up and down the deck together. They would go up one way, round the companion hatch and down the other way. It was then that they would pass Aunt Emily. She would nod at them and smile, a nod of cheerful companionship, a smile of zest and enjoyment. Once she had pointed at some porpoises: that had been an unwise thing to do: it had been sheer bravado. Aunt Emily regretted the gesture as soon as made. Eirene stopped. "Yes, Aunt Emily? What is it?" she had asked.

"Sleepy," was all Aunt Emily could answer: Eirene smiled at her: "Oh, it will be better soon: we shall soon be under the lee of the shore: in twenty minutes there will be scarcely any swell at all."

Eirene had no tact. The girl had no tact whatsoever. Nor, for that matter, had Tenterden. He had asked her whether she would like to go to her cabin. She had shaken her head. It was too long to explain verbally what happened to people when they went below. And then he had murmured something about being more comfortable if she had a bucket. Aunt Emily hated coarseness in any form. Tenterden had been coarse: his success had not improved him. Aunt Emily looked up again at her stationary object It was nearer now, and it no longer slipped up and down behind the awning. Perhaps Eirene had been right. Aunt Emily raised herself and looked over the bulwarks. Yes, it *was* much calmer now: they were getting near. "Very sleepy," she volunteered, quite loudly this time, when Eirene passed her. It would be over soon. It would be better coming back; the swell would be behind them. It would, perhaps, have abated. She would be back by midnight in her little, blue silk bed. . . . "Oh, we had such a delightful day on Thursday in the Embassy yacht: we went across to Yalova. A perfect day: just enough motion to make one feel one was in a boat. . . . Mr. Tenterden was so kind: so considerate."

How angry Miss Wrightson would be about it all! Aunt Emily pushed the bandage off her eye. She put the dressing-case upon the deck beside her. She hoped that they would not have luncheon before two o'clock. It was one now. A little nap, perhaps, before luncheon. . . .

The Director of the Casino had sent a carriage down for them to the landing-stage: it was a full hour's drive from the shore to the little *Station balnéaire* up among the pines. High up it stood clustering among the Bithynian mountains: a white hotel, the Casino, and the baths. There were rhododendrons and acacias, and a great deal of pampas grass: there were geraniums in little beds, and revolving water-hoses upon the lawns.

And rose trees. It had been a speculation, this absurd settlement in Asia: not a successful speculation. In fact, the establishment, the Compagnie des Bains Thérapeutiques de Yalova was on its last legs. But it was determined not to admit the fact: quite determined. The gardener was bedding out the geraniums when Tenterden and Eirene reached the little, tidy plateau among the hills: the revolving water-hoses were throwing sprinkled rainbows upon the lawns. The flags flew bravely over the hotel and the Casino: the British flag in honour of Tenterden. The parquet floors were clean and cool, and smelt of Europe. There were Evian bottles on the tables in the dining-room.

"What fun!" said Tenterden.

"What a funny place!" said Eirene.

Aunt Emily had remained behind.

They had tea at a tin table on the terrace, and then they walked through the pine trees beyond the hotel, and up the hill to where the trees stopped: a high and rugged clearing among the pines; granite boulders, flat cushions of saxifrage mingling with the grey leaves of santolina. The gulf of Ismid shimmered below them, and across the sea, beyond the Islands, hung the haze where twenty miles away the great city steamed and rattled in the sun.

Eirene walked lightly in her rubber shoes: she outdistanced him and climbed the granite boulders on the summit. She wore a coloured jersey and she stood on the rock looking out across the sea. He laughed as he came up to her: "You look quite English to-day, Demeter; you look like the cover of an English magazine."

She smiled at this: she smiled, but she did not

turn to him. She stood there straight and slim as a cypress tree against the sky, looking out upon the sea, the lapis sea below her, noting its change to malachite where it touched the shallows. She looked beyond to where the distant haze hid the city of her girlhood, the city of her past.

Eirene's girlhood! She rose above it now; perched above it. She could see it shimmering below her, the shrouded remoteness of it, the closeness, and the distance. It changed in colour there where it approached. She was on dry land now; high land, dry land, above the miasma and the mist. Firm land. Clear air. Vision. Reality. There to the left was San Stefano, a mere lip of land upon the sea. And in the centre, Pera. The little brown room; the voices of people talking; the smell of beeswax on the staircase; the switch of the electric light beside her bed. And to the right, behind the hills, Therapia. The frogs at night; the soft propinquity of water; magnolias; music; soft music; her felt slippers upon the matting.

And further to the East, Chataldja. . . .

To-morrow she was going to the front. It was mean not to tell him. He would be so angry when he knew. But she would keep to-day apart: to-day was different: a loose sheet in her life, it did not belong to what had been or what was still to come. The mountain side below her sloped down to where the sea began; mulberry and poplar, peach and vine; luxuriant to the very lips of the sea. The flat and gentle sea: an edging of malachite among the rocks; the lapis sea.

"You see, Demeter," he began, "you have

your youth before you. And I, have only age. You do not know what youth is, no one knows till they are old. Sun-lit and adventurous, it seems to us: the great, the only opportunity. But to you, to you who have not crossed the shadow-line? Nothing? The life of every day? Their life. Themselves? Just the beginning of what will continue. A thing that does not matter much, not over-much. There will be so much time, you think, in after-life to add, to alter, and to make amends. That time, Demeter, never comes: the moment never comes when we can make amends. You see your course before you, you see it straight across the sea. There will be so much time, you think: afterwards, you think, there will be so much time. And so you linger here in little bays and valleys or where the meadows and the peach trees hang above the shore. You do not put to sea. And then the evening comes: the shadows lengthen. One does not want to travel then: nor does one want to linger by the shore. What *does* one want when one is old? Nothing. Do you understand? Nothing, Eirene—or too much."

She sat down upon the boulder, her arms locked about her knees. He looked up at her: "or too much, Eirene!" he repeated. She did not answer him. He leant against the rock below her: "Tell me, Eirene," he said slowly, "are you happy in this life of yours?"

She started round upon him, a faint flush upon her cheek: the sudden light in her eyes died slowly back to reticence.

"Oh, yes," she said, "I think so. And you?"

"Oh, I—I am no longer young, you see."

Eirene hesitated. "I see," she answered.

Sweet Waters

(II.)

Edhem was very strange that evening; certainly he was very strange. They were dining in the back room at the Hotel Modern. Edhem had insisted on going there. "It is my last night," he explained. "I go, to-morrow, to Gallipoli. Who knows when I shall return? We shall eat this last meal together, Angus, and talk about other things; about the Symbolist movement, and about ourselves. We shall not mention the war: I want you particularly to avoid all mention of the war." He had begun by drinking vodka out of a tumbler. "It is a pity," he had said, "that you are not better educated. You speak French well, I admit it. But then your mother was from Lausanne. But your culture is superficial. I am sorry to say so, Angus: but so it is. There are many facets of life, and art, and literature to which you do not respond. You have a little knowledge, my dear Angus. It is a dangerous thing. And then you know so little about music. I should have liked this evening to speak only of music. Now music is the thing that really matters. The only thing that really matters."

He talked feverishly for twenty minutes about Ravel, and about Stravinsky. It was thoughtless of him: it was more than thoughtless, it was unkind; there was something deliberate about it. Angus was disconcerted: generally Edhem was such an easy person to dine with; a little egoistic, perhaps, a little too inclined, perhaps, to treat Angus as an inferior; but easy and amenable, with flashes of insight if not of sympathy, of understanding if not of friendliness. To-night he had been different. He *looked* different. There were purple pouches underneath his eyes, and the eyes themselves were bloodshot. And then his voice was so odd: it grated up into a falsetto suddenly, and it trembled out into a laugh: a loud, quavering laugh, louder than was necessary. So loud that the people at the other table looked across at them curiously. And what was worse, he drank too much; he was forcing Angus to drink too much. Angus felt bewildered and unhappy: quite early in the meal he wished he had never come: Edhem was saying things on purpose to provoke him. Angus objected strongly to being provoked: it was such a difficult state of mind to cope with. It made calls upon the very qualities which Angus felt most lazy about: upon dignity and self-respect: all those qualities which were so apt to land one in a scene. He loathed scenes. Scenes were only tolerable if there had been ample time to prepare the stage. On this occasion he felt acutely that the stage was totally unprepared.

"Yes, you must come to Paris," Edhem was saying. "You must come in the autumn. There is a little room in my flat which you can have. You will be discreet, I know, little Angus. And we'll educate you. We'll educate the young barbarian."

"She had encouraged me," Angus continued, "I am quite sure that she had encouraged me. And then suddenly, like that, she snaps her fingers. They are a paltry sex, Edhem, one as bad as the other."

"Oh, you must come to Paris, little Angus. I shall take you to see Marthe de Laversine. What a woman! Imagine to yourself a little blonde with dark eyes, and of an intelligence! And then such luxury, everything of the best. And the people one meets there! I tell you, Angus, I dined there once: there were only four of us. There was Anna de Noailles and Forain. Just us four. Imagine it! And what a temperament! She laughs the whole time. It is most entertaining. She would like you, Angus: you would have to pull yourself together, of course. Oh, Angus! You and Marthe together, what a joke!" And he laughed stridently.

"But, Edhem," pleaded Angus doggedly, "you're not listening to me. *Please* listen. I tell you that . . ."

Edhem was plunged in sudden gloom. Angus embarked a second time upon his story. "You see, her mother," he continued, "you know her mother, Edhem? La belle Madame Davenant? Well, her mother . . ."

"Oh, be quiet, Angus! For God's sake, spare me your sugar-water stories! What do I care about it all, or about you, Angus? To-morrow I go to Gallipoli. Early to-morrow. Come, Angus, we shall have some more brandy; we shall have some of the best brandy here, and then we shall go together to Parisiana."

An hour later they were sitting at a table together, Edhem and Angus, at Parisiana, the café concert of Pera. They were drinking sweet champagne; they had been drinking a great deal of sweet champagne.

"Now this is very important," Edhem was saying, his finger swaying towards Angus. "Very important indeed. The boat leaves the bridge at seven to-morrow morning: I am to go with the general. It is a yacht, you know, one of the Sultan's yachts: the 'Ertogrul.' We start for Gallipoli at seven. That is very important. I rely on you, Angus. I shall come back with you to-night. I can't face Ortakeui again. I will send them a telegram. No, I shall come back with you, and I can sleep upon your sofa. And you must wake me at six. That is very important."

"Very important," repeated Angus dreamily. He had not been listening. It was better if one leant forward, over the table, like that. But if one looked up, the light in the roof would wheel and circle in the air. And on the stage there, that square of garish light, it was as if a vast propeller revolved in front of it, so quick as to be invisible, so quick as not to hide the mincing, mouthing figures on the stage, but wheeling there with the dim noise of distant waters. It made his stomach turn. He felt sick and cold. It was better if he leant forward: he could bend down his head and count the olive stones upon his plate. Two, four, six, eight: he could arrange them in groups. Then people would not notice.

"You are looking pale, my little Angus. You have not the *vin gai*. Consider me! I have drunk more than you. I have drunk much more than you. It has made no effect. I could get up this moment and walk straight across there to the table by the door. You see that table there with the Russian woman, and the fat man next to her. You see it, Angus? Close by the door where we came in. You see it? That fat man?"

Edhem had raised his sleek head to look across the café: "That table over there," he repeated, and his voice dropped suddenly, "that fat man over there. You see, my little Angus? He has got one of his hands behind her chair. He is smoking a cigar. You see, Angus? That fat man, with the roll of his neck above his collar? He has not seen us yet: no, he has not seen Edhem Bey. He thinks I am at Charkeui, do you not, Lukacs Bela? At Charkeui. Safe at Charkeui, eh? On the way to Charkeui?"

The words hissed between his teeth; the glass in his hand rattled upon the table.

Angus was counting his olive stones again: "At Charkeui!" he echoed. "Yes, of course." Two, four, six, eight: they went in twos: or one could do them in threes, but then there were two over. There were eleven stones.

An Italian tenor was singing on the stage. Edhem rose slowly in his seat and swayed a moment, gazing across the room. The man was singing: he took the high notes and squeezed them with his voice: he took the low notes and shook them gently. It was very effective. He was singing the "Musica proibita." . . .

"Vorrei baciar i tuoi capelli neri,
Le labbra tue e gli occhi tuoi severi.
Vorrei morir con te, angelo mio,
O bella inamorata tresor mio."

Edhem stood there beside the table, swaying a little and cutting patterns on the cloth with the table knife. He was looking across the room: his nostrils quivered like a frightened horse.

"It was like this," Angus continued: "you see, Edhem, she was beautiful to me as the sun, and lovely as the moon. No, gentle as the moon, and lovely as the sun. That was it. And she had encouraged me. I defy anyone to say she had not encouraged me. It was I that hesitated. Up there at Therapia: oh, that will interest you, Edhem; listen to this, Edhem. . . ."

He looked up from his olive stones. Edhem was no longer beside the table. How the lights reeled and swirled above the tobacco smoke! The man was still singing: he was singing about someone with severe eyes: Eirene's eyes were severe: "her imperial and disimpassioned eyes." Angus clapped his hands suddenly. But the man hadn't finished yet: it was at the end that one clapped. One could join in the chorus. One could . . .

What a noise they were making over there, all of a sudden, in the corner. There was a woman screaming. What bad manners! The poor tenor, there, on the stage. People were standing on chairs. Angus clapped again. No, one only clapped at the end, one sang the chorus now:—

"Vorrei baciar i tuoi capelli neri
Le labbra tue e gli occhi tuoi severi. . . ."

Angus lay back in his chair and hummed it tremulously at the ceiling. He paused for a moment: what a noise there was! Everybody seemed to be screaming and shouting. Something must have happened. The man had stopped singing. The manager was on the stage. He was waving with the palms of his hands. "Calmez vous, mesdames, messieurs! Calmez vous." He was shouting at Angus. What impudence! A dirty Levantine manager to shout at him like that! And people were standing on the chairs. Really, something must have happened. Anyhow, he would show them that he, Angus, didn't care. He leant back upon the chair and looked up at the ceiling. He would show those lights up there that he didn't care either. He would show Eirene that he didn't care. He would show Edhem that he didn't care.

Someone came and tapped him on the shoulder: it was Antrobus from the Embassy. "Come," he said, "I'll help you. We must get out of this at once."

Angus rose unsteadily: he was used to obeying Antrobus. It was all very puzzling; they passed out by the door: a waiter was sprinkling sawdust upon the floor by the table. "What a lot of claret," mumbled Angus, "what a lot of claret."

"Come," said Antrobus, "we must get out of this before the police come. There has been a murder: don't you understand? Someone has stabbed old Lukacs in the back. Came up behind and stabbed him in the neck. He's got away all right. He got away at once."

Angus was not listening. He allowed Antrobus to lead him into the street. He followed, swaying meekly: he was murmuring: "Must say good-night to Edhem: good fellow Edhem: must say good-night to Edhem."

(III.)

Tenterden signed the last of the despatches with a flourish of his pen. The Secretary beside him leant across and blotted the signature, gathering the pile of type-written papers together in his hands.

"Well, so that's all, is it?" Tenterden asked.

"All the despatches, sir. The bag leaves at four if you have any private letters."

"No, nothing more from me."

Tenterden sat on there for a moment, the pen still between his fingers. His last bag. Next fortnight they would come up again and stand beside the chair; blotting each paper as it was signed. But it would not be his signature! By then he would be in the train speeding back to England. In ten days from now he would be leaving for England. The Ambassador would have returned. But what luck, all the same! Five months in charge at such a crisis! He had done well, of course: he had increased his reputation. It would mean the next vacant Legation, probably; what did it matter? What did anything matter? He was old now: yes, she had sat there with her tennis shoes flat upon the rock. She had hesitated for a moment: "I see," she had said. She had seen that he was old. Not old for work, of course; oh! young enough for that! He was still one of the young men of the service: he would be the youngest minister. At forty-two? No, one was not old at forty-two, not for work one wasn't. Only too old to go back; to re-make; to re-adjust one's values. His values? Had they been so wrong? So very wrong? They had given him amusement, reputation, success. They had carried him, a gentle, easy tide, to where he was. Hugh Tenterden. *The* Mr. Tenterden. Scarcely a drawing-room in Europe in which the name was unfamiliar. And his work? Was that also a mistaken value? After all, he had done things: certain things would not have been done if it had not been for him. At Petersburgh, and here in Constantinople. There were many people who would envy him what he had done. His reputation! His mother would be pleased: she thought him a boy still. She would be very pleased. He laughed bitterly. He understood, now, what was meant by moss: the moss that the rolling stone omits to gather. Well enough for the twenties; well enough, even, for the thirties: but then the forties come and the poor stone, cold and bleached, has rolled beyond the realm of moss: only grey lichen, perhaps, to cover its nakedness and its old age.

Yes! she had been right, Eirene. It had been kind of her to let him see so clearly. A little more, a little less, and it would have been too late. It would have hurt her so to have been asked, and to refuse. She was so gentle and so generous. She would have been sorry for him, sorry to have hurt his pride. He was paying now for all the pleasures he had sipped so thoughtlessly. Well, he would face it decently: it was the only balanced thing to do. She need not fear again: never again would he approach the subject. He would go back to the old relationship: to the old, easy comradeship of the last few weeks. She would be grateful for that; she would understand and be grateful. After all, at forty-two, it would be something to have earned her gratitude. Sanity, balance, reason! They would pull him through. And there must be no hesitation: that was morbid. It must begin at once: to-morrow. Why to-morrow? Why not to-day? This evening? He would go and see her now.

He rang the bell: "The victoria," he said, "as soon as possible." Yes, he would drive down there and ask her to come out with him to the Sweet Waters. It was warm that afternoon.

Perhaps she would drive out with him to Kiatkhane. That would show her that there was no difference. He would tell her of other things: they would not speak of Yalova; nor even of Kent. No, certainly not of Kent. But of Paris they would speak, and Petersburgh. He could tell her about the Caucasus.

He found Mrs. Davenant sitting by the stove reading a French magazine. "Eirene?" she answered him perplexed, "but Eirene has gone to the front with Dr. Williams. Didn't you know? She left yesterday at daybreak! And she had slept so badly! She takes no account of her health, that naughty girl. And how strange that she should not have told you! Why, she was with you on the yacht the day before!"

"She mentioned something," said Tenterden. "Of course she mentioned something. I did not understand that she was going so soon."

He said good-bye to Mrs. Davenant. She did not press him to remain. "I shall walk," he said to the coachman. The wind had turned suddenly to the north: a few heavy drops of rain were falling on the pavement. Tenterden shivered, and turned up the collar of his coat.

(IV.)

"It was mean of her," said Tenterden, "yes, it was mean of her to go off like that without a word."

Aunt Emily's little eyes flicked malignantly for a moment. "But she *is* mean, Mr. Tenterden. And thoughtless. She is, she is, isn't she? I have always said so: 'Eirene,' I have said, 'my niece, is a thoughtless girl, I fear. She has no consideration for other people.' And then she is deep, Mr. Tenterden. Still waters, they say, run deep. Eirene runs very deep. One never knows where one is with her."

"I do not think," said Tenterden, "that she meant, exactly, to deceive me. Women are like that, especially these gentle, impassive women. They do not like to see pain, and if circumstances force them to cause pain to other people they prefer not to be there when it happens. It is not duplicity."

Aunt Emily snorted: she was angry with Eirene.

"Believe me, Miss Davenant," there was a note of anger, mingling with a note of half-entreaty, in Tenterden's voice, "believe me, it is not duplicity. It is not even selfishness exactly: not exactly thoughtlessness. Women, all women, are cowards about the consequences of their actions. They are cowards and optimists: they shut their eyes. 'Something will turn up,' they think: 'he will understand,' they think: and within themselves they add: 'and, anyhow, I shan't be there to see.' Truly, Miss Davenant, I do not think it was worse than that."

Again Aunt Emily snorted.

"And then there is another side," continued Tenterden, "the practical side. After all, she knew that I would stop her going. I had told her so; or, rather, I had told the little doctor so. But the little doctor was mesmerised. I don't blame him: poor little doctor. You see, Eirene knew that I would prevent her going. She is not up to it, in the first place: she is not strong enough. And there is a second thing which she does not realise. I am afraid. Williams has pushed his hospital across to Kalikratia. It is very exposed: there is only the bridge behind it: it is the first line of retreat if the Bulgars attack. They *will attack*. They will attack any day now: the fall of Adrianople is, I take it, certain. I am only telling you things that everybody knows. There is to be a diversion these days: to-day, perhaps: a landing somewhere on the coast of the Marmora. If that fails the Bulgarians will attack at once. They need not worry any more about Adrianople: it will fall to them as a ripe fruit. They will throw all their reserves upon the Chataldja line. And then? It was foolish of Williams to establish himself at Kalikratia. Only one swaying bridge, a congested bridge, a bridge congested perhaps by a defeated army. And under shell-fire, perhaps, Miss Davenant. They will forget the little hospital out there at Kalikratia." Tenterden struck his palm with his clenched fist. "Of course," he concluded, "they will forget it."

Aunt Emily's eyes flickered nervously. "Then you mean, Mr. Tenterden," she faltered, "you mean that Eirene may be in actual danger of being hit by something, of being captured—cut off, I think they call it. I do not understand politics, but you really mean, do you, that her life there is in danger?"

Tenterden stared gloomily in front of him. "Her life, yes. And more. I could telegraph to Sofia, of course. But what good would that do? You see, I am powerless. It is no use sending a message to Eirene. She would not listen. She would think I was being official. It is no use ordering the doctor to return. He would not leave the hospital: he would say that he is in Turkish service. No, he can be obstinate enough, the little doctor. He is a monomanic." He spread out his hands. "You see, we are powerless, Miss Davenant. Quite powerless."

Aunt Emily was becoming flustered. Her little dimpled hands fidgetted with the black lace about her throat.

"But, Mr. Tenterden, surely you can do something? You don't seriously mean to tell me that nothing can be done? You don't expect me to think that a girl like Eirene, a British subject, is in any danger, any personal danger? And she is in Red Crescent uniform, too. So becoming. My poor little Eirene! My dear Henry's daughter. Of course, she has been badly brought up. My sister-in-law—Zoe, my sister-in-law, you know—her mother—well, she's not the sort of woman—and Eirene would not listen to me—she would never listen——"

Aunt Emily was crying nervously. She was making little nervous dabs with her pocket-handkerchief. Tenterden sat there grim and saturnine. He was thinking aloud.

"There would be time," he said, "to telegraph to Sofia. I could send a private telegram. I could suggest that Savoff should be held 'personally responsible.' Poor Savoff! He'll be at Chorlu: he won't know what happens at Kalikratia: not in those first few moments. Or on the bridge. I know the place: I went there once for the duck-shooting. The sea runs up between the lines, and there are marshes at the northern end. At the southern end, where the little harbour is, stands Kalikratia, and the bridge. It is a long bridge, built on pontoons.

A long, narrow bridge. There is no other escape from Kalikratia.

"Except," said Aunt Emily, "I suppose the sea."

"Except, of course," Tenterden added absently, "the sea."

"Well?" said Aunt Emily.

Tenterden did not answer. He sat there gazing in front of him.

"Well?" Aunt Emily repeated. Her breath jerked inwards at intervals: an inverted sigh, like a child who has been crying.

"Well what?" said Tenterden irritably.

"Well, the sea," said Aunt Emily.

"Useless," barked Tenterden. "Once they reach the heights, they'll shell the steamers."

"Not the British flag, though; not *your* flag, Mr. Tenterden."

He rose and looked at her: the little, huddled, nervous woman in the chair. "Out of the mouth of babes and sucklings," he murmured to himself.

"Thank you," he said aloud. "Thank you, Miss Davenant. You are right. There is the sea."

(V.)

Angus was sitting at his desk in the little archive-room in the Chancery. The door into the larger office was open, and through it came the click of typewriters and the desultory conversation of the Secretaries. It was cold in there on the ground floor of the Embassy: for two days now the north wind had blown across the

Thracian steppes, shaking the blossom from the trees. Angus lit the little oil stove in the corner.

"What a climate!" he murmured. "A week ago it was June, and now January. What a climate!" He opened the wide ledger on his desk: he would be very busy to-day. For four days now he had remained in his room lying upon the sofa. The papers had accumulated during his absence: the two tins there on his table were full of papers He must register them and put them away in the green canvas boxes that lined the walls. It was tedious work. He selected a pen and scraped the dried ink from the nib. "What a climate!" he repeated. And then he set to work: on the left side one wrote the papers that were received, on the right side those that were despatched. One entered the telegrams in red ink, and the other papers in black. It entailed changing one's pen the whole time. It was tedious work.

They were talking about it in the next room. Angus strained his ears to listen. "Poor old Lukacs!" one of them had said; there had been more, but it was drowned in the click of the typewriters. Angus laid his pen back upon the tray: he could not write this morning: his hand was trembling. He was seriously unwell. He must go for a week to Broussa; it would be easier now. The typewriters in the next room had stopped for the moment. It was Antrobus who was speaking. "I was only two tables off," he was saying. "It happened so suddenly. It was a Turkish officer: I am sure of that. He dashed out of the door. Quite an ordinary table knife: you know the sort. Oxidised silver handle: right under the left ear. Lukacs fell forward on to the table: there was a white cloth. It was like putting blotting-paper into a pool of red ink. And the handle stuck out all the time. How they screamed! You know that little Russian woman? It got all over her dress. And then they carried him out: the waiter pulled out the knife carefully, so as not to hurt. I do not think Lukacs was alive then. His hands had scrabbled a bit at first: but he made no movement when they pulled out the knife. What a mess it was! I did not know that people had so much blood. Like a pig being killed. I saw Field on the other side of the room: our archivist, you know: he was terribly upset: bright green he was. He could hardly stand. And then . . ."

The typewriter had begun again. They had heard the story before, the other Secretaries. Antrobus was telling the story to someone else, someone who must just have come in. Angus wondered who it was: he must go and see. He tried to rise, but his legs gave way under him. He sat down again upon his chair and put his head within his hands. How cold and damp his forehead was! He was going to be sick again. He pulled a flask from his pocket and gulped some brandy: it had been a good idea of Hamsa's, that flask.

The door in the next room opened again: the typewriter stopped suddenly: there was a chorus of welcome.

"What! Back again!" they said. "We thought you were at Gallipoli."

"Oh," the voice answered, "I transhipped at Chanak: there was a torpedo-boat coming up. It was no use staying longer. The show had fizzled out two days before we started. Besides,

I was sick of the 'Ertogrul.' I never wish to see that filthy boat again." It was the voice of the Assistant Military Attaché: Angus recognised it. He pulled the papers towards him, and began to work again. He felt better: what a good servant Hamsa was!

"You have heard the news," began Antrobus. "You have heard about old Lukacs?"

"Yes, I have just been to the Ministry of War. I stopped there on my way from the boat. They have found the assassin. He is an Arab officer, it seems, called Haddad. They had been looking for him for other reasons. He confessed: they were able to extract a full confession. He was living with a woman, whom Lukacs had got hold of. He had been drinking, and when he saw them together it was too much for him. He was hung this morning at the Hippodrome. The Austrian Consul attended in full uniform: they are paying compensation. The thing will be hushed up, of course. There has been nothing in the papers. The Turks are marvellous hands at hushing up. Besides, it is not a pretty story: I don't think the Neue Freie will relish much publicity. They called it 'cette histoire doublement pénible' at the War Office. They were distressed and nervous about it, but the Austrians seem satisfied enough. He was a Hungarian, Lukacs: I always thought he was a Jew."

There was a pause, and the typewriter began again. "Have a drink, Colonel?" someone shouted.

"Thanks, I will. I was waiting for that."

Angus was working better now: the whole of one side of the ledger was already covered with his neat, grammar-school writing. He would get up soon and go into the next room to see who Antrobus' friend had been. He got up and went to the door. It was only the messenger. The Military Attaché was sitting by the table drinking whiskey. The typewriters clicked in the silence. Angus went back to his chair: he turned the page and pulled another paper towards him. "Acting Consul-General Flecker," he wrote: and, in the next column, "March 8." "No. 42." The next column was a wider one, and he wrote: "Import of textiles into the Lebanon." This he underlined: the last column was the widest of all. He glanced at the despatch, and wrote: "Forwards statements for financial year 1912-1913. Draws attention to marked increase in imports from Austria Hungary." He shuffled the remaining papers in his hand: no, there was no more from Beyrout. He had better put this one away at once. He rose and ran his finger along the rows of green boxes.

The typewriters had stopped again. It was the Assistant Military Attaché this time who was speaking. "Yes," he was saying, "they are a curious people, very curious. You see, the whole Charkeui business depended upon surprise. It was *not* a surprise: the Bulgars had been warned. Even then, however, the Turks managed to land and to occupy the village. The Bulgars must have underestimated their transport capacity: they forgot the Bosphorus steamers. Yes, they landed all right and occupied the village: they captured a Bulgarian Colonel and all his papers. And then the enemy brought up their reserves and turned them out. They lost heavily."

He paused, and there was the tinkle of glass and the hiss of a syphon. "Yes, they are a curious people. Among the papers that they captured was a little piece of white cardboard. I have seen it: I will tell you later how I came to see it. It was a menu card, about ten days old, from Tokatlian, and on the back was written in pencil the word 'Charkeui' and the date: the date of Tuesday. They had made enquiries: the Chief of the Police had made the most successful enquiries. Yes, they are a curious people. A grim sense of humour. They knew about it already when the wretched fellow came on board. They did not tell him at first: they pretended that nothing had happened. He was aide-de-camp to the general. His name was Edhem Bey. You knew him probably; he was the drawing-room type of Turk. I think he knew already that something was in the air: he crawled on board, all unshaven, looking as if he had spent the night upon a dust-bin. That's why I noticed him. We all had luncheon in the grand saloon: you have seen it, haven't you? Plush and mirrors. They put the menu in front of Edhem's place there at the table: they watched him pick it up. I must say I admired the man at that moment. He took it up, and turned it round to see the back. He merely raised his eyebrows. And then he propped it up again in front of him against a vase of tulips.

"They court-martialled him in the saloon after luncheon: he was taken away by the sailors. I did not understand quite what had happened: they came up on deck while we had coffee. We were passing the Marmora Island. It was that fat fellow, you know, Hillal Bey, who sat next to me. I asked him what he was laughing at. He held up a fat finger: 'Listen,' he said,

'Listen and you will hear, perhaps!' The ship had stopped, we were rolling there in the swell off the Marmora Island. They sat there smoking their cigars: waiting for something. I asked them what it was: it was Hillal who told me. 'A little experiment,' he said, 'a little experiment to beguile the tedium of the journey. You did not hear, I think, the argument that Raouf Bey raised at luncheon. He was telling of his experiences last year at Adana. He was saying that when a man is burnt alive there is a moment, towards the end, when his head explodes with a report like a bomb. He said that if a dead body is burnt it merely pops: but if the man is burnt alive it explodes with a report. Like a bomb. It is an interesting point. Very interesting. And to-day we have, by chance, the occasion of ascertaining whether what Raouf has recounted is true. We regret that we have had to stop the engines for a moment: only a moment. We wish to use the furnace for a moment. For our experiment, you understand. I assure you, Colonel, it will not be for long.' He held up his finger again. 'Listen,' he said.

"I did not understand at first. The whole ship was listening, some of the sailors leant against the side grinning but silent. A puff of yellow smoke gushed from the funnel.

"I realised it then. I jumped from my chair. 'You do not really mean—you cannot mean . . .'

"They held up their fingers at me. For a moment I hesitated. A muffled detonation reached me from below. They laughed.

"'No, not so loud as a bomb, Raouf,' Hillal laughed, 'not quite so loud as a bomb.'

"In a minute or so the engine had started again. At Chanak I transhipped." He finished and helped himself to another whiskey and soda.

They found Angus unconscious, with his face upon the open ledger.

CHAPTER X.

April

(I.)

THE city of Stamboul, the old Byzantium, slumbers upon the ridge that juts between the Marmora and the Golden Horn. For fourteen hundred years its boundaries have stood defined and changeless,—on three sides the sea, and on the fourth the walls of Theodosius; five miles they run, a double line of battlement and turret from Eyub to where that tower of marble glitters in the sea. A tattered coronal; a decayed antiquity. Toothless and blind, the city croons and mumbles, a little shrunken in its shabby clothes; resigned, inglorious, and silent; the plane trees sighing in the breeze of evening, the voice of the muezzin calling to the dawn.

And over there, across the walls, clang the new cities which have sprung from this decay. Pera and Galata, Chichli and the rest: stucco and asphalt, urinals and little stilted trees: the smell of tar and petrol, the shrill insistence of the yellow trams. At their best, when the eye is blinded by the quiver of the sun, Marseilles perhaps. But at their worst, when the plaster dampens in the rain, some squalid quarter of a French provincial town; Cherbourg, or Tourcoing, or the drab environs of Brest.

Sweet Waters

Concealed within this clangorous stuccoed world there lies a Turkish quarter, a wooden village, as it were a self-sown seedling strayed across the harbour from Stamboul. One leaves the streets of Pera, turning down the hill: a narrow European street at first, and at the corner a curtain of wisteria drooping from the roof. The noises of the town are deadened when one reaches it, and, as one turns, the silence falls suddenly with the hush of some secluded cloister. A sleepy street opens to the left; a street of wooden houses and uneven paving. The cats lie blinking in the sun; the cry of the pedlar echoes from the lane below: and at night will come the tapping of the watchman's stick, the shuffle of a slippered foot upon the pavement.

The house of Nouri Pasha stands on the right, a little down the hillside, with its garden wall upon the street. Three terraced gardens tumble round it down the hill: some stone pines by the house, and below, a water cistern and a group of pomegranates. It was not difficult to find the house: Tenterden had been walking quickly when he stopped beside it. He pulled the bell there by the iron gate: its tinkle echoed from the house below. The sharp call of a woman's voice, and then an old negress panting up the steps. The Pasha was ill, but he would see the gentleman; the Pasha had been very ill. There was a great deal to say about the Pasha's illness.

Nouri was lying on a divan in the wide-windowed room on the first floor. He was lying by the open window in the sunshine: beyond him sparkled the sea and the minarets, and in the background the blue mountains of Bithynia and the white, suspended cloud of Olympus. There was a table by his side with papers on it. He clapped his hands and called for coffee.

"Well, it has failed," he said, "the expedition has failed. They had received warning and they were prepared for us."

Tenterden sat on the divan beside him at his feet. "Tell me," he said.

"You know," said Nouri, "you know by now. But there is something else you do not know, my friend." He rose with an effort and pushed a paper towards Tenterden. "Adrianople," he said, "this morning at daybreak. It was inevitable. Inevitable once the expedition failed. We are keeping it dark as long as possible: there would be panic. It would affect the army at Chataldja. There will be one more attack." He sank back upon the cushions. "Only one," he panted.

"So it is the end?" said Tenterden. "It is all over now. You cannot hold out longer now that they have taken Adrianople." He laid his hand upon Nouri's knee. "I am not sure that it is not for the best."

"It is over. Almost over," said Nouri. "They will attack again at Chataldja. They will drive us back to the lines: we have advanced beyond them, you know, in the south at Buyuk Tchekmedje."

"I know," said Tenterden.

"But they will get no further. We shall ask for peace. Yes, it is over, my friend, but it is not for the best." His eyes flashed. "Defeat is never for the best. It means discouragement for the moment, but afterwards it means revenge. We cannot afford revenge."

He was silent for a while, looking out upon the waters, upon Stamboul and beyond to Asia

There was a tense and fevered look upon his face. He pointed with a thin and trembling hand across to the Seraglio.

"There was a time," he murmured, "when the Grand Signior could sit there in the Baghdad Kiosk and count his provinces as a man counts pearls. A time when we were masters from the Adriatic to the Caucasus. And more than that; Tripoli, Egypt, Greece, and all the islands; the gates of Vienna, the mouths of the Danube; the Iron Gates, Belgrade, and Temesvar. You feared us then: even in your cold seas, my friend, you feared our caravels. Your Ambassadors would creep before the Grand Signior upon their knees. You feared us then. You only fear each other now: and so we live: on sufferance. Oh, I know; I know." He held his hand in front of him and gazed at it against the light. "The Sick Man," he muttered with a bitter smile.

He pointed again below him over the pomegranates to where the city shimmered in the evening sun. "I know! I know!" he said. "It is this that has ruined us. Byzantium. If the conquerors had but fixed their capital at Broussa, or later, even at Belgrade! Then history would have been a different thing. It is always the same on these seven hills, beside these gentle waters. It will always be the same: Greek, Turk, or Russian: a soft, a gradual decay." He rose stiffly from his cushions: he pointed over across to Asia. "We shall be back there one day," he concluded. "We shall go back to our rugged home. And then we shall recover: then, once again, we shall be Osmanli." He paused: there was a note of hatred in his voice. "But here," he said, "we rot, and fester, and decay."

There was silence between them: a sweet-seller in the lane below passed slowly playing on his flute: a sad refrain, a wistful lilt.

"And now," said Tenterden at last, "and now there will be peace."

"In a week or two. Only a week or two at most."

"You will be better then; you will have the leisure to recover."

"I do not hope for it, my friend. I do not wish to see that day." He sighed, and then he smiled. "I know. I *know*, my friend, I shall not live to see that day."

The outline of Stamboul turned purple as the sun slipped behind it to the west.

"Eirene!" Tenterden was thinking. "Eirene there at Buyuk Tchekmedje. I must be prepared."

(II.)

"You will leave," Tenterden was saying, "by the Orient Express to-morrow. I have written to the Foreign Office and explained. I have not explained it away, Field, do not think that. But I have explained. They will transfer you to the General Consular Service. You will not come back to the Levant. You are not, I gather, particularly anxious to return to Turkey?"

"I am not, sir," Angus answered.

"Perhaps you are right in that," Tenterden continued. "Perhaps you are right. It is a pity, though, in some ways. They tell me that your Turkish is above the average. It would be a pity if that were wasted. Mind you, Field, I am not saying that you have behaved well in all this business. You acted foolishly from the first, and in the end you seem to have lacked courage. You see, I know the story now: the whole of it: they have pieced all the broken bits together up there at the Porte. The Chief of the Police was here this morning. It was he, in fact, who suggested that it would be better if you went on leave. You see, it was foolish of you to have told Lukacs about Edhem having deserted. You must have known from what I said to you, here in this room, that it was a matter which required reticence. And then you go and tell: tell Lukacs! Lukacs Bela, of all people! Yes, it was foolish: it gave him the weapon which he required. He must have used that weapon to frighten Edhem Bey, to frighten him into writing those two words on the back of the card. Yes, it was foolish of you; but we all do foolish things. But later, Field, at Parisiana. Surely you should have told me of that? Immediately? You have placed me in a difficult position: you realise that nothing happens here that is not known? You realise that? It would have saved me some discomfiture if I had known—if I had known in time—that one of my staff had been with Edhem at the moment of the murder. It makes no difference that the Turks should have chosen to hang another man for this murder. It is their habit to kill several birds with one stone. They have disposed of Edhem in their own peculiar way. It was convenient for them to hush up the incident. It was convenient for the Austrians. But they told me the truth there at the Porte. I did not know the truth. You did, Field. It was your duty to have told me, but you failed. I do not know, of course, what explanation you can give. Was it your loyalty to Edhem, a mistaken loyalty, that prevented you? Tell me, Field." He balanced an envelope in his hand: "You see, my letter to the Foreign Office has not gone as yet."

Angus stood there pale and speechless beside the fireplace. It was like being at school again: absurdly like being at school. For a moment the impulse came to him to burst into tears: Tenterden was so big, and hard, and angry. The sixth-form bully: he had always seemed that to Angus. He reminded him of that beast Hargreaves, at Tonbridge: Hargreaves had pushed Angus's face through a briar fence. It came back to him: he felt the thorns. And then Hargreaves had tried for that scholarship at Oxford. He had failed. Angus had not failed: he had been a scholar of Wadham. History was repeating itself. That very morning Angus had been asked to become a contributor—"a regular contributor"—to a London weekly. What London weekly would ever think of Tenterden as a contributor—a *regular* contributor? The pen was, after all, more mighty than the sword. One day even Tenterden would understand. There would be poetic justice, recognition, and revenge. But meanwhile silence, wounded, dignified, and uncomplaining. The Alfred de Vigny attitude: the picture of Dionysus at the court of Pentheus.

His mind worked in this way: within him: instinctively, subconsciously; but as it worked his lips were moving.

"I was drunk, sir," he was saying. "I was very drunk. I did not realise what had happened

Even afterwards I only half-remembered it. I wasn't sure: there was nothing in the papers. If I had been sure, I should have come to you, I really should. I should have been afraid. But it was all like a nightmare. I couldn't remember what had happened. It was only yesterday that I remembered. And then I fainted. I fainted in the Chancery." He stretched behind him to the mantelpiece. He felt giddy again. He had not meant to answer Tenterden: and then it had come from his lips as if someone else had spoken. He felt relieved: the room was spinning round him, but he felt relieved.

And Tenterden was laughing. "Oh, you were drunk, were you, Field? Well that's human, anyhow. A healthy vice. So that's the explanation. Well, it's honest, anyhow: and healthy."

He took the envelope and tore it into little pieces. Angus looked at him surprised: "Oh, I'll tell them something: don't worry, Field: it will be all right. But remember, Field, to-morrow you leave Constantinople by the Orient Express."

Angus mumbled something and walked unsteadily to the doorway. "Come, Field," said Tenterden, "don't slink away like that. It will be all right in the end, I promise you. It will have done you good. Go home; into the country somewhere. You will forget all this. One does forget things, you know; at least, one thinks one does. You see, you are young, Field: you are very young. You are younger than your years, Field. But it is different with me: I am old: I am much older than forty-two."

He passed his hand across his forehead: and then he laughed again buoyantly. "So cheer up,

Field, see? You will go home to England. It is all over now. You will go home—— Where is your home, Field, by the way?"

"In Kent, sir."

"Kent? My county? Where, in Kent?"

"At Tunbridge Wells, sir."

Tenterden laughed again: spontaneously, this time. He held out his hand: "Well, good-bye, Field. And remember, if you want help later, with the Foreign Office or something, let me know."

"Good-bye, sir," said Angus.

(III.)

The defences of Chataldja, the last defences of the capital, had been drawn across the peninsula, some eighteen miles from Constantinople. The line runs as a succession of fort and trench across the barren uplands from the lake of Derkos, on the Black Sea, to the lagoon of Buyuk Tchekmedje, on the Marmora. A natural defence, spanning the tongue of land where the two inlets to the north and south have pinched it to its narrowest, and cover the flanks of the position with water and with marsh.

The lagoon to the south is entered from the Marmora: a little fishing port at first, only a little bay upon the sea, backed by the breakwater of the pontoon bridge which bears the long, slim road to Adrianople. Behind the bridge the inlet widens out, more lake than sea: some rushes by the water's edge, the trail of wild duck against the sunset. Five miles it runs, a glint of water among the Thracian downs, and then a mile or two of marsh again, and then the railway.

The lines of Chataldja as at first established reach the Marmora at the eastward point of the lagoon, commanding the little bay and the bridge that spans it. There had been an attack one night in January, a surprise attack: the Bulgarians woke to find the Turks established on the western side of the bay, the side furthest from Constantinople. A precarious bridge-head here: two kilometres deep, and not more than three in width: and only that one vulnerable bridge for their communications. "We have advanced from Chataldja," ran the headlines in the morning papers. It was true; they had advanced. But they advanced no further. Three months now they had held that point beyond the lines: for three months had they clung to their wire over the brow of the little hill. It had its advantages, this bridge-head, practical as well as moral. The little steamers could creep up from Constantinople and stay for a few flurried hours unloading into lighters in the bay. They were unobserved. That was the advantage. The night attack had robbed the enemy of direct observation; and in the little village under the hill they had established a field hospital: the hospital of Doctor Williams.

From each house in the village floated the white flag with the red crescent: there were only five houses in all, yet the village had a name, the name of Kalikratia. It was months since the inhabitants had been evacuated: Dr. Williams had the village to himself. He organised. The larger house became the hospital: a rough dressing-station beside the quay. The smell of lysol and iodoform: the japanned tin boxes with the red crescent painted over the red cross: some stretchers upon trestles in the corner. It was primitive enough: this was the advanced station. There was a large boiler in the other corner of the ground-floor room, and another in the little garden behind. The wood crackled day and night, the smoke drifting pungently across the water. And in the middle stood the operating table which the Society had sent out from London, a white and glittering object against the dark wood walls. Upstairs there were two further rooms: white tables, basins, towels, rolls of lint. It was here that the walking cases were treated: they would sit waiting in a row upon the bench. A row of dazed and muddy peasants. This was Eirene's sphere of action: she helped the matron and the two orderlies. She would hold basins for the young assistant surgeon from St. Thomas's Hospital. She would speak to the soldiers in their language. She spoke it well: it served to soothe them. A smile would flit across their puzzled eyes. "This will make you well," she would say. "It will hurt at first because your shirt has stuck: we will put this soft white cloth upon it and tie it tight." She would say these things to them calmly; so gently she would say them: with such calm conviction. They would whimper sometimes at the pain, and they would look at Eirene with the trusting eyes of a retriever. And she would smile at them standing there with the basin and the lint. How deft she had become at bandages! Her firm, cool fingers, and the safety-pins ready in the other hand. Tightly she would roll the bandage: she would speak to them as she did so. "It is over now: you will sit on the other bench now, by the door. They will tell you when it is ready. And then you will walk with the others to the landing-stage. There will be a little boat. It will take you to the big hospital at the Court of Happiness." "Dersaadet," she called it: she did not say "Stamboul." And sometimes through the rough planking of the floorway would come strange smells and noises from the room below. The sweet pungency of choloroform: the grating of the saw.

Dr. Williams would shout up to her through the ceiling: "We're through down here," he would call, "any more in your little lot?" "There are four more here," Eirene would answer, "and it will not be long."

The last boat would leave at sunset. It was seldom that cases came during the night. There was no shelling this end of the line. They were waiting for the fall of Adrianople. Eirene would go back to her room in the smaller house. She would drop exhausted on the bed. No time for thought: slowly she would drift into sleep, soothed and troubled by the memory of dazed and grateful eyes. A shot would ring out from time to time over there beyond the hill. An isolated ping in the darkness. The noise of the water came to her, breaking against the little quay. It was so like Therapia: it was so unlike Therapia. Eirene would rise and slip into her dressing-gown. Yes, it was better than Therapia. It was clean, and cold, and hard. That's what she wanted. Tenterden had said that she was sane. She *felt* sane. Sane, confident, and happy. Yes, happy in the midst of all this suffering. Physical, not mental. No torment of the mind.

And then one did things: neat, tidy, unpleasant things. It was concrete. It was clear, and cold, and hard.

Her mother's letters came to her: long, rambling, ill-spelt letters in a sloping hand. She had sent her telegram to Paniotis, the telegram she had shown to Eirene. He was staying at Biarritz till the end of May: in June she was to join him in Paris. They would be married. Meanwhile her mother had opened the house up at Therapia. She was going there at once: she wanted to be alone and quiet. "Il faut," she wrote to her daughter, "me refaire une virginité." How strange to write such things! How unlike mother, the mother of her childhood, the nervous, fussy mother of whom she had been afraid. Afraid of little mother! Mother had been so particular, so prim. So particular. And then the ice had broken; suddenly, that evening in the drawing-room when Paniotis had been afraid. After that mother had not tried any longer to pretend. Poor little mother! Poor foolish little mother! Eirene was glad now that her mother could write things like that. It *helped*. Yes, it was more natural than what had gone before. It was more sane.

Eirene's nights were dreamless there in Kalikratia.

(IV.)

It was the 31st of March: the bombardment began at daybreak. Eirene dressed hurriedly and lit the little spirit lamp. The familiar, homely smell of methylated spirit cheered her as she dressed in the bruised and shattering glimmer of the dawn. Dr. Williams was calling from outside. He was calling the assistant surgeons and the nurses. Eirene was the first to be ready: she ran out on to the quay, the white apron of her uniform glimmering in the half light: the low clouds streamed dark across the downs, their black bellies lit from time to time by the sudden flashing of the guns. The rain was falling in big, sullen drops.

"Is it you, Eirene?" called the Doctor. "Go up to the house at once and light the boilers. The attack has begun."

Eirene hurried along the quay-side in the rain. The little sticks for the fire were kept under the staircase: and there were old newspapers there: the "Gazette de Pera." She lit the fire in the operating-room under the great boiler in the corner; that was easy enough. It would be wet in the garden: perhaps the fire would not light: and the attack had begun. She gathered the dry wood and paper in her hand and hurried to the garden. She held the paper underneath her apron to keep it dry. She had forgotten the matches: she must go back for the matches. She pushed the wood and paper under the wall: it was dry there; that was a good thing. And the pile of logs there were not drenched as yet; not the underneath ones. She would start the fire going with the lower logs. She went back into the lower room to fetch the matches. Dr. Williams was prancing up and down giving instructions to the nurses. It was getting lighter now: the bare windows gaped upon the growing light. The white table in the centre stood out stark and shining in the dawn.

"We're in for it this time," said the doctor. "House full, and no mistake. First boat won't come till nine. Cases any moment. Crowded out. Hurry up with your show upstairs. Tell 'em to bustle."

Eirene took the matches and ran out into the garden. The paper lit easily and the wood crackled. She pulled out two of the lower logs and they were dry enough. She hurried back into the house and up to her room. They had tidied up the night before: there was little to be done until the cases came. It was half-past six. She went to the window and looked out upon the lagoon. "Oh!" she exclaimed, "Oh!" And she drew back startled. A pillar of water had sprung up into the air. "A shell," she added.

"Yes," said the matron, "they are shelling behind the line."

"They are shelling over our heads. We are in no danger, so the doctor says."

A gust of rain rattled against the window. Eirene wished that the cases would begin to come. It was unpleasant, this suspense. It was better to roll bandages: or to make some tea? Yes, that would be best, she would have no time later.

The cases began to come. They limped down from the hills in little twos and threes. And then the stretchers came. The light widened into the chill of day. Eirene was too busy now to listen to the guns. She stood there holding the bandages. She was thinking of other things: she was up there on the rock above Yalova looking down across the sea. It had been warm that day, and the sun had smelt of the cotton lavender. She had felt the rock warm and smooth through the rubber of her shoes. He had asked her if she was happy. It was that which had set her thinking, thinking back upon the secret, and the Angus agony and San Stefano. It had been a discovery; that's why she had not listened really to what had come after. A discovery that she had been happy at San Stefano, more happy in all that nightmare than in the safe, secluded home at Therapia. He had said something about being old, and she had agreed with him. Listlessly and absently she had agreed, and then she had seen the pain spring to his face as at a lash. She had been a coward not to explain afterwards; and the next day she had come here without telling him—against his wishes. He would not speak to her again. He was a person who was used to obedience: who deserved it. He would not speak again to Eirene.

The doctor was calling her sharply from the room below: she gave her basin to the orderly and went quickly down the dark and mildewed staircase. She opened the door. A man was lying upon the operating-table: Eirene winced away from the sight. The doctor stood there in his white and splattered coat: he wore his india-rubber gloves. There was an officer in the room. The doctor was irritable.

"Oh, Sister," he said curtly, "ask this fellow what he wants. Man can't speak any civilised language."

The officer saluted Eirene as she turned to him. He wore tidy dog-skin gloves. He gave his message in Turkish.

Eirene translated in a level voice. "It is a message," she said, "an order from the Commandant. We are to evacuate the hospital by four o'clock. Not later than four. They are attacking in force. The bridge-head is to be abandoned."

The doctor snorted: "Last boat doesn't come till five or six. Tell him that."

Eirene turned to the officer. "The hospital," she said, "will be evacuated as soon after four as possible. You will understand," she added, "that we must evacuate the wounded first. We cannot say, as yet, how many there will be."

"It is understood," the officer answered, and swung from the room. The doctor turned again to the table: "Upstairs!" he said. "Thanks!" Eirene left him and recovered her basin from the orderly.

Yes, she had not meant to be cruel. She had been absent-minded, that was all. Perhaps Tenterden would not understand that. Perhaps it was better that he should not understand. She liked him for not understanding. No, even if ever again he spoke to her, if ever again he held his hand to her and looked down so protectingly, even then she would not explain. She would keep that as her secret. Her new secret. He would never know that she had not understood. That she had not listened. How warm and silent it had been up there. Surely the noise above the hill was getting louder! She glanced at the sea beyond the window: another pillar of water rose suddenly and subsided on itself. Not spray exactly: it took a strange, heavy shape upon itself: it collapsed upon itself suddenly as some heavy thing. It was like what one saw in pictures of naval battles. Cones and pillars of water dotting the sea like African ant-hills. They gave a wrong impression those pictures: it was not the cone itself that was so surprising, it was the spurt with which it rose, the sudden way that it collapsed upon itself.

She was dressing a shattered hand. The man groaned as she pressed in the wad of wool. "It will be better now," she said mechanically. "It will hurt you less. You will sit upon the other bench by the door. They will tell you when they are ready. And then you will walk along the quay to the little boat. It will take you to the big hospital at Dersaadet. You will get well there. It will hurt no more. You will go home. You will not fight again."

He smiled again at her, with glassy eyes. "Hanoum Effendi," was all that he could say.

They ate there at the table; biscuits and more tea. And the day wore on. She glanced at her watch. It was three o'clock: the second boat had gone at twelve. They had sent a message that the last boat must come earlier. It must be here by half-past three. The room was crowded: there were soldiers sitting on the bench. They were smoking, some of them. And some lay on the floor with frightened, staring eyes.

The doctor bustled upstairs in his rubber gloves. "I don't like it," he said. "Have you seen the bridge? They are taking back the guns. The stretcher-bearers have come in. They say it's no use waiting. The line has given higher up. Finish off this lot—we must be ready when the boat comes. I've got ten downstairs."

Feverishly they worked for half-an-hour: it was four o'clock: a quarter past. Yes, that was the boat coming round the corner. They had just finished in time.

"Stretcher cases first," the doctor's voice came ✱

through the ceiling. She could hear the tramp of the orderlies as they bore their burdens along the quay below. "Now walking cases," called the doctor, and the dazed line of bandaged soldiers began to shuffle off the bench. The little steamer hooted nervously in its impatience. The doctor bustled in again. He had taken off his coat and was rolling down his shirt-sleeves. "Hurry up there," he said. "Not got much time."

The last case was limping along the quay-side. Eirene hurried into the little living room to get a coat. No time for her possessions. The steamer hooted pitifully: the doctor was standing by the gangway.

Eirene came up to him. "Well," she said: "I am ready."

He clapped his hand to his pocket: "I have left my instrument case up at the house. Hold on a second. Won't be a second."

Eirene stood there by the gangway while he ran back into the house: his voice came to her: "Eirene," he was calling, "Eirene, come here a minute." She left the gangway and hurried across the quay. He was in the lower room, leaning over the table.

"Quick," he said, "this poor fellow. Finger blown off. Wandered in here all alone. Saw the flag, I suppose. Just time to patch him up. Give a hand. Some oil cloth in the cupboard. Here's the lysol."

He worked quickly: they could hear the little steamer hooting panic-stricken by the pier.

"That's done it: there, my man. Bit rough, I fear: no time for delicacy. Give a hand, Eirene: man's faint."

They helped the man up on to his legs: between them. Eirene worked her shoulder underneath his arm to support him. They staggered slowly to the door.

Eirene paused there on the threshold, and her eyes narrowed. "I don't understand," she said. And then, very slowly: "Doctor," she said, "the boat is no longer there. Look, doctor, can you see its smoke there disappearing behind the Point? The boat has gone without us."

Slowly, between them, they let their burden slip to the ground. He sank there with a sudden whimper of pain. Eirene stooped to him: "All is well," she said. "It will get better soon," she said. "You will be taken in the steamer," she said, "to the big hospital at Dersaadet, to the Court of Happiness." He looked at her with tired eyes. He sank back against the wall.

The doctor turned and gripped her by the arm. "I have let you in for it, Eirene. My damned optimism. Always trusting people. Who but I would have trusted that skipper man with the shells lumping around like porpoises. Oh, Eirene!" . . .

He looked at her in dumb apology. "We must try the bridge," she said. They looked at it simultaneously: there were men walking like flies across the outside of the parapet, trying to jump from pontoon to pontoon: a sea of struggling heads: an ox-waggon had got jammed across the fairway: frantically they were trying to push the oxen into the sea. There was a man on a white horse in the middle of the bridge: he was hitting with his sword upon the heads of the crowd: he was screaming at them: the sound of his high voice reached them across the water:

people were jumping off the parapet into the sea: their heads showed like the bobbing floats of nets upon the water.

They were firing now from the other side: it was the Turkish guns that fired. A spurt of water shot up beside the bridge, and then another. "We must be quick," the doctor shouted. "We must try the bridge."

Eirene stooped to the man lying against the wall. "All is well," she said. He looked at her with the eyes of a frightened dog. She turned to the doctor. "We must take the man with us. Give me a hand." She stooped again. The doctor took her by the arm: "Don't be absurd, Eirene. Don't you understand, girl? Don't you see, that it's you, you who are in danger? Not that man. He's a *man*. He'll lie there till they come. Not that man. He'll be all right. They'll not bother about him. But you, Eirene, *you*. Don't you understand?" He was pulling nervously at his hair, and his voice rose tremulous in his agitation. Eirene looked at him. She understood.

"We must try the bridge," she murmured, and she hurried towards it. A hundred yards or so: that was all they had to go. A shell from the Turkish guns moaned over them and spluttered down into the soft hill beyond. "Be quick, be quick," she mumbled as she ran. The crowd of soldiers at the end of the bridge streamed out upon the road: how silent they were! Only the voice of the man on the white horse screaming halfway across the bridge: "Let me pass, you sons of pigs!" he was screaming, and waving with his sword. But the crowd was silent: they pushed and pulled at each other silently: slowly, silently they pulled and trampled: the weaker had gone down already. There, where the space narrowed for the entry of the bridge, there was some obstacle: the crowd stumbled as it reached it, and then climbed something, and for a moment their heads showed above the rest.

Panting they reached the outskirts of the crowd: "We must try. Doctor, let me link your arm." Together they approached the outskirts of the crowd. For a moment they hesitated, and in that moment came a spurt of flame, and then a crash rending and terrible. The air shot up in dust, and flame, and splinters: and then settled again silently: only the splash for a moment of bits, and bars, and splinters falling in the sea. The crowd swayed backwards now: violently: the slow torrent had set the other way. "Come," the doctor said, "we must get out of this. Quick as you can, back to the house. They are shelling the bridge. The Turkish guns are destroying the bridge." Back they ran along the quay-side. They paused there by the landing-stage, looking behind them. Slowly the bridge swung open and apart, its battered edges jagged as broken posts.

"They have broken the bridge," Eirene murmured.

"We had better go in now," said the doctor. "There is the red crescent, that is our only hope. Fetch the man, Eirene, by the wall. We can do him properly this time." His face was jerking in a ghastly smile.

The guns were silent now: even the rifle fire had subsided: a shot now and then, and now and then the sudden rattle of a machine-gun. "They are coming down the hill," said the doctor. "Rats in the trap, Eirene. That's what we are. And it's my fault. Oh, Eirene . . .!" his voice ended in a wail of helplessness.

She took his hand: her fingers trembled: she looked out towards the sea. "There is a boat coming," she said slowly, "a little boat. It is not our steamer."

The doctor looked to where she pointed, and then he laughed. A clear note of laughter in the darkening rain. "It is the launch," he said. "I am half-blind, but I can see better than you. It is the Embassy launch. You see, Tenterden knows. He always knows."

"Whew!" he concluded, and mopped his dripping forehead.

Eirene stood there motionless for a moment. "Come," she said quietly. "We can help this man to the jetty. There is so little time to lose."

They were standing there, the two of them, with the man lying beside them on the quay when the launch arrived. A machine-gun rattled close to them for a moment behind the dressing-station.

"You must be quick," said Tenterden.

She took his hands, she held them tight within her own.

"I was so afraid," she said, "I was terribly afraid you wouldn't come."

(V.)

Eirene sat there silently in the well of the launch, looking out upon the darkness. The rain had stopped, and a bar of primrose sky stretched in the west, below the bank of clouds. The sun had set.

Tenterden leaned down towards her: "We are

passing San Stefano," he whispered. She saw the line of lights upon her left and roused herself. She went into the cabin. The doctor was sitting there, writing feverishly. He was writing his report. He had promised to show it to Tenterden before he sent it in. They must devise some explanation. It would not do to say that Tenterden had come himself: they would not relish it in Downing Street. If he had been hit, if the launch had been hit! The complications of it! Most injudicious. Eirene sat down beside him and took his hand:

"Doctor," she said, "supposing that I had not been frightened. Supposing I had refused to leave that man beside the wall. What would you have done?"

He looked at her for a moment above his glasses.

"Chloroform, Eirene. Heaps of it. Only way to have rendered you reasonable."

She pressed his hand, and laughed. "Dear doctor!" she said, and she went out to Tenterden.

She sat beside him. "Supposing," she said, "supposing I had not been frightened. Supposing the house had been full of wounded and I had refused to come with you? What would you have done?"

"I should have stayed," he answered.

"You would have stayed?" she murmured.

There was silence between them: the lights of Constantinople glimmered ahead, a little blur of light fringing the dark sea.

"And your career?" she added.

"Oh, my career," he laughed, "of course, is everything."

She did not answer him. She was looking at the lights.

"You know, Eirene," he began, "that I am leaving to-morrow?"

"Leaving?" she echoed in amazement. "Leaving Constantinople? Leaving for home?"

"Yes: it is unlikely that I shall return."

"Oh, but how mean of you!" she cried, turning upon him suddenly. "How mean! You should have warned me. You have not given me time."

He leaned towards her. "Time, Eirene? Time for what?"

She hesitated for a moment: "The wind has changed to the south," she murmured; "it is April."

"Time?" he repeated, leaning down to her. "Time, Eirene? Time for what?"

The lights showed brighter now. The high light in the Seraskerat tower, the little, humble lights by the water, the line of lights across the sea.

The wind from Asia came softly across the waters, laden with the scent of cistus and of thyme. The scent of spring.

There was no longer any silence between them.

(VI.)

She spoke to her daughter in the languid French of the Levant. She said: "Eirene, you must come in now, you must come in, and you must close the windows."

Eirene stepped back slowly into the room. She closed the upper half of the window and pushed home the bolt: she then released the lower half from the brackets which supported it. The murmur of the water was hushed suddenly as the sash rattled home in its socket. "There is a breeze to-night," she said; "it comes straight across from Kavak: it is cool upon the balcony."

"Yes, it is still cool at night," her mother answered, "but that window always makes a draught and the lamps smoke. Why, even now the shade is shaking——" and she pointed to the silk fringe swaying gently against the light. "You do not mind, Eirene? You do not want to stay upon the balcony!"

"No, mother," Eirene answered, "I want to talk to you. It is better with that window closed. We can leave the others open upon the garden. The magnolia is not even in bud as yet."

Her mother was lying there upon the sofa with the lamp behind her. She was reading an illustrated paper, and the light cast upon the page the oblique shadow of her piled and tidy hair. Eirene stood for a moment looking down upon her. "Poor little mother!" she murmured, and she knelt down beside the sofa.

"Mother," she said, and pressed her cheek against her mother's shoulder. "I have something to say to you. Put down your paper and listen to me. Listen, mother!"

"I have proposed to Hugh Tenterden."

The little white thumb that held the paper jerked in surprise. Eirene laughed a cool and gentle laugh that filled the room with music.

"Yes, mother, I have asked Hugh Tenterden to marry me. He has agreed."

THE END.